© Willy Somma

Anna Solomon

The Book of V.

ANNA SOLOMON is the author of *Leaving Lucy Pear* and *The Little Bride* and a two-time winner of the Pushcart Prize. Her short fiction and essays have appeared in publications including *The New York Times Magazine*, *One Story*, *Ploughshares*, *Slate*, and more. Coeditor with Eleanor Henderson of *Labor Day: True Birth Stories by Today's Best Women Writers*, Solomon was born and raised in Gloucester, Massachusetts, and lives in Brooklyn with her husband and two children.

Also by Anna Solomon

Leaving Lucy Pear

The Little Bride

Labor Day:
True Birth Stories by
Today's Best Women Writers
(coeditor)

THE BOOK OF V.

THE BOOK OF V.

A NOVEL

Anna Solomon

Picador
Henry Holt and Company
New York

Picador
120 Broadway, New York 10271

Originally published in 2020 by Henry Holt and Company
First Picador paperback edition, 2021

The Library of Congress has cataloged the Henry Holt hardcover edition as follows:
Names: Solomon, Anna, author.
Title: The book of V. : a novel / Anna Solomon.
Description: First edition. | New York : Henry Holt and Company, 2020.
Identifiers: LCCN 2019028705 | ISBN 9781250257017 (hardback) | ISBN 9781250257000 (ebk) | ISBN 9781250756459 (international)
Classification: LCC PS3619.O4329 B66 2020 | DDC 813/.6— dc23
LC record available at https://lccn.loc.gov/2019028705

Picador Paperback ISBN: 978-1-250-79844-2

Designed by Meryl Sussman Levavi

P1

To my mother, Ellen Rachel,
and for my daughter, Sylvia Risa

I have always regretted that the historian allowed Vashti to drop out of sight so suddenly . . .

—Elizabeth Cady Stanton, *The Woman's Bible*

I have come to believe over and over again that what is most important to me must be spoken, made verbal and shared, even at the risk of having it bruised or misunderstood.

—Audre Lorde, "The Transformation of Silence into Language and Action"

THE BOOK OF V.

Part One

Exile

BROOKLYN

LILY

Esther for Children and Novices

Close the book now. Close it. Look. The story's simple. Persia, once upon a time. King banishes queen. Queen refuses to come to his party and parade in front of his friends—naked, is what most people think he wanted!—and he sends her away, or has her killed. No one knows. She's gone. Vashti, this is. Her name's Vashti. You know this! And then the king gets sad and wants another wife so he calls for all the maidens to come and win his affections. A maiden? A maiden is a girl. Or a woman. A woman who isn't married. Kind of. Right. And the maidens come and put on lots of makeup and smelly oils. But when it's time for the beauty pageant, the king chooses the maiden who doesn't try too hard, the one with just a dab of lipstick, or whatever they used. Esther. She also happens to be Jewish, though she doesn't mention that. She's very pretty, yes. No, she's not a princess. She's an orphan, with an uncle who looks out for her, but then this uncle also winds up getting her into trouble because he refuses to bow down to the king's minister, and the minister gets mad, really mad, and decides it's time to kill all the Jews. And then things get kind of messy, but the details aren't that important and most of them contradict each other anyway, which is why I'm tired of reading you this book and why we are going to put it away for a while. I know you like it, but I need a break.

Okay, so the new queen winds up being really brave and going to the king without his permission, which is a big no-no—remember what happened to the first queen when she did the opposite? And the new queen asks the king to save her people, and then the king—even though, a few minutes before, he was fine with having all the Jews killed—gets really mad at his minister and has him killed instead. Also, he thinks his minister might like his wife, like Daddy likes Mommy, so that makes him kill him, too.

But I can see this isn't making sense. That's why we're done with the book. It's not simple at all, I don't know why I called it simple, and twice a day for a month is too much—it just is—and we're done. Really all you need to know, and all anyone ever remembers anyway, is that the second queen, Esther, is the hero.

Lily tosses the book out of the girls' bedroom, into the hallway. It's a children's book, the biblical story dumbed down, but still it's convoluted, full of plot holes and inconsistencies. After they're asleep, she'll drop it in the recycling bin, then later, admitting to herself that it won't be recycled, she'll shove it deep into the kitchen trash. Her husband may or may not be home by then. He is deputy director of programs for Rwanda at a major humanitarian aid organization. She is his second wife.

So tomorrow, girls—ushering her daughters into their bunk beds—I'm going to learn to sew, so I can make your costumes for the Purim carnival. Remember? We dress up like the characters and then they act out the story and everyone boos at the bad minister and cheers for Esther? I don't know what happened to

Vashti. The book doesn't say. No one knows. Heads on pillows. If you don't want to be Esther, tell me in the morning. Otherwise, you'll be Esther, like all the other girls. Good night! Sweet dreams! No more words tonight! Love you to the moon and back! Eyes closed, mouths closed, stop talking now! Good night!

WASHINGTON, DC

VEE

Royal Preparations

It happened in the days of Nixon—that Nixon who presided over fifty states, from the Florida Keys to the Aleutian Islands. In those days, in the fifth year of Nixon's reign, when the scandal that would undo him was erupting in Washington and beyond, a great, unspoken license was given to any official who was not he. A veil of distraction fell over the capital's swampy fortress and a lustiness took hold, an appetite for drink and women uncommon even among that time and people. It followed that a banquet of minor scandals, insults, and crimes was enjoyed in the town houses of powerful men. There were floor-to-ceiling drapes of heavy velvet, and there were couches of Italian leather on sheepskin rugs. The wineglasses were nearly invisible, the lowballs weighty as a man's fist. The rule for the drinking was, *Drink!*

Among these men was one, Senator Alexander Kent of Rhode Island, who gave no fewer than five parties in one month, displaying his home, his wife, and his good taste in scotch. To the fifth party, which would be his last for a very long time, Senator

Kent invited not only those colleagues and donors he counted among his friends but also one man who was obscure in the capital but famous in Rhode Island for the suitcase-manufacturing empire his family had built. Kent invited this man to address a quickly spreading rumor he hoped to learn was untrue: that Suitcase Man was planning to endorse Kent's opponent in the following year's election.

And so to the fifth party the senator added a live band, Rhode Island scallops and littleneck clams on the half shell, as well as a conceptual twist: a second, concurrent party upstairs, for the women only. His reasoning, as he told it to his wife, was that such an arrangement would feel at once traditional yet fresh, old yet new, comfortable yet enticing, and would give him a chance to talk plainly to Suitcase Man. His other reasoning he did not tell his wife: it happened that once upon another time, when Kent had still been called by his father's name, O'Kearney, of County Offaly across the ocean, he had known Suitcase Man's wife.

Senator Kent's wife, Vee—born Vivian Barr, daughter of the late Senator Barr of Massachusetts and granddaughter to Governor Fitch of Connecticut, as well as great-granddaughter to a soft-spoken but effective suffragette, all of whom, though dead, would be helping to pay for the party—protested: Weren't separate events antithetical to the spirit of the Equal Rights Amendment, which Rhode Island ratified one year ago and which Senator Kent claims in his official platform to support?

A sound enough question. The senator had responded by giving her a foot massage, a rare offering, and Vee had yielded.

And so in the year 1973, on the second day of November, a day as mild as June, Senator Kent returns from his affairs of state to find the house crawling with caterers and cleaners, bartenders and a flower arranger, and, deeper still, in the kitchen—all the old, noble town houses of Georgetown had their kitchens in the deep, dark backs—his wife, on her hands and knees, working at a spill with a ragged beach towel.

It is *the towel*, striped red and blue and white like a barber pole, faded and frayed yet still festive, the towel he had in his dorm room when they first met and which they kept for sentimental reasons and continue to use for any and all things unclean. The senator loves this towel. He steps on it now, the toe of his shoe grazing his wife's hand. "Excuse us," he says to the caterers rushing around, and they jump quick as sand fleas and are gone.

He locks the swinging door, hook to eye.

"Why hello," he says.

She looks up at him slowly, bangs in her eyes, blouse hanging open to reveal the shadows of her bra.

And though everything about the moment—the towel, the bra, the reluctant, obscured gaze—seems to him a calculation, her end goal being his seduction, in fact Vee moves slowly because she is tired from a day of list checking and directing and emptying the second floor of personal effects for the women's party that she doesn't want to give in the first place; and her bangs are in her eyes because she still needs to shower; and her blouse hangs open because it is not a blouse at all—that is only what he sees—but a stretched-out T-shirt from a Jefferson Airplane concert Vee went to with her girlfriends before she and Kent got serious.

"Get up," he says.

"I'm almost done," she says.

"Then I'll get down."

She smiles, understanding. "Oh no."

"Oh yes."

"It's almost five o'clock."

"I know what time it is."

"Our guests are . . ."

"Not for a while yet."

He drops behind her and starts to unbutton her jeans.

"Alex—"

"Vee . . ."

"Alex." She flips over and wriggles backward. "Stop. I forgot my pill yesterday."

He walks on his knees to her, laughing. "What pill?"

"Sh." She eye-points toward the door.

He grins and stage-whispers: "What pill?"

"*The* Pill."

She expects him to stand, walk out, go cold on her as he does when he's insulted, as her father used to do to her mother and her grandfather to her grandmother. They will finish the conversation tomorrow, after the party has been a success. But Alex is on a roll. He is the youngest senator in the US Congress, if not elected exactly—instead appointed by the governor after Senator Winthrop died—then popular, and deemed likely to win his seat legitimately next year, assuming no twists like Suitcase Man standing against him. Today he aced his first high-profile press conference, at which Ted Kennedy announced he'll cosponsor a bill that Alex introduced, then he left the Hill nearly skipping and walked the four miles home, paying homage to Mr. Lincoln on the way. He is on fire, on pace to rise. He pushes Vee back onto the floor, holds her by the wrists, and presses a knee between her legs. In her ear he breathes: "I thought we were going to make babies."

Feet shuffle outside the door. Vee nods. A twinge of heat splits beneath his knee—a kind of revving she can't control. Words spin uselessly in her gut—*Of course, just maybe not yet*—words she has managed to say only to a doctor, and even then her eyes averted, her face blazing. This was a few months ago, when Alex stopped using condoms. They waited years longer than most of her friends because of his political ambitions, but now, as far as Alex knows, they are no longer waiting. Vee is twenty-eight, thinking of waiting until twenty-nine, maybe thirty, not for any particular reason, nothing she can argue for, even to herself, only a want, to wait, a barking inside: *Wait!*

In her ear: "Weren't we going to make babies? Wipe up their spit with this towel? Maybe you'd sew the ends up a little, make it nice for them, yeah?"

The caterers' shuffling grows louder. In the sweetest, sexiest voice Vee can conjure she says, "Let's reconvene tonight," but already Alex is loosening his belt, then Vee's back hits the floor and he is inside her, and she doesn't fight him, not because within her in some squishy feminine core she is all right with having a baby (she isn't) and not because she knows her fighting him wouldn't matter (spousal rape—if that's even what this is—being legal in those days) but because his not listening to her, his force, turns her on. She will hate herself for this fact as soon as it's over. She will think how ashamed she would be to admit such a thing to the women's group she has been attending once a month. But for now, her pleasure grows, she a caught thing, and now, because at the last meeting of the group a radical thing took place, a lesson in female orgasm, now, once Alex is done, she makes him do what she learned to do herself: she grabs his hand and guides him into place. He looks quizzical. She repositions his fingers. Like this, she thinks at him. Like that. She watches his confusion turn into annoyance but refuses to stop—instead she moves his hand faster and turns her face to the side so she won't have to look at him. In his place, though, filling her vision, is the towel, with its faded stripes and tangle of threads. Goddamnit, I'll sew it! she thinks and closes her eyes. She must concentrate. But girls' voices trill in her head, a thing they used to say at Wellesley, Vee included, feigning courage and pep: *You can't be forced if you don't resist!* Other voices hiss back, the women's-group women: *Tsssk.* Vee shakes her head and returns to Alex's hand, and to the point between her legs, but as her pulse starts to quicken and her thoughts relax, the point is also a sewing needle, its eye glinting in the sew-on-the-go box her grandmother gave her when she turned ten, its point shoved deep inside a pink foam cushion in the box, the box shoved deep inside Vee's stocking drawer, unopened for years. Vee has softened on Alex's hand—she has lost her channel. If she loses, he wins. Again, she shuts her eyes. Alex is giving off an impatient heat but she steals it and drives his hand until at last the heat flares and she is satisfied. Then she pushes him out of the kitchen, wipes up his mess with the towel, and lets the help back in.

SUSA

ESTHER

The Shapely and Beautiful Maiden

The camp is as you imagine—which is not to say that it is as it was. Heat and sand and rock. Bare feet. Brown tents. Sand. What grass grew in the low swells has been ripped up and woven into pallets. A damp, dark track shows the way to and from the river, trampled to a sheen by heels and hooves. They are hundreds, but not a thousand. They drain the red river mud to clay, bake the clay into brick, use the bricks to mark their fire pits. They attempted a wall once but gave up within a day, understanding that if it could save them, it could also be their trap. So their only wall is the one they threw the camp up against when they first arrived: the outermost palace wall, a tree-high, tongue-pink slab of boundary that curves away infinitely—like any circle—in both directions.

In summer, when the sun is so hot a pebble can burst into flame and the far sands send up smoke, they wake and begin to walk. They walk slowly, following the palace wall and its shade. They carry their water and wares and infants, working as they walk, returning, by sundown, to where they began. Each time a crude place is left and returned to it appears a little less crude. In this way the camp begins to settle in their bones, not as home—they are not that naïve—but as a place they will stay for however long they can.

Some hunt, while others grow fruit in groves a day's distance away. A few dozen keep sheep, at a farther distance. Most stay in the camp, making things out of the clay, which they sell at the city market; a select few, like one woman who makes necklaces out of bird and fox and mole bones, sell to the palace. A small group makes magic, but it is crude magic—each time they are banished from a place, their strength is diluted, so that the granddaughter of a woman who could grow a shade tree in a month now takes six times as long. And so on. This generation can make two yolks grow in one egg, they can spin twine out of sand and water, they can summon a goblin from his hole in the river.

The goblin is not a sure bet. Sometimes he spits up true Persian coins and sometimes he spits up counterfeit, and it takes a sharp eye to know which is which. But he answers their summons and allows them to play master and what choice do they have? He is their goblin. They bury the counterfeit in the sand.

They have been here for decades, some say a century. Sometimes they send two boys to climb up the wall and tie a tarp to the jagged fort. The boys throw the tarp down and the people, arms raised, walk backward until the tarp's limit. The tarp is many tarps sewn together. They stake it into the sand with daggers and twine and luxuriate in their pitch of darkness until a palace guard severs the boys' knots and throws down the tarp. Often this occurs within minutes, but occasionally they get a few hours of reprieve. Years ago, when a new king and queen were named and the guards fell over, sick with wine, the people remained in the tarp's shadow a full week.

They are tolerated here. Which is more than they can say about most places.

Then a kid, barely nine, digging a hole to bury one of his baby teeth, finds a few of the goblin's counterfeit coins and, not knowing the difference, sneaks off to the market to surprise his mother with a new spoon. He lost her old one in the river last week. His sister had cleaned it and laid it on the bank. He only wanted to see if it could float. But the river took the spoon faster than he thought possible, faster than the river itself moved, and by the time the boy, waist-deep, scrambled to the bank, the spoon had disappeared around the far bend.

At the market, the boy chooses the wrong stall, owned by a Persian whose family has fallen. The man's bitterness is clear to the boy, it shines in his eyes, but once the boy has spotted the spoon—cypress and the length of his arm from elbow to middle finger, just like his mother's original—he cannot be put off. He is a soft boy, according to his father, and might even choose the bitter stallkeeper with an unthinking urge to make him less bitter. The man takes his coins and hands over the spoon and the boy departs for the camp, triumphant. But within seconds, the man looks down and sees. His muscles twitch to action. He moves to run after the boy, but his wife grabs his arm. She knows he is capable of more. No one—not even her husband—knows the wife's story, but her bitterness is deep enough to make her husband's taste sweet. That boy is from the camp, she says. Swindler of the first degree. You'll let him get away with a beating around the ears?

So it begins. The man gathers other men and they move on the camp like a wind. They kick over pots, stamp out fires, pull up stakes. They do not touch the people. They don't even look at them. They sweep through as if the people are not there at all.

The Hebrews move. They know how to move. After the men have left—they come frequently now, once or twice a week, though never at the same time—they make their camp again, farther along the wall. This is like chasing the shade but different: they do not go far, but their work is hard. They must remake their tents and pallets and pits. They have little time to form their bowls and beads, or pit their dates, or wash their sheep's guts. Some want to go west, or east, but others want to wait—the Persians will lose interest, they argue. They take turns hiding the boy who made the mistake with the coins. A few believe he should be sacrificed, laid out before the Persians, to save the camp. They are ignored. The boy, called Itz, is wrapped in rugs, or buried in sand, or hidden at the river behind rocks and sheets the women pretend to wash again and again.

The boy's father, Marduk, who was already angry at the boy generally, for his softness, is now angrier because the boy is useless to him. Itz is his oldest child—the others are one and two and four and five and six and eight—yet he can no longer be sent to carry water or taken on the journey to work the family's fig trees. And Marduk cannot go as often as he should, because he is needed to help remake the camp. When he does go, he finds fruit rotting on the ground. His anger swells. He can't afford to pay a boy from a neighboring tent to help, and he can't bear to beg for help, and he can't even bring the one person who would help him along to help, not because she can't do the work—she can, far better than a nine-year-old boy—but because he cannot allow himself to be alone with her. She is seventeen. She is Marduk's niece, left in his care when his brother died, and she is the source of Marduk's holiest anger, the frustration that heats his blood until it hurts. Her name is Esther.

Esther will not be beautiful always. In some other time, her tall nose and brown lips and ferning eyebrows that touch between her eyes will not be considered the pinnacle of beauty, but now, in the early summer of 462 BCE—and now is all Marduk has, unable as he is to go back to when his brother was alive or forward to when the girl will be old enough to marry respectably among the Jews, let alone far enough back or forward to reach an entirely different pinprick of civilization—now her face contains nobility (a lank, tall angle to the nose and jaw) and sex (a pink shimmer to the eyelids, glimpsed at each blink) and mystery (even Marduk, who knows perfectly well the tribes from which she descends, looks at her and wonders, What *is* she?).

And only seventeen. And a late bloomer, which is why it's taken so long for her to smoke up Marduk's tent, swell his brain and nether parts, obscure his wife, who is or at least was beautiful, too. Only Marduk's children are innocent to Esther's menace: to them she is a second mother, more patient and less tired than their own.

Marduk thinks of selling her into slavery. He thinks of killing her. He loves his niece, he hates her. He loved his brother, he hated his brother. Harun. Favorite from the age of three, barely up to Marduk's waist and already sitting with their father in shul. This was when they lived in the city still, within four walls. While Marduk rolled marbles, Harun taught himself to read; by four he spoke three languages; by five he recited Torah, though he couldn't look you in the eye. Later he was celebrated in Bashan for opposing the old synagogue's opulent renovations and starting his own services in a former stable. He stayed a dreamer even after his wife died; he was carrying an armload of books during the Four Day Raid when he turned down the wrong street. Marduk cannot kill his brother's daughter, and he cannot sell her into slavery. He can't even climb on top of her, though he knows most other men would. He is a good man, Marduk. This is what his wife says to his children when they run from his flexed palm. And he is. How could a man who was not good grow such sweet, perfectly formed fruit?

"Let me come," Esther says to Marduk, balancing the baby on her right hip as she chops figs. Esther's left-handedness is her one ugliness, but even that Marduk wants to eat.

"I can help pick," she says, and it's clear that she offers freely. Her black eyes are flecked yellow, like a night sky. He would swim into them, if he could. He would hide there, safe from her body.

One day, the answers to Marduk's many problems seem to come all at once, in the form of a command sent out from the palace: A pageant! Bring the most beautiful virgins from across the kingdom! The king will choose one for a new queen!

What happened to the old queen—who was herself newish—Vashti? No one knows—certainly no one in the camp. The command is not meant for them. But they are not deaf. *We are not deaf!* Marduk shouts silently. His ire fists, then coalesces into a thought. It's like a ball of mud suddenly turning to clear water.

Esther will be the queen of Persia.

Ha!

He knows it's impossible. She is a Jew; she is a no one. She'd go up against girls from as far away as Greece. If he spoke the idea outside his tent, the people would howl.

And yet. Maybe it doesn't matter that she doesn't have a chance. Maybe the idea is smaller, and more practical: Marduk sends her with his figs—his most succulent, sweet enough to make a man moan—and the king, though he cannot choose her, chooses Marduk as his new fig vendor. He cancels his existing contract and takes on Marduk and then, at the right moment, Marduk tells the king about his son. (For the purposes of optimism, Marduk ignores the question of whether the king's fig man would have access to the king's ear.) He is honest. He confesses to his son's mistake with the coin. Then he tells about the marauders. The king, understanding—or at least fig-loving—orders them to stop. Itz will be a boy again. In a year, Marduk will have made enough from his figs to marry Esther off to Nadav, the boy she says she loves.

With fewer words, he consults his wife. Complaints he has only grumbled about he lays out with force. Esther costs the family too much. The girl's ideas of herself are outsized. What orphan decides to want a boy from a family so wealthy, albeit in the past, that they demand a true dowry even in a camp, so full of their own worth the mother calls herself a *créative* and then—the gumption—manages to sell to the palace what she creates? (Nadav's mother is the one who makes the bone necklaces. She already has what Marduk wants.) The family has given Marduk and Chura one year to come up with the dowry—after that, they say, it will be another girl's turn. There is another girl already picked out, they say. It's a betrothal, as far as they're concerned.

All this his wife must see. But she has been a mother to Esther. When he tells her about the pageant, she eyes him with disgust.

"No," she says. "We made a promise."

He nods, a little disappointed but mostly relieved; she has done it for him, taken away the choice.

But she finds him the next day. His arms are raised to the sky. He is stretching after a session of pit building with a neighbor and watching, while pretending not to watch, his niece, in the distance, rolling the children in a barrel. Esther's cloth slips as she bends; her back is narrow and dark; the children's squeals lift the camp into momentary peace. He doesn't notice his wife approaching until she takes his beard in her hand and pulls him to look at her: purple under her eyes, the line that's grown between them since Itz went into hiding. Her hands are nearly black from pitting and chopping figs. The ones they collect now take twice the work, to cut away the bruises and the rot.

"She's a good girl," she says, in the dry voice she uses when she has arrived at a decision. "She'll be treated well."

"Is that right?" Marduk swallows back bile.

"She won't become queen, but she'll be taken care of."

Marduk waits, to be sure she's sure.

"It's good," she says.

He perseverates for a week. His wife is talking about the night station, he knows, though she will not name it. Neither will he. The night station is the place the king's concubines are said to occupy. The station is rumored by his friend Jebi to be a sordid place, a labyrinth of flaking tunnels where girls are rarely virgins by the time they meet the king. Esther may be raped if she is unwilling, or beaten even if she is. Marduk suppresses thoughts of the moods of a man who has lost his queen. He tells himself that the station may in fact be what most people in the camp assume it to be, a largely restful place of boredom and guitars, grapes and fans. Maybe, too, his wife is wrong—maybe there will be no station for Esther, but some better fate. Or maybe she will simply be returned, and Marduk will be the king's fig man, and all will proceed as he has planned.

He sees his niece braiding the loaf of challah. This week's bread is eggless—the camp's chickens are hungry—and will be low, and hard, but Esther braids as if it will be perfect, her mouth open in concentration, her tongue tensed against her bottom lip, the muscles in her upper arms dancing.

He cannot send her away.

He sees his niece looking at Nadav. A fire rises in Marduk's throat, a desire to rip them apart and smash their heads against the wall.

He has to send her away.

She resists. She won't go. She'll work for her keep—why won't he let her work for her keep? Her uncle has lost his mind. What could a poor Jewish orphan possibly be to the king of Persia? He won't pick her, and then what? So maybe he likes Marduk's figs. He might sell Esther, or kill her. Her uncle laughs and says, Unlikely. What, then? Esther asks. What? But he won't answer, and her aunt doesn't meet her eyes. Please, she says, gesturing toward the tent's open flaps, as if bickering in the camp is ever done in private. Itz lies meekly in one corner. He was down by the river earlier, hiding in the women's washing, but then the Persians marched through, overturning buckets and barrels, and Itz was rolled home beneath a pile of bedclothes. His skin, which used to be brown, gives off a green pallor. Esther unties the flaps—made of bright, beautiful fabric her aunt's mother's mother wove—and lets them fall. The tent goes dark. "The night station," she says, as it strikes her.

No one speaks.

She can't believe at first what she's hearing. She wants to shout, to tell them that her father was teaching her to read when he died, that her mother, when Esther was very small, tried to teach her a little magic. Her parents imagined that she would be like them—learned but modest, unconcerned with status or wealth. Better, in other words, than most people. But that will sound like boasting—it will only make her uncle happier to send her away. He doesn't like her. How has she not realized this before? She feels ashamed, for herself and for her parents. She says, more quietly now, "This isn't what they wanted."

Still, no one answers.

Esther stamps her foot and her uncle slaps her.

A little while later, Esther and her aunt sit by the river as her aunt, humming, holds a wet rag to her niece's cheek. It's swollen already—Esther can feel the extra weight of fluid building under her skin. She scans the camp for Nadav. The sun has started to fall. Miles away, at the horizon, a red shimmer stands up off the sand. The last women doing washing today pack up their bundles and heft them back toward the camp. Her aunt stops humming to say, "I wish it were different."

"Then make it different," Esther says.

Her aunt resumes humming. She dips the rag again and wrings it, but this time, without warning, she pulls Esther's head into her lap. Her hands are at once gentle, which is like her, and also firm, which is less like her, and Esther regrets her rudeness. Her aunt has been nothing but kind to her. She made space on her pallet for her, fed her, taught her to cook. When Esther began to bleed, a few months after she arrived, her aunt showed her what to do. She was simple but, unlike Marduk, she did not seem to resent that Esther was not. Esther understands this about her uncle now. Thinking of it heightens her shame. Water drips from her aunt's rag into her mouth, and she swallows it helplessly, thinking of other people she may have misread. Maybe the other girls her age whisper behind her back: an orphan, unwanted. Maybe when Nadav kisses her he is mocking her, and she is too lustful to realize. Maybe he mocks her *for* her wanting, for the fact that she kisses him back without any official betrothal—maybe, when she tells him what her uncle is making her do, he won't be surprised. Maybe the pride her parents instilled in her has made her blind.

Esther seizes when her aunt begins to stroke her forehead. It doesn't seem right to allow herself this when tomorrow she will have to go. But her aunt's fingers feel good, almost embarrassingly good, and she lets herself stay for a moment, curled on her side on the bank, and then, because she is so tired, she stays for another moment, and then another. Soon, she is sinking. She is swimming in a river, not this river but the river of her childhood, in the city; she is underwater but breathing, as easily as a fish, and seeing, through the sunlight that falls into the water, a pair of feet, illuminated, her father's perhaps, or her mother's. She is swimming fast for them when her aunt's voice cuts in, silky and, for the first time, false. "Don't worry. You are beautiful. Anything is possible."

Of course, this is not true. Earth cannot turn into water. The sun cannot be caught. (Not yet.) Dust cannot be banished from the desert, only blown and swept into a different order.

She doesn't sleep. Tomorrow, her uncle told her, he'll take her to the palace gate. She should be ready, he said, in her aunt's best cloth. She should comb her hair. He didn't look at her. Then he looked. A feeling of some kind washed through his eyes: doubt, or maybe fear. Then he walked away, calling back, Comb your hair!

Esther twists on her pallet. She pulls her sheet down, then up. On either side of her, the girls breathe. Across the tent, the boys lie like cats, curled around each other, except for Itz. Itz is still lying in the corner by the flaps. Esther watches the long, still rope of him. Itz has always been her favorite. He reminds her of her father, his way of wandering, occupied by some idea, how little he cared what others did or thought. She has assumed a quiet greatness in Itz, something that will reveal itself as he grows older. Above him, on a clothesline, is her aunt's muslin cloth, and draped next to that a linen belt. In Esther's hand—gifted to her before bed—her aunt's good comb, cut from a turtle's shell. *Please*, her aunt said. And then her uncle was back, crowding without touching, his very breath like a rope. *Hadassah*, he said, using her Hebrew name. *You don't have to say what people you're from.*

She snorted. Any duty she'd owed him she did not owe anymore. *What will I say?*

They may not ask. If they don't ask, don't tell.

Esther closes her eyes. She rocks her head against her pallet. As a little girl she did this to help herself fall asleep and her mother would scold her, warning of tangles, but now she does it for the tangles, to snarl her hair so irretrievably that it won't be salvageable with the comb.

She reaches back to check the damage and decides it's not enough. On tiptoe, she finds the basket where her aunt keeps her tools: her knives, her thread and needle, her saw, her scissors. Esther holds a fistful of hair away from her head, spreads the scissors slowly to prevent the blades' high-pitched rasp, and cuts. She cuts until her feet are buried in hair and the hair left on her head is jagged and short. She touches her bare ears, her neck. Then she decides, again: it's not enough.

She stays as close to the tents as possible, sliding her feet where the sand is loose enough to allow it. The night's fullest dark is already fraying, pale threads splitting the sky's edges. She hears a shifting, then a light clang, and drops to the ground. It's the night-duty guards, her own people, but not wholly, of course. They're men. Every one of them would drag her by the ear back to her tent. Or maybe worse—how can she know, given how little she has turned out to know?—maybe they would drag her somewhere else, push hands up her nightshirt, take advantage of her need to stay quiet. She changes direction, swallowing back tears. They've blocked the path she planned to take, past Nadav's tent. She went to see him before the sun went down, but before she could call his name his mother appeared at the flap; *he's not here, out of camp, a neighbor's sheep*, and so on. Esther didn't believe her. She doesn't believe her now. But she can't risk being caught, and she doesn't believe she could wake Nadav without waking his mother, and another part of her, the vain part, doesn't want him to see her with her hair like this. She crawls to the palace wall and, staying close beside it, begins to make her slow way forward until the camp begins to thin. Here, at its far northern boundary—the boundary this week, anyway—is a small subcamp, only five tents large, where the magicians hold their own society. Even in the city, with everyone crushed up together, the magicians stayed apart, in their own dead-end side street. Her mother said it was to protect their powers, to keep their children among their children so when they were old enough to mate, they chose their own kind. Esther's mother knew because her own mother had been one of them before she defied her family and married out, and then Esther's mother had defied her own mother, who by the time she was a mother saw that magic might do more for a girl than love, and married Esther's father, and by the time Esther came along, her magic was likely a trickle, at best. Esther remembers holding her breath when her mother spoke of this, feeling as though she was being told that she might have a tail, or a secret name, or a fate none of them could imagine. She absorbed all the details—the names of the purest, most formidable families, the Tolous and Ibrahims; the mix of respect and bemusement in her mother's voice—yet in her alarm forgot the actual lessons her mother gave her. She retains only an image of a knot being tied without her mother having moved her fingers. But what help is that? She feels angry now, regarding the magicians' tents, thinking of how calmly her mother accepted her loss of power, and her work as a seamstress, how unworried she seemed to be about Esther's future. Her mother would cup the back of Esther's head in her hand, look at a pile of garments waiting to be hemmed, and say, Go on then. As if Esther's returning were a given, as if her mother's being there, when Esther did return, were guaranteed. Even before her mother got sick Esther had a sense of foreboding. She was the only only child she knew—maybe that was part of it. She would grab her mother's hand sometimes, forcing her mother to dislodge her. She would dig her nails into her mother's skin. She feels a nausea thinking of it now: her mother's large hands unknotting her small ones. Her mother's hands were larger than Esther's father's hands, a fact her parents joked about, over Esther's head. As the sky lightens over the circle of tents, she wishes that she had at least inherited those hands, if not the magic. Her own are petite and stubbornly soft—no matter how hard she works, they don't callus. Nadav has commented on their softness. He has called them beautiful. Twice, he has taken one of her fingers and bitten down on it. This shocked and pleased her. But thinking of it now, she is afraid for what it revealed: a certain force she exerts, whether she intends it or not. Her hands are beautiful and won't help her.

She crawls on them toward the largest tent, which is known to belong to some Gadols—the most legendary of all the magician families. She lifts the flap and crawls in.

The next morning, she joins hundreds of other girls in the courtyard outside the palace gates. Marduk is next to her but not hovering or blustering—he is shrunken, hands clasped behind his back, hunched like an old man. This morning, when the tent woke, the children—all except for Itz, who knew where she was going—laughed at her hair. Her aunt gasped and began to snip, trying to somehow salvage what was left, while Marduk turned a raging garnet. An hour later, as they walked out of camp in what Esther had assumed would be a quiet departure, for Marduk had not even allowed her to go to Nadav to tell him she was leaving, her uncle turned toward the tents and, as if possessed, began to shout: *I am bringing Esther to the king! He will put a stop to our suffering!* Esther watched in horror as families poured out of their tents to hear Marduk's boast. How had saving his fig business turned into saving his people? She banishes him to her peripheral vision now. Most of the other girls have come alone. The sun rises quickly as they wait an hour, then two. A third hour passes without movement from the guards on the other side of the gates. A few girls faint. It is hotter than the day before, hotter than any day in recent memory. Or maybe it only feels that way because of the crowding? No one knows. They are girls. Everyone is afraid to complain too loudly so instead they whisper, and shift, making in sum a thundering hiss. Esther sets down her basket of figs. She stretches her fingers, rubs at the lines the handles have dug into her palm, ignores Marduk beside her. She touches her linen belt and the pocket her aunt has sewn to it, a small purse containing the comb and a pot of pomegranate paste. Esther intends to drop the paste—meant to color her lips—as soon as the gates are opened. She will toss it to the trampling feet, pick up her basket with purposeful clumsiness, letting figs spill in all directions, and begin to walk without so much as a glance at Marduk. She will resist in every way possible.

Then the gate opens. It's a shock, though they've waited for hours—when it actually happens, there's a collective gasp. The crowd surges, and Esther, pulled and pushed by the current, finds that she doesn't have space to reach for her paste and discard it. And she cannot spill the figs—the basket is pinned to her leg by the tightness of the pack. She turns her head, but Marduk is already lost, far behind her now, and as she's carried forward with the roar of the girls' feet on the royal stones, she hears, or rather feels, a strange rattle in her throat. She is humming. It's her aunt's habit, taking abrupt root in her. There is no melody. It's the vibration she's after, the echo of herself that steadies her as she walks.

BROOKLYN

LILY

The Second Wife

She hums to ward off panic, time running out to pick up one child from school while the other, smaller one throws her boots against the apartment wall. No boots, no boots! They are such nice boots, not hand-me-downs like the rest but a gift from Lily's middle brother, brand-new fuzz-lined boots in a pine-green suede. Lily would like to have such boots. She almost says this—*If I had those boots I wouldn't throw them against the wall!*—but she knows it won't help, and it's mean, too, the kind of lording over that Lily's grandmother did incessantly, according to Lily's mother, Ruth, which is why, she says, Lily herself was rarely scolded as a child. Reparations, her mother jokes, though her leniency has eroded: now that Lily is grown, Ruth scolds her all the time, albeit passive-aggressively, for Lily has not become the type of woman she was supposed to become.

"I hope it fulfills you, taking care of the children all the time."

"What a variety of sponges you have!"

"You were so driven when you were younger. But maybe you're happier now. Are you happier now?"

Lily hums to ward off her mother's voice, though it's Ruth's favorite lullaby she's humming, *Oh the fox went out on a chilly night* . . . She squats behind her daughter, pins her under the arms, and attempts to work the boots back onto her feet, thinking of Rosie being herded into the cafeteria with the snotty, sorrowful clump of abandoned first-graders.

This child, June, whose preschool "day" ended hours ago, at 11:30 a.m., kicks and kicks. June, that warm and pliant month! Lily begins to sweat. Her coat is already on, her hat, her scarf. *Oh the fox* . . . June's boot flies off again and Lily makes the mistake of going for it, which gives her daughter the chance to squirm away and run down the hallway toward the bathroom, where she will, in her newest favorite rite, rip off her shirt and throw it in the toilet. *And he prayed to the moon* . . . Lily sheds her coat and runs after her, telling herself to take a breath, get a little perspective, no one will die here—at least not today. This isn't war, or revolution. Right? If Ro sits in the sorrowful circle, so what? She'll look at Lily with that look, the one that seems to see into her. But so what? So she waits a few minutes, so the world is not going to end, so lots of kids have it far worse, so she'll learn resilience, and resilience is the latest . . . *and the moon* . . . As she rounds the corner into the bathroom, Lily reminds herself to smile. She doesn't want to scare June. If she scares her, they will never make it out. Lily hangs her face in a grin. But June isn't looking at her, she is deep inside her shirt, wrestling to get it off, and Lily makes the mistake of glancing in the mirror, where she sees that her grin is terrifying. She drops it, yanks off her slouchy wool hat with the hideous pink "ponpon" she let Ro talk her into, and stares at what she understands to be her face but which appears, under the stuttering, chemical fluorescence of their rental apartment's bathroom light, to be that of an old, gray witch. *Because, because, because, because, because! Because of the wonderful things . . .* The tune changes as Lily enters a kind of derailment in which time goes one way and she goes another, into her small makeup box—small so as to deemphasize its importance to the girls, though there is more makeup, much more, hidden in Lily's underwear drawer. She begins to dab and swipe at herself, thinking of the other mothers, the women who will be at the party this afternoon, a party for Lily, to teach her to sew. Lily doesn't know any of the women well. She didn't intend for them to throw a sewing party in her honor. But the hostess, a woman named Kyla, overheard Lily talking to another mother at preschool pickup about how she wished she could make Esther costumes for Rosie and June for Purim this year, *if only she knew how to sew*. This was true, in a sense. Lily did wish that she could sew. But she wished it as she wished for sleek hair or a triplex apartment: certain it would never happen and not really caring. Sure, she had a vision of herself, by herself, at a table in front of an open window, sewing. But didn't every woman? It was a fantasy she might once have tried to parse, in a paper, theorizing about its origins in popular and literary culture and arriving at an idea, or a way of articulating an idea, that was semi-original. There would be a lengthy bibliography, the production of which would give Lily a deep, almost rabid kind of pleasure.

But to actually sew?

She should never have spoken the wish aloud. It was an empty frill of after-school chatter. Lily knows that she will struggle at sewing, just as she struggles at disconnecting tiny Lego pieces. But before she could take it back, Kyla had invited her and the other mother and some other women, too. *Why not make it a party?* she'd said. *I'll have wine, and snacks*, and she will, Lily knows, because Kyla is always wearing boots with heels, even at the playground, and she sent real, paper invites to the thing: *A Sewing Fête!*

What does one wear to a Sewing Fête? Not baggy underwear, certainly. Not sweat.

Lily, smearing concealer under her eyes, spots a new gray hair in her left eyebrow, tweezes it, and feels instant remorse, not only for the hole she has made but for the pain. It's enough to make her eyes smart with tears and to make June, whose shirt is off now but still in her hand, think that her mother is crying. She wipes her face with her shirt, as if demonstrating, then offers it to Lily, and Lily, who has again forgotten to stock the bathroom with tissues, accepts and wipes her eyes, remembering too late the concealer she just applied.

"Momma?"

But time! After a five-minute grace period, the school asks for a "donation" of a dollar a minute to cover care. It's not required—the school is public, after all—but suggested, and the understanding is that you pay if you can, and Lily can in the sense that doing so will not make her homeless, and her daughter has the boots to prove it. So if she's twenty minutes late? Fifteen dollars. Fifteen dollars is a cocktail shaken by a man in a vest, or take-out pad thai plus a couple spring rolls, or overnight diapers for a month, or one-sixth, almost, of a haircut in Park Slope, which is where Lily lives, of course. It is a lot and not very much, though if you fail regularly in this way it becomes, undeniably, a lot. Besides, there is simply no good reason for Lily to be late. She begins to hum again, thinking of Adam in his office, his youthful messenger bag leaning against his aging calf, talking and typing and directing and greenlighting hygiene drops for families that don't have toilets, let alone lights capable of sputtering, and everything else he does to keep money climbing into their bank account and set himself up to be promoted, not to mention help people. Adam and Lily are trying to save to buy an apartment so they can stop paying through the nose for rent, but they're paying through the nose for rent so it's impossible to save—an old story—and then there are things like late pickup, or the occasional parking ticket, also Lily's fault as she's in charge of moving the car from place to place to outrun the street cleaners, that eat up their nonexistent "cushion."

Lily and Adam have discussed her going back to work. But their conversations always circle back to the same grim reality: adjunct teaching—and adjunct is all she'll get within a hundred miles of New York City—barely pays enough to cover childcare. They know because Lily did have a gig for a while after Rosie was born, at a college up in Westchester, and there was one day alone, when a snowstorm turned her usual ninety-minute return drive into a five-hour highway crawl, that ate up one-tenth of her semester's salary in babysitting costs *and* gave her mastitis. Then, when she was seven months pregnant with June, she finally got a campus interview for the kind of tenure-track job she'd once assumed she wanted, at her alma mater, Grinnell College, a job that paid nearly as much as Adam was making then, but in Iowa, which meant it paid the equivalent of three times as much. But the instant she finished the last of her two days of lectures and talks and interviews and lunches, knowing that she had aced every one, knowing that even in the grotesquerie of her "workplace" maternity outfits—the least offensive ones she could find still involved ruffles and Easter hues—she came across as intelligent, committed, and not insane, Lily knew she was done with academia. When she was offered the job, she took twenty-four hours to make sure, then turned it down before telling Adam, who flushed and said, *Really? Wow. Congratulations. Really?* He was happy, because he wanted to stay in New York, but he was visibly frightened, because he wanted her to be happy. *Are you sure?* he asked for days. *Are you sure you won't regret it?*

To her mother Lily lied. She told her the job had gone to someone else. To which Ruth said, *It's because you're pregnant! You should sue.* To which Lily replied, to end things, *I just might.*

"Momma, your cock?"

Lily's watch—her "clock"—is beeping. It's her first digital watch since 1984, a gift from the kids, i.e., Adam, who insisted that Ro and June picked it out but also took it upon himself to walk Lily through the device's many alarm functions.

How long has it been beeping?

And if it hasn't been beeping for a long time now, why not? Shouldn't it have been beeping half an hour ago? She must have set it wrong, which means she's lost her ability to perform basic math. Or maybe she didn't mean to set it at all, and the fact that it's beeping now, at the moment when she should be arriving at school, is merely a coincidence. Ha.

"Momma?"

Lily presses buttons, and the watch stops beeping. She wonders, not for the first time, if there is something wrong with her that she can't deal with what is in fact a completely manageable situation of her own choosing. She is not captive. Sure, if she had some extra cash or could give up those cocktails she might sign up for a fiction or playwriting workshop, try her hand at actually writing one of the stories that rumble around in her head. But she has two healthy children, an apartment free of leaks and mold, a park nearby, no hunger, no rickets, no physical abuse. An excess of education. She can buy what she needs and vote and get an abortion (for now, in this part of the country) and is married to a man who likes to say it makes him happy to see her happy. Every day, it becomes clearer that most men are pure dick; they're selling ten-year-old girls and stealing and raping even younger girls and drugging women and reaching their hands up women's skirts and tugging on choir boys and forcing people to look at their stuff, which makes Adam, in comparison, a very good man. If, for instance, Lily and June wind up thirty minutes late to pick up Ro today, and owe twenty-five dollars, and Lily were to tell Adam, Adam would tell her to get her shit together, but then, because he does not want to be a man who says things like that to his wife, he would kiss her and insist he's happy, because she's happy. This was the plan, he likes to say. Enjoy this time. Enjoy the girls. *Enjoy me.*

This last bit he never speaks aloud, but the sentiment oozes from him, his longing for Lily to be not only present but satisfied. His first wife, Vira, was neither. She worked for a different, scrappier aid group and was always running off to war-torn places. She wanted to keep doing this, it turned out. She didn't want children. She didn't want, he says in summary, or used to say, when he spoke openly of Vira: *She didn't want to be a wife.*

When June grabs her shirt back and drops it in the toilet, one part of Lily's brain ponders appropriate reactions. Time out? But they are late! A slap in the face? But that's not allowed . . . Yet the rest of her is motionless, staring at her reflection. Her makeup effort has halted, her hum has fallen off. Her thoughts have wandered from the party and the other mothers to Vira, whom she has never met, Vira with her flawless brown skin and flat stomach and lustrous black hair. No matter that somewhere, Vira is aging, or that she may have changed her mind and had three children by now. For Lily and Adam, Vira will always be as she was when she left (Adam's version) or he threw her out (hers): thirty-one and childless. Her skin will forever bounce back when poked; her female parts will be fresh and tucked in. Lily hates the jealousy she feels, thinking of Vira—she is jealous of her eternal youth but also of what looks from here like freedom, and clarity. Why is she still hanging around? When Lily and Adam fell in love, they talked about Vira all the time, and it seemed a bold, smart tactic, a way of declaring that they weren't afraid. Or Adam talked, and Lily believed, about how over time Vira grew angry about almost everything Adam did: the new job he took, which she considered to be "establishment"; the J. Crew catalog he dug out of the recycling bin to which she'd exiled it in protest of its knock-kneed, starving models; the praise he heaped on her very occasional bouts of cooking, traditional Gujarati recipes she'd learned from her mother that he just actually, genuinely loved! She accused him of passive aggression and said he was trying to get her to cook more. In the end, Adam told Lily, when fighting was their main activity, Vira said she'd probably married him to piss off her parents, who'd had an idea about her marrying a fourth cousin from Ahmedabad. Which was when Adam told her to go, though he had not meant go as in forever but *go, get some fresh air*. But that was that. She was gone. Adam and Lily used to joke about how Vira was like Lilith, that other angry first wife, which was funny, both because Lily's name was so close to Lilith and because Adam's name was Adam, and fun because it made Lily into Eve, which they both found sexy. Then they got married and immediately started trying to conceive, because Lily was not young, but they were lucky and within a year Rosie came along, and soon Lily no longer seemed like an antidote to Vira's mercurial moods. Also, she was even less young than before, she was forty-two, so they tried again and got lucky again and June came, and as the years passed and dwarfed Adam's three-year marriage to Vira, her name didn't make them laugh but caused them to feel exposed. They are no longer a beginning. They don't talk about her anymore. But sometimes, without warning, she swings down and hangs in Lily's vision, pries at her fears, throws a cruel light. Is Lily too pasty, too frizzy, too compromising, too bougie? Vira's questions, perhaps, are not so different from Ruth's. As Lily reaches into the toilet now and squeezes June's shirt to avoid drippage, and elbows the shower curtain out of the way to avoid contamination, and tosses the shirt into the tub, she sees for the first time that her hands have grown sunspots. She scrubs at them. She is still scrubbing when June runs out and down the hall and Lily hears her call, "Momma, just one time?"

Lily grabs her hat and follows and finds June standing on the couch, holding *The Book of Esther* above her head like a trophy. Lily snatches the book away. Her attempt the previous night to throw it out was thwarted by the building's porter, who, having found it in the trash, knocked on their door this morning, cheerful in his blue jumpsuit: *One of your girls make a mistake!* Lily wanted to scream. She hates the book, and not only because her mother gave it to the girls in her pushy, be-more-Jewish way—though she wasn't even born a Jew herself; it was Lily's father, long dead now, who'd been the Jew—or because the girls quickly grew obsessed with it. She hates the book because after going through three stages with it herself—she was entertained briefly, then bored, then bewildered—she has entered a fourth stage in which she recognizes that the embattled queen Esther, like Lily, is a second wife.

Lily drops the book into the dark crevasse behind the couch cushions. Tomorrow afternoon, but not before then, she will dig it out and leave her mother to read it to the girls. Every Thursday, Ruth comes over so Lily can have a little time to herself, though what Lily does with this time she cannot exactly say. Mostly she walks, sometimes through the park, sometimes through stores, touching things, feeling fizzy and weirdly burdened until the time has passed. Tomorrow, maybe, she will do something more productive: purchase supplies for the girls' dresses, practice the stitches she will be taught tonight.

Ignoring June's squeals, Lily throws her into the stroller and, with a knee between her legs, manages to strap her in, buckle the tiny, injurious buckles, and maneuver her out the door. June is shirtless and bootless but they make it, somehow, into the elevator, which causes Lily to remember that she was doing laundry in the basement earlier and that her wet sheets are still waiting in washing machines number one and number three—what will the super do with them this time?—but time is chugging along and look, she managed to grab a fresh shirt for June as well as the boots and also her own coat and hat and by the time the door opens into the lobby they are, a miracle, ready. June smiles sweetly, and Lily pushes them out into the yellowing winter sunlight, and they join the river of other women and strollers and children on Eighth Avenue, heading to this school or that, or home from school, or to laundromats or piano lessons or nitpickers or playdates. There are no men to be seen. It is 2016, four days into a new year. Lily breathes. The cold air wicks her sweat. The sky is blue, the bare trees make it appear bluer, the skin beneath her eyes appears smooth and bright. She will pick up her other child. She will go to the party. She will learn to sew.

WASHINGTON, DC

VEE

Ablutions

For obvious reasons, Vee chooses a bath over a shower. She is not naïve enough to believe that she can save herself with a good scrub, but it's impossible not to try. And who knows? Her mother believed women could only get pregnant during the full moon, because this was the circumstance in which her own child was conceived and she was a particular kind of lucky person—drinker of gimlets up and down the New England coast, sailor, wearer of pearls—who assumed, despite all evidence to the contrary, the steady bestowal of her luck upon the world. Other people believe other things, about positions or douching or poison. No one seems to understand with any certainty how any of it works.

She runs the water scaldingly hot, pours in enough bubbles to give an elephant a UTI, opens her legs, and flutters her hands, trying to pull the soapy water into her pussy. Vagina, she corrects herself. This is what the women's-group women insist on calling it. Vagina, she thinks dutifully, though the word disgusts her.

She closes her eyes and envisions the water flooding her interior, reaching every crevice and crack, washing out any trace of Alex.

"What are you doing?"

The door makes a solid thwack as it flies open and hits the sink.

"Vee! Look at me."

She doesn't move. "I'm bathing," she says in a delicious monotone. "You're making the room cold."

"The party starts in less than an hour."

"I realize."

"Well?"

"I'd be further along if you hadn't attacked me."

"Oh come on. You loved it. Are you getting out, or what?"

"I don't know." Vee sinks lower, up to her ears. Maybe she did love it, in the end. Still, she does not want a baby.

"No! Don't get your hair wet! It takes you an hour just to do your hair!"

"Then I won't do it," Vee says. "Why should I, for a bunch of women?" She widens her eyes for emphasis, thinking of the women's-group women with their unblown hair. Only a few wear makeup, several go without bras, and the older ones, in their late thirties, are letting themselves go gray. They are meeting tonight, a meeting Vee will miss. But why shouldn't she bring a little of the women's-group vibe to her own party? If, as they claim, the beauty standards that enslave women are set by men, why shouldn't Vee's party of women, left on their own, wear blue jeans, or housedresses, and allow their hair to do what it will?

"Vee—"

But she is gone, fully sunk. Alex's voice beyond the water sounds like a distant foghorn, and Vee, holding her breath, thinks of her childhood friend Rosemary, who lives year-round now in an old, comfortable house on the water and who might be feeding her children dinner at this moment, or drawing their bath. Vee, her lungs aching, is startled by the longing she feels for her friend. She pops out of the water and sees Alex's hands gripping the side of the tub. He is leaning over her now, saying something about how the president of the suitcase-manufacturing company is known for being unfashionably on time to parties, how it's a Rhode Island thing, and what would she, from distant Massachusetts, know about that?

She giggles, but he doesn't join her. In another moment, in the time before he was a senator, Alex might have laughed at his own nonsense. Instead, his voice keeps pouring onto her, along with a faint, sour scent, and as she gives in and looks up, she knows what she will find, beyond the freshly shaven jaw and the Roman nose and rich brown eyes: he's afraid.

He sees her see it and walks out. Then he returns a moment later, flinging the door into the sink again. She would like to mention this, the door-sink situation, because she finds it funny that after a $4,500 renovation the bathroom door slams into the sink, and she would like him to find it funny, too. The money came from her family, after all, just as her family's money had paid for them to buy a place on Dumbarton, three short but significant blocks east of Wisconsin. But Alex does not like to talk about this, she knows, and he is pacing the length of the tub. "You have to get out now," he says. "I'm not leaving until you get out," and Vee thinks, the poor boy, the frightened king, with his nervous, bad breath. Perhaps she has been unfair to him. She rises from the water, and lets him stare, and wonders at how easy it is, to give him what he wants. Why does she make it hard, then? Why resist and demand? Why make him touch her as she did, when he so clearly disliked it? Why keep going to the women's group? She'd been cajoled the first time, by a fellow Wellesley alum, but no one pressured her to go back. Why not be more like Rosemary, who didn't hem and haw over whether to have children; who no longer indulges herself with late-afternoon baths, let alone uses them to purge and hide from her husband; who is soft and glad in her warm house? Or like Vee's mother, who until she died kept clipping her favorite columns from *Redbook* and *Ladies' Home Journal* with titles like "Five Ironing Secrets You'll Wish Your Mother Taught You" and "How to Please Your Husband." That was the title, on numerous occasions. Vee chose Alex for reasons that are still apparent to her. He was smart, ambitious, a dignified drinker, a great kisser. He could give her what she'd always known, forever. He was like home. She liked home. Why not be like Rosemary, or her mother, and be content?

Could it be so easy? As if in answer, Alex salivates audibly. For a moment, just by standing here, she has relieved his fear. It should make her glad, or proud. It does, in part. His hormonal response dominates him, and she dominates his hormonal response. But in another part, a drawer deep inside, Vee vibrates with anger, and something harsher: she hates that her power has nothing, really, to do with her; hates that it's a passive, humiliating power; hates that she uses it anyway.

Coldly, she says, "Hand me a towel."

Alex's spell is broken. He obeys, then goes to check on the party, leaving Vee staring at herself in the mirror. She drops the towel and looks at her white breasts, her flat stomach, her thick whorls of pubic hair. The hair is dark now but will fluff out a reddish blond when dry, the same as the hair on her head. Her waist is a little thick, her hips a little narrow, the overall shape a little straight, boyish. The longer she looks the plainer she appears—a body, made of the requisite parts, each with its own function. She sees one hip bone, and another; two fleshy knee joints; two feet with their ten toes. From the knuckle of each toe, she sees, grow a few wisps of hair, like grass from a hillock. The wisps of toe hair match her pubic hair, which matches her head hair and her armpit hair, and all of that probably matches her nose and ear hair, though she has never bothered to investigate.

Vee tilts her head back to see if she can see inside her own nostrils. This behavior should repulse her, she knows. But she finds it oddly comforting: herself before the mirror, divided into crude parts, inspecting herself with dispassion—perhaps because none of what she sees in the mirror at this moment correlates with sex, and sexiness, and all the problems they cause.

She's working to find the right nose-to-mirror angle when a crash returns her to the thing she's meant to be doing. A tray of silverware, from the sound of it.

She moves quickly now, plotting. Her green dress, her pearl necklace. She glances at the clock. Alex was right, of course—she doesn't have nearly enough time. She pours herself a thumb of bourbon—apologizing silently to her mother, whose only rule regarding drinking was that you didn't start alone—swallows it down, and begins. Lotion. Stockings. Her new bra and girdle set, meant to lift and separate. The dress, which zips up the back—she secures it above her hips and leaves the remainder for Alex, in the space of a second noting that this will please him, wondering if that's what she wants, and worrying that she might be pregnant. She sets her hair, then positions herself at her vanity, picking up her powder and brush only to put them down again a second later, her hand drawn instead to an envelope tucked behind her jewelry box. Vee begins to thumb it open, then puts it back and begins to powder her face. Someone is shouting downstairs.

She watches the letter as she powders. She's read it three times already, savoring Rosemary's fat letters—Vee imagines Rosemary's children look like her handwriting, plump and hearty—and her matter-of-fact narration: she's bought a new-model washer-dryer set, with an extra rinse option; a new stop sign has caused all kinds of upset among the village elders. This letter is like most of Rosemary's letters. Or it would be—if it didn't contain a disturbance, related to Rosemary's husband. Rosemary is of similar stock as Vee, descended from judges; as girls they went to the same preparatory school in Boston, then graduated together from Wellesley. But the weekend after graduation, Rosemary married a Jewish lawyer, Philip R—Rosenbaum? Rothblum? Vee can never get his last name straight; no matter how many letters she addresses to Rosemary, each time she has to consult her address book. Whatever his name, Philip, for reasons Vee doesn't understand, agreed to move with Rosemary to the same seaside street on the same exclusively Protestant point where Rosemary and Vee's Protestant families once summered. The brokers balked. There were rules on the point about which colors you could paint your clapboards—white—and your shutters—black—and about permissible fencing and noise and lawn care, and it's been understood since the Indians "died off" which people are welcome and which are not. But Rosemary's mother stepped in with some kind of bribe, and until now things have seemed to be going smoothly enough. Philip has hung his shingle in the small city's downtown and is building a client base among the ethnics. Rosemary thinks she's pregnant again, with a fourth. She is hunting for new wallpaper and experimenting with the boys sharing a bedroom because she feels certain that the new one is another girl, and shouldn't girls have their privacy? She writes about this and then, suddenly, she is writing about a cross. She doesn't even begin a new paragraph, just describes coming home one afternoon with the boys, and it's almost dark, and she is thinking about dinner when, pulling into her drive, out the corner of her eye, she perceives a flame. It takes her a few seconds to realize what it is. Then she pushes the boys into the house, fills a bucket with water, runs to put the fire out, and drags the cross into the garage.

Someone burned a cross on Rosemary's front lawn. Her letter returns to the wallpaper for the baby's room, then asks after Vee and signs off.

Vee turns her face to one side, then the other, checking that her powder is evenly applied. She's been writing a response to Rosemary in her head, but apart from the usual—she'll mention a party or two and a book she's been reading, and she'll fail to respond to Rosemary's questions about whether she is having trouble in the pregnancy department—Vee doesn't know what to say. If she mentions the cross, should it be to extend her condolences? Is that appropriate in such a situation? It might sound like pity. And Rosemary's account was so sparse. Maybe she wanted Vee to leave it alone. Then again—Vee leans in toward the mirror and begins to line her eyes—maybe Rosemary was just being shy, not wanting to trouble Vee but secretly hoping Vee would ask all the questions Rosemary had left unanswered. Which was basically everything. How did Rosemary know what to do, in that moment? Did the children watch her as she quenched the flames? What did she tell them when she came inside? What did she tell her husband when he came home? And before that—how long had the cross been burning? Was it charred? Did she think that whoever lit it meant to actually hurt Rosemary and her family, or just scare them? Not that Vee would condone such behavior either way, but it did seem, to her, important. Intent had to be important—didn't it? But it might be unwise to get into that. Vee puts down her eye pencil and picks up her mascara, refusing to look at the clock—if she looks, her hand will start to shake. She would like a cigarette but settles for a little more bourbon, then paints her lashes from the inside out, as her mother taught her, thinking maybe, if she writes back about the cross, it should simply be to express her outrage. But she worries that could land wrong, too, first because Rosemary herself didn't sound all that upset—*don't fan a flame that's not lit*, as Vee's mother used to say, a terrible metaphor given the circumstances, but still, apt—and second because Vee is not in fact outraged. Outrage requires surprise. Vee is not surprised. Nor does she imagine Rosemary can be, not entirely. Rosemary is not a simpleton or a Pollyanna. She knew what she was doing when she married a Jew. Vee has met Philip twice, and though what Rosemary said about him is true—he appears *modern*, and doesn't strike a person as *religious*—he does have an obviously dark, foreign appearance. Vee respects Rosemary for doing what she wanted. Even Vee's modest acts of defiance—the Pill, the women's group, her arguments with Alex—fill her with guilt and a kind of dread. She doesn't have the courage it would take to go against her family's wishes or the stomach to live as an outsider, never mind to deal with a burning cross. Rosemary is brave, Vee thinks, dabbing at a bit of lipstick that's bunched on her top lip. But that doesn't rule out the possibility that her marriage was a mistake.

Vee's face is done. She lifts her eyebrows to see how she will appear in conversation, checks her teeth, her nails, the angle of her necklace, and so on, a series of minute actions as natural to her as swallowing. In this sense, Vee is ancient—she belongs to the millennia. She blows her hair, unpins it, sprays it, pinches it to relieve the slight helmet effect. She has her finger on her perfume mister when Alex walks in.

"Ready?"

His brow is filmed in sweat, his jaw already showing signs of stubble. He is afraid again, she thinks. And he is handsome. He is an objectively handsome man who knows how to wear a suit, his thighs big enough to fill out the trousers, his hands strong, well veined. She kisses him, hard, then turns away, and Alex zips her, and their wordlessness makes her happy, because this, after all, is the point. Isn't it? They will throw their parties. They'll have sex again, drunk and a little wild, but this time with a condom. Maybe he'll tie her to the bed—he has done this a couple times—and Vee will come without his needing to touch her. She'll go crazy, and in the morning the house will be put back together and they'll sit in the dining alcove and read the papers over coffee and marmalade toast.

Alex spins her around. He nods. He toggles a finger at the buttons on her collar, which she has left open.

"Button up," he says.

"I like it this way."

"Me, too," he says. He cups his hands around her breasts and squeezes. "Button up."

Vee turns back to the mirror. "Get out."

Behind her, Alex picks up her empty glass and smiles. He assumes Vee is joking, even flirting, and for a moment she doesn't know herself. Maybe she is joking. She wants it to be so, wants to lift again into their moment of grace. She didn't think hard about the buttons. She could say this, and point out that her necklace, a gift from Alex, is more visible this way, but his eyes meet hers and Vee sees that his position is firm: He wants her to look like a virgin. He wants to defile her and he wants her to be new, again and again and again.

"See you downstairs in five," he says. "Buttoned."

Vee buttons her collar. The bourbon gnaws at her stomach. She stares at herself. She feels like a piece of ice in a shaker. *You look perfect*, her mother would say, and Vee can see this, that she is well armored and lovely, but it doesn't solve her rage, and now she is digging through her stocking drawer, all the way to the back, filled with an absurd and mounting fear: What if it's been stolen?

She digs frantically, her nails scraping wood, until she finds it: her sew-on-the-go box. "Every girl needs one," her grandmother said when she placed it in Vee's hands sixteen years ago, and Vee has brought the box everywhere, to college and on every trip she's taken, but she has never opened it, and for a second the profound, undisturbed order visible through the clear plastic top—three white cardboard spools, each neatly wrapped in six colors of thread—makes her hesitate. Then she pries off the top. She tosses the thread aside, pulls up a layer of paperboard, and finds a thimble, a packet of needles, a needle threader—for cheaters, her mother would say—and a miniature pair of scissors. She is looking for something else, a thing one uses to *remove* thread, a ripper, it might be called, but the box is empty now, so she grabs the scissors and with them returns to the mirror.

Vee works swiftly, unbuttoning her collar and snipping off each button. She uses her fingers to flick out the remaining thread. Then she flushes the buttons down the toilet and goes to join Alex for the welcoming ceremonies.

SUSA

ESTHER

More Serious Ablutions

This is where belief may prove difficult—the lengths to which the girls go to prepare themselves for the king. They don't just soak in oil for a few hours, or exfoliate their heels with razor blades, or spend days practicing the art of hair towers. They spend months doing these things, scraping and scrubbing and oiling and perfuming though it's never clear, on any given day, if this will be the day that the king at last wants to see them. A heel that's shaven to the pink needs shaving again two weeks later. One of the Greek girls compares their lot to Sisyphus, and the mood is a little like that; after their initial excitement—they are the final forty, whittled down from hundreds—the corner of the palace where they're kept has grown heavy. Rumors have trickled in about other night stations, higher stations, where the women are trained in harp and dancing, and higher still, where the women are made wives and given apartments and servants and courtyards where they can walk outdoors. Some stations are moved, in chariots, when the court moves north for summer. Not this one. Half-underground, it is perhaps the lowest; the girls' only duty is to prepare.

Esther tracks the days on the wall beside her bed, scratching lines into the stone with her thumbnail. She is up to sixty-three the morning she returns from the hand room—where she's been chastised for her ragged thumbnail—to find her tally marks rubbed away. Swallowing tears, she turns to face the room. "What do you know about this?" she asks two girls standing nearby. They look at her, then walk away. Esther has gained a reputation in the night station. She scrubs herself apathetically, refuses the oils and perfumes, does nothing to ameliorate her hair situation, though it's growing out more quickly than she'd like and she can't get Mona—the night-station mother—or any of the eunuchs to bring her scissors. Early on, when she was still begging them on a daily basis, another girl lay down on her bed without asking and said, *Don't bother, of course they won't allow scissors, they're afraid we might hurt ourselves*, and Esther, seeing that she was honest, befriended her. She is Esther's only friend, a Babylonian named Lara whose problem—the extent of which was discovered only after she was chosen for the final forty—has been deemed her excess of hair. Her hair is like a fur, running from her nape to her crack, and from her navel to her cleft. Esther finds these warm paths beautiful, and knows that in the camp they would be objects of envy, but here, Lara is shaven. Her skin burns from shaving and every day she is shaven again. Lara and Esther have in common one language, Farsi, and one goal: neither will become queen and both will go home. They decided this from the start, when the rest of the girls were still high from being among the chosen and still besotted with the comforts of the night station. Every one of them is from the traveling, impoverished tribes. The families of means understood that when a man in power is done with a noble queen he is done with nobility—he wants a woman accustomed to some degree of suffering, a woman who can't afford to question. They understood that they didn't want their daughters following Vashti. So it was left to girls from desperate places and peoples, orphans and daughters of whores and daughters of slaves and daughters of failed rebellions and daughters on the verge of being sold into slavery.

In the early weeks, even Esther and Lara had to admit that life in the station was easier in most ways than the lives they lived outside. They were given as much food and wine as they wanted. They slept on mattresses as thick as four pallets. There was no work required of them, no hauling or washing or planting or cooking. They walked only as far as the dressing room, the hair room, the face room. All they had to do was prepare. All they had to do was keep living.

But even the most enthusiastic of the girls now understands that this particular sort of ease can be unbearable. They understand that they are essentially slaves—and that only one of them will be freed. Their response is to fight, like dozens of crows going after the same bone. They hoard wires and ribbons and animal hair and bird feathers for their hair towers, whatever the eunuchs will smuggle in to them for whatever services they'll perform for the eunuchs. This, too, they understand: they do work in the night station, albeit a particular kind of work, the oldest kind. They hide, they steal, they sabotage one another. They also braid each other's hair, and take turns putting on finger-shadow plays about the king and Queen Vashti, and make each other laugh. They have to, or they'll go crazy. Another old story. They have to despise and depend on each other.

The night station is not as Marduk thought: a brutal prison

or a luxurious bathhouse. Evil or pure. Like nearly everything, it is neither, and both.

Lara and Esther are different from the other girls in that they believe that the one chosen as queen won't actually be free. Lara's tribe is anarchic and violent—anyone who tries to lead, man or woman, is swiftly killed. The palace, she says, is nothing but a facade, with the queen at the center of its hidden misery. Esther's view, while less extreme, bears similar fruit: as a Jew she was raised to mistrust people who are worshipped, and as the daughter of her particular parents, she was taught to judge those who aspire to wealth and power. Both girls believe themselves superior to other people, subject to different rules, or in Lara's case no rules at all. Between them they have created a third option, an alternate plot in which they will be released. Each has begun cultivating her own eunuch; she gives him something, but not too much. Esther's is tall and too thin and has heavy eyelids and a soft mouth that make him look perpetually half-asleep. She lets him watch her. They meet in the room where the sheets and towels are stacked and she touches herself while he watches. One breast. That's all, for now. Soon, she'll introduce a second—later, she'll lift her cloth. The eunuchs are nothing like girls, it turns out. Their voices aren't high, despite what historians will report. They are not sexless. She has watched them hold a girl down until she licked another eunuch's asshole, stick fingers into any place a finger can be stuck, make girls lie beneath them on the floor in the defecation room. Her eunuch is not like that. Baraz is his name, and she chose him for his fealty, perceived it in him as palpably as a scent. Though she doesn't trust him fully yet, she trusts this. He touches her only with his eyes. The idea is that little by little, Esther will agitate and titillate him to such a degree that eventually he will do whatever she asks. The idea is that after the king has finally chosen, and Esther is not queen, she will go to him and say: *Get me out. Do anything you want to me. I'll do anything, if you'll bring me back to the camp.* And by that point his anguish will be such that he'll do anything to have her.

Lara chose her eunuch because he's very pale skinned, so pale it's as if he's not fully formed. She guessed, correctly, that he would like her fur. She lets him lie with her on her bed, his chest against her back or his back against her stomach. That's all; they lie together. Already she has gotten him to sneak her tea, which Lara is not allowed because Mona says it stimulates hair growth. Like Esther, she has her plan.

The girls understand that their "plans" may be overly optimistic. They have no experience in these matters—does anyone? No special knowledge has been imparted to them, nothing beyond a belief in their own exceptionalism, and this was granted to them by two people who are dead and two others who live in a cave. Mostly, though, they are able to ignore their doubts, just as they ignore the despair that subsumed them when they first arrived. They have to. But sometimes, like now, as she sits in front of her patch of newly blank wall, her despair hits again—the erasure of her tally marks is like a blow to her ribs. Questions tumble through her mind, questions she has asked and tried to answer every day since she arrived. Why didn't she run the night her uncle told her what he would do? (Because she did not want to go out into the desert alone.) Why, the day she left Marduk and the palace guards took his figs without a word, why didn't she do something in that moment, shout or scream as she wanted to, to get herself kicked out? (Because she feared she would be killed.) Why did Marduk think Esther's problem would be her Jewishness, a laughable notion now that she's lived among half-breeds and mutts, many of them tribeless? (Because he believes in the exceptionalism of his own oppression.) And why would the king, after a queen like Vashti, of noble birth, known to be educated in archery and hunting, decide to choose from the streets and sands, the lowest of the low, when all they have to offer is their bodies? (Because all they have is their bodies.)

"What are you looking at?"

Lara is back, her jaw red from a shave. She lies down on Esther's bed. Esther lies next to her. "My tally marks," she says.

"They're gone?" Lara is on her side, facing Esther.

"Look!" Esther says, nudging Lara's knee with her own—*turn over*. But Lara shakes her head. "I'm too tired. I believe you."

Esther watches as Lara's eyes close—she observes the now familiar pattern of veins on her lids, the angry skin at her upper lip and jaw. Once, privately, Esther asked Mona why Lara wasn't just sent home, a question that required every ounce of selflessness she possessed, for if Lara went, Esther would be alone. Mona answered as if she'd been asked where to find a chamber pot: *It would be to admit failure*, she said. *Also, the king's minister prefers a round number.*

Esther cups a palm around Lara's chin and presses as Lara has shown her, rocking from the heel of her hand to the tips of her fingers. Lara is quiet for a while. Her face relaxes. "Thank you," she says without opening her eyes. Her knee finds Esther's and nudges it back. "Sorry about your marks. How far had you got to?"

"Sixty-three."

"Counting today?"

Esther thinks. The days run together. That was the reason for the marks in the first place.

"I don't know," she says.

Other girls walk in, laughing and talking. One asks another why she's limping and the girl says it's from a foot treatment and then another says no, it's because she's drunk, and they laugh more loudly than before. Lara opens her eyes and rolls them and Esther giggles. They watch each other as the girls continue their banter, which turns soon enough, as Esther and Lara know it will, to Queen Vashti. She is the one subject no one tires of, the story that gets told and told because no one knows how it ends and everyone who tells it gets to arrive at a cliff, look around at her audience, and smile. Then the speculations begin.

"But do you think she's actually alive?"

"No."

"Yes! They mated her with a donkey."

"No! They decapitated her."

"She was impaled."

"How do you know?"

"My brother said—"

"What's he, the king's minister? I thought you come from Farna."

"No, no, no. She was buried alive."

"Can you imagine?"

"I think she was stoned."

"You think everyone's stoned."

"Haaaaaaaa!" Everyone laughs. By now they've all either drunk opium or watched others drink it. Esther and Lara belong to the latter category. But they giggle, too. Lara jounces her chin in Esther's palm and rolls her eyes back in her head, making Esther giggle harder.

"I heard something different," someone says. "From Mother Mona."

"Mona? She barely opens her mouth to eat. What did you do for her to make her talk?"

"Shut up."

"What did she say?"

"It's not about her punishment. It's about what she did."

"So?"

Lara's eyes are closed again. She thinks she's sick—from the shaving, or the lack of sunlight. She says she feels like an old woman, and sometimes, like now, Esther thinks she looks like one, too. Her lips are so dry they've begun to peel—tomorrow, maybe, they will be slathered in yet another paste, made of a different animal's hoof. Esther looks past her, out the one window, which gives a view of the palace wall and a narrow strip of purpling sky.

"I thought it was leprosy," says another girl.

"That's a myth, spread by the lepers."

"I heard that, too. She slept with the king's minister! Obviously."

"She took a eunuch into the royal bed."

"And told him a state secret!"

"My mother said she tried to poison the king."

"She said that, then sent you to be his queen?"

No one talks for a moment. Esther watches a black bird with yellow wings light on the wall, then fly out of sight into the dusk.

"Doesn't anyone want to know what Mona said? She said he threw a weeklong banquet and, days in, asked Vashti to leave the women's banquet and come appear in front of his men—in her crown."

"So?"

"Don't you get it? *In her crown.* That means naked."

"How does that mean naked?"

"That's what Mona said. She said he asked her to come *in her crown* and she refused and—"

"That's stupid. Why wouldn't she just ask first, like, what do you mean, *in my crown*? Maybe he didn't mean naked. Maybe she heard what she wanted to hear."

"She'd want to hear that?"

"Maybe she was jealous."

"But maybe he did mean naked."

"If I'd been her, I would have just done it."

"Me, too. If I knew I'd be killed otherwise?"

"Who says she knew?"

"I'd just do it."

"But you're the queen! You can't just do that, like a whore. You'd be punished."

"She was punished anyway."

"What do you know of queens?"

"She had a tail. That's what I heard."

"A tail?"

"Like an ass."

"She couldn't bear children, is what I heard."

"That's not rumor, it's true."

"Then maybe it's also true that the king doesn't have a cupful of royal blood. Vashti was the noble. He worked for her father, a high-up something but still a something."

"If that's true, why would anything be up to him?"

"Where did Mother Mona hear this about the crown, anyway?"

As the girls veer into another story, Esther nudges Lara's knee again. "You awake?"

"Mm."

"Is it better?"

"Mm."

Esther removes her hand from Lara's face. "I think she knew everything," she whispers. "She knew he wanted her naked and she knew what would happen if she refused. She refused anyway. She got away. We're going to get away, too."

Lara shrugs. "If us getting away looks like her getting away . . ."

"No, silly! I didn't mean that. I meant—"

But Lara is rolling over. She nestles her backside into Esther's front and lets out an emphatic, silencing sigh.

WASHINGTON, DC

VEE

He with Gourds and His Wife with Cucumbers

Dusk here, too. The senator and his wife preside at the top of their front steps in the weirdly warm November air, kissing and shaking, directing: men downstairs, women up. No one appears irritated by this arrangement, or even surprised, though in a crowd of professional expression-hiders it would be hard to tell. The light on the northern side of Dumbarton Street is fading. Vee watches the women's powdered faces absorb the purple hue and her heart falls a little further. It's already fallen from her earlier, button-snipping high because at the last second she faltered and knotted a white kerchief around her neck, and now it tumbles to a new low as she hears herself call *Hello, good evening, hello!* The women's-group women will be gathering soon with their hard embraces. There will be none of this restrained smiling, no lacquered hair or painful shoes or chit-chat, just a headlong launch into self-realization. If Vee were there, they would applaud her button flushing and cringe as she described the women at her party.

But soon, Vee forgets. The greetings complete, Alex goes inside, unsubtly chasing the suitcase man—did he even notice her missing buttons?—and Vee goes up and the rule, after all, is, *Drink!* and Vee's upstairs parlor has been transformed with drapery and flowers and a jazz trio playing in one corner and golden-haired boys serving gin and tonics and punch on golden trays, and within half an hour Vee is floating around feeling just fine. The party is more charged than she imagined, the women smoking and circling each other like boxers, their dresses shorter, she thinks, than at the last party, and one woman, the wife of a congressman from Dallas, is wearing a white pantsuit and clearly a new kind of underwear, if she wears underwear at all, and four-inch heels when she's already as tall as many men, and it's scintillating, this pantsuit—it knocks something loose in Vee. She unknots her kerchief and drapes it over the curved elbow of a sconce and just like that, the familiar fixture is made exotic and Vee feels powerful again, like a queen. She accepts a lit cigarette and explores her altered realm, enjoying the prerogative of the hostess not to settle anywhere for long. Excuse me, she says, when she is bored by a conversation, excuse me, and moves on. A golden-haired boy takes her empty glass and hands her a fresh one, and she drinks deeply and laughs out loud, then finds that she is listening to a debate about the ERA, not about whether it will ever make it into the Constitution—that is the men's subject, the tally; someone's husband has heard that Maine may be next to ratify—but what difference it will in fact make. One woman contends that *Roe v. Wade* was far more consequential and the ERA merely symbolic, another that symbolic change comes first, a third that the opposite is true, that symbolic change placates the oppressed and precludes any real progress. Vee, drifting on, is lifted on a current of joy. It's not only the gin, she thinks—though she must pause for a second to touch a nearby chair. It's the fact that the women are arguing. It's the way they jab and paw at each other as their cigarette smoke swirls through her parlor. This is where she belongs, she thinks, not among the women's-group women with their circle talk and their red wine and unmade faces. They seem impossibly distant to her in this moment, as gauzy to her as their skirts, as ineffectual as their marijuana. Ugly, too. Vee floats past two more women in heated debate and thinks of the first time she met them, at a welcoming luncheon hosted by the Senate Wives Club. Vee was twenty-five, the other two older but as meek as she was; together they sat through the afternoon as quietly as dolls. Look at them now, wiggling at odd moments to the music and yelling to be heard. They are dazzling, these wives of politicians and company presidents, these tigresses who openly disagree with each other. They don't protect each other's feelings or pretend they don't love their power, their direct means of manipulating the leaders of the free world. Vee's grandmother was a governor's wife and her mother was a senator's wife and Vee is a senator's wife. Why should she think she might be anything else? She drifts from one argument to another, stirred to a smoke-swirled paroxysm of pride and satisfaction, thinking, perhaps aloud, Look at these women! They are not cross-legged on couches talking about liberation. They are already liberated, and she is one of them.

The mood shifts. Vee's ribs ache for food. Her thoughts paddle around: *If gin is to ecstasy as food is to joy as a baby would be to . . .* Where have the golden boys gone? Some of the women are outright dancing now, but Vee can't join in; she is too hungry, and maybe drunk, and starting to feel claustrophobic. She feels a cramp in her abdomen, close to her groin. Fear ripples through her. She knows what the woman said about *Roe* is true, knows two women who since January have ended pregnancies not in hotel rooms or in New York but in doctors' offices nearby. One a congressman's wife, one a woman from the women's group. But legality is not the only problem for Vee. The problem is that Vee would not permit herself to do it. She has a husband, money, health, no children—she has no excuse. A glass breaks behind the bar and a golden boy comes running, but he holds no tray of food. Vee spins aimlessly. She stares at the boy's ass as he prances away, feeling like she might pass out, and coaxes herself to remain upright with a promise: later tonight, when she's sober, she can write to Rosemary and turn this evening into a tale.

"Hello."

Vee smiles, then turns. Standing in front of her is the wife of the suitcase-company president, the man who might be Alex's undoing. Vee smiles harder, horrified to find that she has forgotten the woman's name. She and Alex rehearsed. Mark Fiorelli and his wife, so-and-so. She is tiny in a blue dress, her white-blond hair a shining helmet. Vee holds the little hand for a long beat, still empty on the name front, baring her teeth with what she hopes looks like warmth and not hunger. "Thank you so much for coming!" she cries.

"We wouldn't have missed it," the woman shouts back. "Congrats on the ERA!"

"Yes!" Vee cries, raising her glass. She clinks, and drinks, and tries to focus on the woman—who is attuned, evidently, to Alex's platform—though in Vee's peripheral vision she searches desperately for a golden boy with a tray of appetizers. "Yes! My husband is very committed to equality . . . He's ready to go to the mat . . ." A tray of food floats by and Vee lunges. Quince tartlets. She grabs one, then another. "For women," she continues, trying to talk, smile, and eat all at once. "You know. Ready to go to the mat for women."

"Mmmmm," says Suitcase Wife, and Vee feels a flush of

anger. Why didn't this tiny woman reintroduce herself? That's what people do at these parties, say their names over and over. You assume people forget, assume they're drunk. You play the game. This woman is playing some other game. Vee opens her mouth to ask about this woman's family—she is 82 percent sure the suitcase man has three children, though it might be two—then thinks of a rule her mother used to have: *Policy before person.* She said if you asked people about their kids and dogs right off, they would call your bluff and think you insincere—you had to go straight for the gullet, reveal your agenda, to get them to trust that you weren't merely politicking. It was a tactic of reverse psychology of which she was proud.

Vee beckons the boy with the tartlets—though another rule of her mother's was never to eat at one's own party—and says to Suitcase Wife, "I understand your husband is having second thoughts?"

The woman's face seems to shrink as she looks at Vee. "I don't think he had first thoughts." She speaks more quietly now, so that Vee has to lean in close to hear. "There's a very strong candidate, an up-and-comer from Westerly—"

"Sounds promising," Vee says sharply as she grabs another tartlet. Dried up a little, she's feeling more capable of thought. "What makes you think he can win?"

"He'll win if my husband wants him to win."

"I see." Vee taps on a nearby golden boy and gestures for a napkin, using the moment of nonengagement to consider what is happening. Why is this woman threatening her like this? And if her husband wants to endorse Alex's opponent, what is Vee supposed to do about it? Vee wipes her mouth slowly, stalling, taking in the room. White Pantsuit is leaning against a wall, talking with the wife of Congressman Haskell. The wife of the ambassador to the United Kingdom is shaking her cigarette at the wife of a UN guy. A golden boy is circling with another tray of drinks. Suitcase Wife is quiet for long enough that Vee thinks the conversation might be over. She begins thinking of how she'll describe this exchange in her letter to Rosemary. *She started out with that kind of sweetness you can't tell is syrup till you're stuck in it: "We wouldn't have missed it! Goo!"*

Then the woman says, without looking at Vee: "A long time ago, I knew your husband."

"Okay." Vee is not surprised. Alex is from Rhode Island; this woman is from Rhode Island. It's a very small state. "Did you go to school together?"

"No."

Vee waits. The woman looks elsewhere, blankly. They had some kind of fling, Vee thinks. Okay. It's not news to her that Alex had girlfriends before he married her. It would not be particularly shocking to learn that he had a lover now. It would hurt—but she wouldn't be able to pretend not to have known it came with this territory. Vee's father had affairs. Her grandfather must have, too.

"Well," Vee says. "It was lovely talking with you—"

"The ERA isn't much of a commitment, you know."

"Excuse me?"

"The ERA. It's not much of a commitment." The woman enunciates as if trying to cut air with her teeth, and Vee sees that what she took for skepticism is hostility.

"I don't know what you're talking about," Vee says. "It's a constitutional amendment."

"Sure. A piece of paper."

Vee is unprepared. All the arguments she's listened to garble. She watches White Pantsuit sliding down the wall and Haskell's wife moving closer and then they're kissing. Vee is almost certain, in the aftermath, that it was a kiss. It was brief. It couldn't be called passionate. But it wasn't merely salutary either. Their lips touched. Their bodies were very close. They remain very close. Vee's blood thumps. Suitcase Wife waits with her tiny glare. You're the hostess, Vee reminds herself. You can walk away. "Excuse me—"

The woman grabs her arm. "Put it this way: your husband—back when we met? Back when we *knew* each other?" Her grip tightens. "He was not a gentleman."

How could Vee know that downstairs, the senator is in a corner with the president of the suitcase manufacturing company, sweating? He has given the man cigars, and kept his glass full of thirty-year Glenlivet, and snapped numerous times for one of the circulating golden-haired girls to bring more scallops. He's been chatting him up for almost an hour, but still the man, Mark Fiorelli, is cold, barely speaking. Alex is superior to him in every way: trim where Fiorelli's gone soft under his suit; half-WASP, half-Irish where Fiorelli is half-Irish, half-Italian; a member of the United States Senate where Fiorelli's greatest claim to fame is as one-time president of the Greater Providence Chamber of Commerce. Smallest state in the nation, and he's going bald in that inarguably pitiful way where the top goes first, before the bangs even, so that he's looking a little like a monk. And yet it's Alex who's throwing adulations at the guy as if suitcases were life-saving drugs, as if the man's two hundred employees produced their own GDP. He hates how desperate he sounds. He never lets himself sound desperate. Even when Vee told him she's on the Pill, he didn't let her see his surprise. He was hurt, sure, but where did that get you? Get caught up in feelings and you forget to act, forget the point is what you're going to do about it.

He tries a new tactic. "Have you thought about expanding?

Know some of those old mill buildings up in Pawtucket? I can't promise free, but I could definitely talk with—"

"Let's be straight, why don't we." Fiorelli has come alive. His jowls light up red, his eyes narrow. He places a palm on Alex's chest. Alex flicks it off. Fiorelli puts it back. "You screwed my wife," he says.

Alex's lungs feel like they're departing his body. Why did he imagine the guy's anger was about something else? But who told her husband that sort of thing? "I don't—"

"And if you ask her, she'll tell you it wasn't what she wanted."

One of the girls stops with a tray, imploring, and Alex has the urge to hit her. They are not gorgeous, not up close. This one is pancaked. She had acne as a kid. Alex shakes his head and she is gone. He doesn't remember Fiorelli's wife not wanting it. Blond, petite, good nails. Diane. Wasn't it what she wanted? She wasn't half as pretty as Vee, wasn't even nice. But Vee wasn't around yet. They met at a hotel, he thinks. Doesn't that mean she wanted it?

"I don't know what you're—"

"Hey." Fiorelli's in his face now, a finger tapping Alex's nose. "Enough with the bullshit. I never got involved in politics before. My old man didn't, his old man didn't. Not our place. Now I'm involved. People wonder what I'm after, what's my angle. My angle is: I don't *like* you."

Upstairs, more women have started to dance. One sits on the knee of the saxophonist. Vee lounges on the sofa. More food has been brought up, at her request, and her stomach is happy now, full of cocktail shrimp and cheese puffs. Out one corner of her eye she watches Suitcase Wife's shoes, but Vee refuses to look up. She has no idea what the woman is so hung up about. *Not a gentleman*. What did Alex do, stick his fingers up her ass? Choke her a little as she sucked him off? Vee doubts it's anything he hasn't done to her. If she isn't always willing, she usually gets into it. More worrisome is what the whole mess might mean for Alex.

Vee smokes a cigarette, drinks another gin and tonic, and talks about nothing with Congressman Flint's wife. Only when Alex's chief of staff kneels on the floor next to her and leans in close does she realize a man has entered the room.

"Mrs. Kent?" His voice is low.

Vee finds herself pinching his cheek. "Yes, Hump?" At thirty, he is her senior, but so cute, she thinks suddenly. A towhead. Freckles. So cute! Hump. Short for Humphrey Sumner III.

"Mrs. Kent, the senator has requested your presence."

Vee laughs. "So formal!"

"That's what he told me to say."

"He wants all of us, I presuuuume?" Her accent is vaguely British. She giggles. "All the madames?"

"Only you, Mrs. Kent."

She hands him her cigarette. "Well!" she says, and heaves herself up off the couch. She rocks for a moment, lightheaded, then sees Suitcase Wife staring at her and pulls herself straight. "It does make one curious," she hears herself say. And then, "Well," and again, "Well," as her grandmother used to say. *Well well well*, her grandmother said, as she moved around the house making the beds, or preparing supper, or—as she got older—looking for something she was ashamed of having lost. *Well*, like a verbal banister. Vee's mother achieved the same effect by humming: *hummm* as she bent for carrots from the refrigerator, *hummm* as she rose, as if to accompany herself through her tasks.

Vee passes her drink to Mrs. Flint. "Well." She meets Suitcase Wife's eye, then, emboldened, crosses the room with a swagger. "Here I go!" she calls. "Wish me luck, ladies! If I'm not returned within an hour, promise you'll come to my rescue!"

BROOKLYN

LILY

A Different Kind of Party

Atop a kitchen island gleams the party's centerpiece: a massive turquoise sewing machine from the 1960s. The hostess, Kyla, repeats the vintage as each guest arrives, explaining that the old machines are superior, if you treat them right. This one was her grandmother's, she adds, and all the women ooh and ahh at this, Lily included, though the machine fills her with fear. She imagined this would be a needles-and-thimbles kind of sewing party. She thought she might cut out some pieces of cloth, maybe learn to sew the edges to prevent fraying, then wrap them toga-style around the girls and call it a day. But Kyla has laid out patterns, which as far as Lily can tell—who knew sewing patterns were in code?—appear to be for dresses that entail sleeves, and necklines, and in one case a pocket. Lily wants to whisper: *Since when did Esther have a* pocket *on her dress?* But she doesn't know any of the other women well enough to trust they'll take to her snarkiness, and she's realizing, as they begin to pepper her with questions, that they know each other very well. It's palpable, the togetherness of women who've stood around like this on countless other occasions, in other kitchens. They are a group. Lily, too, has a group, but she and her friends have never invited a stranger into their midst, their wine isn't as good, the atmosphere they create isn't as cheerful, and they don't have dedicated playrooms like Kyla. On the other hand, Lily's group includes women of various shapes, colors, and hair textures. And they are skilled at using all these facts, from the mediocre sauvignon blancs that ostensibly allow them to spend money on more important things to the squished apartments to the au naturel hair, to make them feel superior—more authentic, somehow? more real?—to women like these. These women, a couple of whom appear no older than thirty-three, which would make them *thirteen* years younger than Lily, ask Lily with near jubilance how long she's been in the neighborhood, and how old her kids are, and whether she works, and what her husband does, and Lily, overwhelmed and self-conscious, answering as best she can, wonders at how easy it would be, if you mixed up these women and Lily's women and stood them in a line, to tell which ones belong to which group. It's a depressing thought, because it suggests that they are all basically in permanent uniform and that their superficial differences—these women's blown-dry hair and diamond rings, etc., as opposed to Lily and her friends with their chunky bracelets and scuffed boot-clogs like something out of *Heidi*—actually portend deeper ones, like what they do with their pubic hair, and deeper ones still, like what they think and feel. One of the women, upon hearing that Lily used to teach at the city colleges, says, "That's so cute!" and Lily, feeling mean and small, excuses herself to go check on the children, half hoping one of them will be sick so that she'll have to take them home, but she finds them cheerfully rolling and cutting homemade Play-Doh with the other children at a low, large table probably made in Finland. Ro looks up first, then June, both girls with almost absurdly happy expressions on their faces, and Lily feels the kind of deep, unadulterated love for them that she experiences when they are asleep, or when she cups the fat arch of June's foot in her palm, or when Ro lets her hold her as they read. This feeling, in this moment, feels as if it could be felt eternally, if only she lived in this apartment and had this table and this particular bespoke Play-Doh. Lily smiles and waves until, in unison, like happy Finnish cows, her daughters turn back to their work.

In the kitchen, Kyla asks Lily to give everyone a brief primer on Purim—*Poor-eem*, she pronounces it, like Adam used to—which causes Lily, who feels at once defensive of and embarrassed by her tribe, and unreasonably irritated by being, apparently, its sole representative at this gathering, to issue forth a brief and conflated account of the holiday and the story that sounds something like "lots of drunkenness and misogyny but also female worship, which you could argue is a form of misogyny, and a so-so king and good queen and evil side guy, celebrated with a play and a big carnival and a pageant and triangle-shaped cookies, and also there's a thwarted genocide of the Jews . . ." By the end, Lily is so turned around she adds a final, ambiguous punch line—"It's kind of a burlesque?"—and then Kyla, undaunted, begins introducing the women to the machine, identifying its various parts and what they do. Lily is hungry. In her nervousness she has drunk too much wine. But the food—cheese and crackers and nuts and something that looks like pickled broccoli—has been laid out at the opposite end of the kitchen, so that to get to it you must walk away from the group and make a thing of wanting it.

As Kyla talks—the machine has many parts, including one called a *feed dog*—Lily's fear mounts. Where are the thimbles? Where is the softcore sewing party? But then Kyla is turning to her and looking deep into her eyes, so deeply that Lily notices the remarkable blue of Kyla's irises and wonders if she wears colored contacts, and saying, "You're up first, Lil; you'll do great," as if they've known each other forever, and her voice is quiet now, and tender, as if she senses Lily's struggle. Lily thinks of the word *cerulean*, for Kyla's eyes, and of the freshman-year poetry class in which she fell in love with that word. "Do you mind?" Kyla asks Lily, and before Lily can figure out what she's talking about Kyla is behind her, taking Lily's hands into her own. They'll start with a straight stitch, she says, and suddenly the machine is purring and Lily, guided by Kyla, is sewing. She feels a pleasurable shock, as if she's jumped into cold water. There is vibration, and fabric, and Kyla's hands on hers, and the satisfied grumble of the machine, and the cheers of the women gathered around to watch, and, at the small of her back, the gentle press of Kyla's belly, and Lily realizes not only that Kyla has a belly, like anyone, but also how long it's been since someone has taken the time to teach her something. Since graduate school, at least, and even then they expected her to teach herself most of what she didn't know. There is a weightless quality about it, something she remembers from childhood, a sense that as long as she follows she will be okay. And now Kyla asks if she wants to try the foot pedal and Lily looks down and sees that there's a foot pedal, and Kyla's foot slides off it to allow Lily's to hop on and instead of internally mocking the five-hundred-dollar boots Kyla is wearing—though noting the fact of them, she admits, may be a form of judgment—she mostly just feels grateful. She is grateful for this woman who is teaching her to sew, grateful that she cares, grateful for her earnest and unabashed domestic ambitions. So what if Kyla is a little too perfect, her cheekbones a little too good, her blouse a little too drapey-yet-lean? So what if her name is Kyla, as if in her spare time she's a yoga instructor? She has been nothing but generous and kind. Lily is sorry for her snarkiness. She is embarrassed, as her back relaxes into Kyla's stomach, at what she suddenly understands to be true: that although her friends, if they could see Lily in this moment, would crack a joke, every one of them would in fact like to be in Lily's spot. They tell themselves they don't care about being good homemakers. But they peek around each other's apartments just the same, commenting on how one person seems never to have any toys on her living-room floor, or how another has managed to put together nonvirtual family photo albums, or how another always manages to buy useful things like that magnetic calendar on her fridge or that cord organizer on her counter. They keep their tone flat, as if they aren't praising but merely observing, and then they move on to other subjects deemed more worthwhile, husbands or politics or the careers they've put on hold. It's in this way that they are different from Kyla's women, after all: not in their actual behavior—for they have all chosen to prioritize their children at this point in their lives, to "embrace" (that word, so redolent with resistance!) motherhood—but in their attitude. Never mind that fridge calendars and organizers and doctor's appointments and school lunches and diarrhea and grocery shopping take up the bulk of their time and energy; never mind that they do feel pulses of pride when they experience success in one of these arenas. They have a phrase that encompasses all of it, "shit and string beans," which came out of an old feminist novel one of them read once, she forgets what it was called, a name they can throw at almost everything they do. *Shit and string beans*, and they laugh at themselves, and pour a glass of wine, and put the kids in front of a screen, and settle in to complaining about things large enough that they can't even pretend to try to solve them that day, like the subway, or the absurd and asinine entertainment of Donald Trump's run for president, or pollution. A husband's infidelity. Their own lusts, which they say they can't imagine actually indulging—how would that even happen? in what space? on whose time?—yet talk about in great detail, for example, the father Lily met recently who looked like he could be a fisherman from her hometown. Granted, half the men in Brooklyn dressed like fishermen these days, but this man, Hal was his memorable name, looked like the real deal and then some: a beautiful, sensitive, sophisticated fisherman with a red beard and strong hands that Lily described to her friends in extravagant detail. She spent a week fantasizing about him, mushy with a kind of lust she hadn't felt since Rosie was born. She and Adam had sex twice in that time. That, too, the women laughed about, because since when was twice a week getting it on? Since a long time.

Back and forth across the cloth Lily goes. It's satisfying, even though she isn't accomplishing anything yet, and totally involving, so that for a time she forgets her hunger and her friends and her laundry and her mother and her daughters and Purim and dresses, until she feels Kyla's warmth depart at her back and realizes that she is sewing on her own. "You're doing great!" Kyla says. "I'm just going to get the kids' dinner together. Keep going!" But Lily's thread snags; the machine growls; the pedal bucks. She hears herself cry out—a desperate caw, as if she's been injured. "Oh, don't worry," Kyla says, "it's been through worse. Here, take a break." She pours wine into Lily's glass and puts it in her hand. "Tell us about Esther, so we can figure out the dress."

The other women nod.

"Esther?" Lily asks dumbly.

"As a character." Kyla opens the door to the refrigerator. "I'm getting the kids' dinner. But I'm listening. What's she like?"

"Well, she's the queen . . ." Lily is unsure what she did and didn't say before, but Kyla nods, so Lily continues: "But she likes things simple. I mean, when she goes to become the queen—because first there's another queen, Vashti, who's banished, and then there's Esther and lots of other women who are brought in, like for a kind of contest . . ."

"That's the pageant part, right?" Kyla uncovers a casserole dish. "What the girls will be walking in?"

"Right." Lily, no longer sewing, eyes the cheese, but the women surround her, waiting for the lowdown on Esther. "So when she goes to the pageant," Lily says, "she's the only one who doesn't go crazy with her makeup and hair. She dresses very simply and ties her hair back with a ribbon." Lily has no idea if this detail is true in the original, which she has never read, but in the children's version Esther ties her hair back with a white ribbon and appears to wear the slightest bit of rouge on her cheeks. The girls love this detail—it's a central focus of their interrogations. *Why not something fancier?* Ro wants to know. *Maybe something rainbow, or glittery?* At which point June parrots Lily: *Because she knows what's on the inside is most important?* And Lily nods, dully proud. It's exhausting, to indoctrinate. And always the truth bleeds through. There would be no need to indoctrinate if there was nothing to cover up. There would be no need for Esther without the whorish girls surrounding her. "Compared to the other maidens," Lily says to Kyla, "Esther looks like a field hand. She's the natural beauty."

"I love it!" Kyla says. "And god, it sounds so relevant. I mean, such a good lesson for our daughters. Even now, they get so much pressure, right? I love the idea of a kind of plain-Jane hero. It's like something out of that book . . . you know . . . *The Paper Bag Princess?*"

Affirmative cries go up from the women. Lily exclaims, too, because she does like that book. Of course she does; she is a woman who keeps the bulk of her makeup hidden in her sock drawer. But plain-Jane paper-bag princess wasn't what she meant by "natural beauty." She meant striking without pretense, attractive with minimal effort. A natural beauty, if you wanted to get nuanced about it—and Lily did, apparently—didn't even have to be beautiful, exactly; it was more that her particular naturalness added up to its own sort of beauty. Lily, for example, knows that she is not objectively beautiful, but according to Adam, she *is* a natural beauty. He says it when they get dressed to go out, and when they spot each other across the apartment in an odd moment of stillness, not wiping a nose or sending a text but standing, for a second, and looking. It's a gesture of sweetness, to stop and appreciate her. It's also an insider reference to their somewhat bizarre first encounter, which Lily, in one of the stories she writes in her mind, calls "How Adam Got Lily for a Wife," the shortest version of which goes something like: Vira left Adam, or Adam threw Vira out, depending on whose story you believed; Adam fell into an abyss; Adam's friend Fred, struck while planning a surprise party for his wife's fortieth birthday by how many of her friends were currently single, decided that the party would have a secondary purpose, which was to lure Adam from the abyss.

Did Adam know? Before the party, as he showered and dressed—choosing dark jeans, a checked shirt that could be interpreted in a variety of ways, and a leather jacket—had he known what Fred was setting up? As he put on his parka, for it was a brutally bitter night, 9 degrees with the wind chill, did he wish for one more stylish, something that said urban woodsman instead of simply L.L.Bean?

By the time the party was in full swing, certainly, he had to have known, because after the surprise for the wife had been pulled off, Fred turned his full attention to whispering in Adam's ear while unsubtly eye-pointing at the various women he wanted Adam to check out. Lily saw all this, of course. She was, at this point, in a corner of the tiny bar Fred had rented out, talking with Fred's wife. They had met over a decade ago in an intense and not great yearlong MAT program, so they were close, in a sense, but only saw each other once or twice a year; Lily did not know Fred's friends. Her first thought, when Adam's eyes landed on her, was that if she'd seen his picture on Match or Jdate, she would have been drawn to him for about ten seconds, then she would have moved on. There was something generic in his handsomeness. She would not have trusted that in real life he would offer more than he did in the picture. But he was good-looking. And she was not looking at him online, she was looking at him in a bar, which meant she could see him move, and she liked the way he moved. Still, she might have dismissed him. She might even have decided to be offended by the overt meat-market situation, though this would have been disingenuous, as she had been on Match and Jdate for a long time. But as Adam's gaze moved on, Lily saw his drink-free hand toggle the zipper on his leather jacket, and in the gesture she saw self-consciousness, a dawning realization, she believed, that he was dressed like every other man in the place, that even their zippers looked like his, oversized and burnished. She saw him shrink a little, and decided that he had not known, before the party, that he was being offered a kind of flock. Or that if he knew, he'd managed to convince himself he did not know. If, after considering his options, he chose her, she thought, she would not be opposed to talking, at least.

So this is not the shortest version of "How Adam Got Lily for a Wife." But neither is it the longest. The further Lily gets from it, the more it fascinates her. Like any origin story, maybe.

In the kitchen, the women wait for Lily's response—plain-Jane paper-bag hero, right?—and Lily wonders what they would say if she told them about the party. If she told how the next two hours passed without Adam making a move, yet how she stayed tuned to him, attentive, would they understand, or think her pathetic? What if she told them how when she was introduced to one of the other single women obviously up for Adam's perusal, she was too busy comparing their respective attributes to listen to a thing the woman said? If she told them that Adam kept looking around at his options with an overwhelmed and innocent expression on his face, an expression she has since seen on him when he does things like look for shirts online, would the women in Kyla's kitchen think that made him an asshole? Did Lily think it made him one? If he felt that way, shouldn't he have picked no one and gone home alone? All the times she and Adam have joked about that night, she has never asked him what took him so long. The party was ending before he made a move. Cold air swept the floor, people threw on their coats, even Fred and his wife were bundling out the door. Finally, Adam walked up to Lily. He chose her because of her hat. He told her this later that night, in bed. He did not delve into the vestigial instinct that must have kicked in, securing him to his stoic, square-chinned, eminently practical New Hampshire forebears. He simply said he'd decided to approach the one woman who had put on a hat to face the coldest night of the year. He assumed it meant things about her, of course—that she was sensible, confident, unselfconscious—things that later would seem less clear, to both of them. But that night he took those things to be true, and so he introduced himself to Lily Rubenstein, in her navy-and-green-striped hat.

"She's not really plain," Lily says to Kyla, feeling protective of her premarriage self. "She's just simple." Or she means to say these things. She is so afraid of sounding defensive that they come out like questions. *Not really plain? Just simple?*

"Okay." Kyla has removed the casserole dish from the microwave and is setting out a large glass bowl of carrot sticks. Not baby carrots, the mushy or dried-out nubs that always remind Lily of dog penises, and then of the fact that her children want a dog, and then that they may never be able to afford enough space in this city to have a dog, but home-peeled, home-cut carrots resting, for some reason, in cold water. Kyla swishes the water with a finger and asks Lily, without a hint of guile, "But their costumes should still be elegant, right?"

Lily thinks of her old hat, with its wide blue and green stripes. Another version of it might have been fashionably ugly, a hat that captured the spirit of a vintage rugby shirt—a *rugshat*!—but the version Lily had was just what it was. It was old even then. Wearing it could only be interpreted as a kind of self-sabotage.

"Or at least special?" Kyla prompts, and her look is so eager that Lily blurts out, "Yes, of course! Definitely special." And it's true, she thinks. The hat was special. Between Adam and Lily it had become a touchstone in their mythology, part of a lapse that included the contest in the bar and which did not reflect upon the basically sane, desirable, kind people that they were. It was a triumph, really, to sail past such a beginning and not only survive but thrive . . . or something. Not until this moment, in Kyla's kitchen, did Lily connect what happened that night with the pageant in the Purim story, let alone see how neatly she and Adam and Vira fit into their respective roles. Had it been so strange, and so obvious, that they simply couldn't see it? Lily had never been Eve, not even for a second. She had entered as Esther—in her plain hat, like the plain ribbon—and stayed Esther. The second wife.

"Definitely special," Lily says again. "But not *that* special, you know? I mean, I don't want you to go overboard, after all you've done. My mother used to grab scarves from the dress-up bin and that was that, I was Esther, ta-da!" Lily grabs her glass of wine and gulps, anything to stop herself from talking for a second. She hates the word *special*. She sounds ungrateful, though she's not. She is not ungrateful, and she does not want to insult Kyla, and she wants—badly!—to do more sewing, with Kyla's help. She takes another swallow, trying to inhale air along with the wine, and makes her pivot: "All I mean is, I so appreciate everything you've done, and I don't want to put you out, but of course you're right, we should definitely make something special . . ." Lily smiles, but Kyla is at the sink with the bowl of carrots, and Lily gets it now: the water will be poured off and the carrots will taste freshly dug. It's a trick—simple, yet brilliant. How had Kyla learned to do such a thing? If Lily's mother hadn't been so involved in her Jewish new-moon ceremonies, would Lily, too, know how to keep cut carrots fresh? Someone points Lily to the cheese board, and it strikes her, as she tosses an inch-thick piece of brie into her mouth, that the only thing her mother ever sewed, to Lily's knowledge, was an embroidery sampler which read: *A Well-Kept House Is a Sign of an Ill-Spent Life.* This was something her mother had read in a feminist advice column she liked, though Lily isn't certain, now that she thinks of it, that her mother actually made the sampler herself, or if she had someone else do it. Which would be funny, really, a joke on the joke, though not on the woman she hired. Whatever its story, it arrived in Lily's house shortly after her father moved out and hung on the back of the bathroom door, so that you read it each time you sat on the toilet, which for Lily, who was nearing eight at the time and lived at home for another ten years, meant she must have read it thousands of times.

Lily tries the pickled-broccoli-like stuff, which is indeed pickled broccoli and is delicious. She tries it on a cracker, then on another cracker with brie, then she finds herself staring at Kyla's ass as Kyla goes to deliver her genius carrot sticks to the children. It's not a perfect ass, Lily thinks, not like her cheekbones or hair. It's not even an especially good one, neither ample nor fit, and Kyla's jeans, neither snug nor loose, don't do it any favors. Yet there is something in the way Kyla walks, at once lighthearted and grave, as if her confidence that she's doing the right thing in the right place at the right time, and her pleasure in doing it, and maybe, too, those unflattering jeans, have imbued her with a kind of holiness. Lily watches until she's gone, wondering how Kyla got like that, if you had to be born that way or if it was something you could learn, like how to sew, and whether Lily herself could learn it—if not holiness, then maybe a little grace? What if it's easier than she imagines, if she could simply decide, right now, to be done with the way she is, done with discontent and done with her mother's voice and maybe done with her friends, too, and their cult of ambivalence? What if she could simply want what she has? Kyla returns, drying her hands on her apron with an ease that makes Lily want to weep. She will get her own apron, she thinks. She will embrace her Estherness. So what if she's the end of the story, the second wife, the virtuous one? Lily is forty-six. She is too old to still believe that she's going to somehow wind up being someone she hasn't already become. She is not a writer or a professor or a singer-songwriter or an adulteress, she is, by choice, a second wife and mother and homemaker. If she is ill equipped to be these things, then she will have to equip herself. If she is not Esther precisely (Esther saves her people; who—whom—is Lily supposed to save???) she will be Esther in spirit. The heroine. The second but lasting queen. A natural, if not terribly sexy, beauty. A virtuous, if not mysterious, wife. A satisfied woman, smiling in her new friend's kitchen.

The children eat and the women eat, and then the children are served brownies and led back into the playroom, where the table is pushed out of the way and music is turned on and the children begin, miraculously, to dance. The women are served brownie *bites*. Lily is eating her fourth when a woman comes up to her, wearing a glow. "I'm Jace," she says, reaching out a hand.

Lily shakes. She has too many questions—*Are you a cowgirl? Where did you get that glow?*—so remains silent.

"I think your older daughter goes to theater class with my son," Jace continues. "Hudson? He says they're friends?" Then, at Lily's blank response, she adds: "He's got red hair?"

"Oh!" Lily cries. "Yes!" She flushes, realizing that Hudson must be the son of none other than Hal the fisherman, of the reddish beard and strong hands, which makes Jace the wife of Hal the fisherman, of course. Lily puts down her brownie bite and says, as casually as she can manage, "I met your husband, I think. At pickup one night? Remind me his name . . . ?"

"Hal! Yeah, he does pickup most of the time. He's a fisherman, so he's out and back really early."

Lily laughs. "For real? He's a fisherman?"

"Uh-huh." Jace giggles. "He's not, like, what you *think of*. He grew up in Larchmont. But then Wall Street wore off, you know? And he got hooked on tuna. Ha ha." Jace babbles on, as if she doesn't know her luck, and Lily, with time to take in how tiny this Jace is, her jean-clad thighs barely bigger than Lily's arms, starts to picture Jace and Hal screwing. Jace is saying, "Maybe we can all pick them up together next time. If your husband can get off work early? I'm a lawyer, but I have some flexibility, like today . . . We could go out for pizza? There's a good place near there . . ." and Lily nods, thinking, Never. Remember the laundry, she tells herself, to quiet the unvirtuous thoughts in her mind. Remember the laundry, and once the kids are asleep, make a real dinner for Adam. Jace—a lawyer! A pencil-thighed lawyer who still makes time for playdates—is still talking about the pizza place, but Lily buries her mind in her cupboards. Make him a real dinner and put on some nice lingerie and give all of what you're feeling for Hal to him, she thinks. Screw him! Last Thursday night, when Ruth was over, she told Lily about a friend who'd just been left by her seventy-three-year-old husband because she wouldn't have sex with him anymore. She said this as nonchalantly as her mother says anything that might shock the person listening, as if to show off her own lack of shock. *That seems harsh*, Lily had said, but Ruth shot back, *Well? Isn't it part of the deal?* Lily didn't have an answer. After she gave up the Grinnell job, she and Adam had made their own deal, she supposed. He would make the money, she would raise the family, at least until the kids were in school. It had felt honest, mature. Post-everything. They knew they were white, heteronormative, and privileged, and they would do their best to be good people while being that. Sex had not been discussed, then or at any point. Making sex part of the deal would suggest . . . what? A kind of servitude, at best. Prostitution, at worst. Still, she knows her mother is right. She also knows that although she and Adam have more sex than her friends do—once a week, usually? maybe?—that it is not enough, and not only in a *Cosmo* sense but in a very personal, Lily sense. She needs more catharsis in her life.

"So, Thursday?" Jace is saying. "We'll meet you outside class?" and all Lily can do is nod. Why is she thinking about her mother again? Why is she thinking of Hal? She is supposed to be where she is, be good and gracious. But in the next room, the music has been turned off and the children are starting to disassemble, turning into rags and beasts. The windows have gone dark. Kyla calls out to her, "So you'll come back next week! Same time?" and Lily takes out her phone to check her calendar but Kyla has turned away, busy gathering people's coats, and Lily drops her phone back into her bag and soon she's stumbling with the other mothers and children down the stairs to the street, the mood jovial and warm as everyone calls good-bye and the family units scatter, each toward its own shelter. Lily, trying to outpace the sadness that laps at her heels, points out to the girls how beautiful the sycamores look on Third Street, lit by the streetlights. But they're already focused on what comes next, whether they will have their dresses soon, and whether they can have screens at home or just a book, and if it's a book it must be Esther, and Lily, after making a halfhearted plug for *The Paper Bag Princess* or *Ferdinand*, her favorite—how utterly the bull embraced his anti-ambition!—says, "Fine, okay, alright," and walks the rest of the way listening to the girls talk and thinking of Adam, wondering what she will cook for him, and of her underwear drawers, wondering what she has to wear.

SUSA

ESTHER

The Original Pageant

She is in the bath when the girls are called. A procession, she's told, a parade before the king, and instantly the number of days she has painstakingly stored is yanked from her mind like a thread. One hundred twenty- . . . what? It doesn't matter now, she tells herself, as she is wrapped and shoved toward the oiling room. Tonight, she will fail to become queen, and tomorrow she will be released. Her grip on Baraz is advanced now, what he has seen of her near replete. A heat is rising in him, like a fever. Esther is confident he'll do what she asks if she offers him more—which is to say, everything.

Is she willing? She is. She is both certain of and disgusted by her willingness. But Nadav won't have to know. The trick for that is so simple it can barely be called a trick.

Esther has seen more, too. Like a plant growing new roots, the night station gains hallways. Esther walks in a direction she has walked before only to find a new tunnel to a new place. Her recent discoveries include one distant room outfitted with eye hooks and ropes where certain girls go to be stretched and whipped, and another outfitted with cages in which girls—often the same certain girls—are locked and prodded. Both rooms are equipped with viewing windows, holes cut into the wall so that a passerby in the hall can stop and watch. Esther stops and watches. It is something to see. It is—be honest—fascinating. Sometimes a eunuch enters a cage with a girl. Other times he stays outside and watches as she puts on a show. Esther—still only kissed—is surprised by the apparent dignity of the proceedings. The girls come to these rooms of their own volition as far as she can tell: unshackled, chins high. Perhaps they are rewarded, or imagine that they will be, in the future, or maybe they're simply bored. They step into the cages as gracefully as birds. They flit and shake and sometimes shimmy like fish, and sometimes they turn without warning into tigers, clawing at the bars, growling. Esther feels heat in her legs but not revulsion, not the shame she would have expected. She remembers her mother picking up speed as they passed the women who stood around behind the market, dragging Esther by the hand with sudden force. Esther remembers thinking that those women were a different species from people like her and her mother, made of a different substance, more like jackals or vultures, but now she thinks the line between them is more porous than she imagined, if it exists at all. In the linen room with Baraz, Esther feels an astonishing ease, an almost out-of-body calm, as she squeezes her breasts and rubs between her legs. She is outside herself, looking on. She waits for the eunuch's moan as if waiting for water to boil, and in this way, like a kettle, he becomes a kind of object for her, domesticated and possessed. He obeys and doesn't touch, though recently he brought her gifts: a square of silk, a fan of peacock feathers, a bone necklace. The necklace nearly destroyed her, a garland of tiny vertebrae sanded to the smoothest white, so clearly the work of Nadav's mother that Esther had to grip her thighs to stop her hands from reaching for it.

In the end, she touched none of Baraz's gifts.

But she did tell him where she's from, and began squeezing him for information. He has told her that the raids on the camp continue, now with an official title: *the king's cleanse*. He says more men, and more violent men, have been recruited. More fire pits have been destroyed, even as other fires are lit, burning tents and tools. The clay vessels her people make to sell are smashed.

Are they leaving yet? Esther always asks, when Baraz is done cataloging the damage. But Baraz's answer is always no. It seems impossible that the camp would have believed Marduk's promise that Esther will somehow save them. And yet—why won't they go? Even her aunt and Itz and Nadav, none of whom would want to abandon her—can't they see by now that it's hopeless?

A part of her, of course, doesn't want them to see. She wants for them to stay. *Wait for me!* she wants to tell them, even as she wants them, for their own sakes, to flee.

Jostling for space in the dressing room now, she slips on her aunt's prized muslin. Other girls laugh, prompting eunuchs—none of them Baraz—to rush over and strip the cloth off her. Esther waits, naked, for whatever robe or dress they'll bring, trying to ignore the battles around her over powders and combs and who will walk first and who last. The smell of balms and oils and cinnabar mixes with the frenzy and heat to produce an overpowering stench. She breathes through her mouth and looks for Lara. And Baraz—where is he? Other eunuchs return to wrap her in a white silk robe; they tie the robe with a gold sash and push a brush into Esther's hand. Her hair is grown out past her shoulders now, a thick, ink-colored curtain that months ago overcame her chop job. She ties it back with a leather string and abandons the brush on a nearby table. Every surface is covered in brushes and paints and pots and somewhere, probably, the pomegranate paste she carried with her that first day. There is enough kohl and cinnabar in the room to paint the girls inside and out, every day, for the rest of their lives. But thankfully Mona and the eunuchs are overwhelmed now, too busy to notice Esther and force her, so she will go before the king as she hoped to go, in her bare face.

A new room. She'll remember it as gilded, and cold, even when she enters it frequently in the years to come and learns that it is neither. The girls walk single file. Esther still hasn't spotted Lara and worries. Has she been punished in some way? Did her eunuch betray her furtive tea drinking? Or maybe Mona, at last facing the day of judgment, has locked her away, not wanting to offend the king with Lara's hairiness, which he would discover if not now then within hours. Esther turns to look, but she is walking somewhere in the middle of the line—the positions deemed least advantageous by the girls' collective logic—and can only see the girl immediately behind her, a Syrian so thickly painted her skin gives off a grayish hue. Esther feels a stab in her thigh, Mona snapping her with her famous forked nails. She faces forward. The hall appears empty but for a stage, the stage empty but for two chairs. The chairs are strange, elaborately adorned with gold tassels and brown leather and tapered legs carved into cat's feet, yet oddly small, as if built for children. When the girls are lined up facing the stage, Mona moves the leader to the rear and the rear girl to the middle, and then she taps and directs the rest of the girls so that soon they're all lined up again in a new order. Esther steals glances left and right, knowing Lara would appreciate the joke, but she sees only girl after girl like the one who walked behind her. They are so shellacked in paints they would be visible from a great distance, maybe even in the dark, but soon they're close enough to the stage that they could spit on it, close enough that when a man mounts it, they can see two parallel creases between his eyebrows, a hint of silver in his beard. He is notably short, with a waddlish style of walking, and for a moment, as he sashays toward them, Esther wonders who he is. A servant, maybe, or an entertainer? But then Mother Mona gives a sharp clap and goes down on her knees, and Esther drops with the rest of the line, understanding. She studies the floor's mosaic. When she hears Mona clap again and looks up, she sees why the chairs are so short: the king, now seated, appears to be a man of significant stature. This trick of perspective is so effective as to be frightening, for Esther saw him standing not two minutes before, saw that he was shorter than the tallest girls, yet already she doubts. She inspects him more carefully: his troubled brow, his pointed slippers, his thickly layered robes, black and purple and blue and finally red, to puff his chest and shoulders. His fingers, curled like sleeping lizards atop the armrests: how very small. On either side of him, a wall of men has formed.

Mother Mona walks the line, prodding the girls from behind. Each is given her moment: she steps forward, turns before the king in a wide, almost laughably slow circle, until, her moment squeezed dry, she steps back. The king wears a mild, steady grimace, impossible to read. His walls of men move only their eyes, raking the girls from top to bottom. As her turn nears, Esther lets her shoulders sag. She rehearses in her mind ungainly steps, dull eyes. At the prodding of Mother Mona's stick she hunches out, her gaze resolutely stuck on the king's tassel-toed slippers. She begins to turn her circle. She moves faster than the others, trying with all her might to erase herself, leave behind no impression. Her circle is almost complete when, facing the line, she sees Lara—or rather, she sees the girl Lara was, now buried beneath a costume. Pounds of hair have been added to her head, heavy earrings have been pushed through her earlobes, oil has been slathered across her face so thickly that the pores from which her moustache grows, opened wide in their freshly shaven state, stipple the smooth facade from beneath. For an instant Lara looks at Esther, her black, kohl-rimmed eyes seemingly depthless, then Esther hears *sk!*—Mother Mona's nearly silent snarl, like a dog whistle for girls—and steps back into line. Her temperature rises as if she's been set on fire, then rises further as she watches Lara turn her turn, a languorous, graceful sweep, as if she might be any of the girls. She might be, Esther understands. Her friend is gone, a stranger. Esther scolds herself for the salt rising in her throat, but her grief is as sharp as when she was ten, being told that her mother was gone. She longs to be knocked out.

Esther is closing her eyes against her tears when she becomes aware of a scratching at her arm and Mother Mona standing beside her. Mother Mona, tall as a man, with her painted jowls and her forked fingernails—the source of the scratching—and her silver eyes that travel Esther now, everywhere but her eyes. "You," she murmurs, in a voice Esther hasn't heard before. "He's calling for you."

WASHINGTON, DC

VEE

The Queen's Offense

She is still swaggering when she enters the room. She stops when she sees Alex's face, his inflamed eyes and pinched nose. On either side of him, men stand, as if part of an audience. They've removed their jackets. Some have removed their ties. They are clearly, as a group, very drunk.

"Vee." Alex smiles. He walks toward her and, for an instant, she relaxes. But his smile is for the men—it dissolves the instant his mouth reaches her ear. "I can explain later," he murmurs, "but I need you to do something. I need you not to ask questions."

"But—"

"Sh. No questions."

The men are talking, fidgeting, glancing at Vee and Alex, glancing away.

She waits. This is some kind of game, she thinks. Alex has made some kind of bet.

"Take off your clothes," he whispers.

Vee giggles; she can't help it. The alcohol is drifting downward now, leaving her head sober, her stomach sick. "You're joking."

"I'm not joking. I need you to take off your clothes, *all* of them, and walk in a circle around the room. That's it. That's all I'm asking for."

"Alex."

"Vee."

"You know I can't do that."

"Just the opposite. I know you *can* do that."

"Not in public."

"This is our home.

"Alexander."

"Vivian."

His hand is on her thigh, lifting her dress. She stops it by taking it in her own and squeezing. She is afraid to swat him away.

"What's going on?"

"No questions. I'll explain later."

"Explain now."

"Please."

Please. His icy voice merging with his sex voice. Vee's head seems to depart her body, float upward into the haze of cigarette smoke. She is all animal. She smells Alex's breath, alcohol gone sour with panic. She sees that the velvet drapes have been hastily drawn, their tassels left askew on the carpet. She sees two choices: play dead, or run.

Alex looses himself from her grasp with one swift pull and he moves around to her back. He breathes in her ear: "Don't think I didn't notice what you did with your collar. Come on, baby. Come on, my little slut."

He starts to unzip her dress.

Vee's eyes lose focus. The bank of men in front of her wobbles. Her dress begins to drop from her shoulders—the fabric peels away, still molded to her shape. The shape of shoulders, the shape of breasts. She is aware of air on her skin, between her breasts. She imagines turning the moment over on him now, walking out of her dress freely, and with grace.

"Yeah," Alex breathes. "Yeah." His voice all sex now, his confidence back; not only will he make her do it, he'll turn her on. She sees her back hitting the kitchen floor, feels his knee between her legs, hears Suitcase Wife's voice, *not a gentleman*. Who is this man? He is everything she's known him to be and he is a stranger. Something snaps in Vee—the deer realizing its camouflage can only go so far, understanding that its life is at stake. She feels her spirit stretching toward the ceiling, reaching for the women upstairs.

In the moment that divides this life from the next, Vee spins out of Alex's reach. *Go fuck yourself*, she says, so quietly she only hears it in her heart. Louder, to the room, she says, "Go fuck yourself." She sees the pull to her zipper dangling in Alex's hand. It's over. She will not wear this dress again.

BROOKLYN

LILY

Another Marriage

Later, when the girls are finally asleep and a puttanesca is simmering on the stove, Adam gets home. He sniffs the air and kisses her. They sit down to eat. She has set the table with adult placemats, the better wineglasses that require handwashing, matching cloth napkins. She is happy with the meal, not only because she was able to pull it off in fifteen minutes and it tastes good but because *puttanesca* means "the whore's pasta," a fact she knows but suspects Adam doesn't. She lights candles, and Adam laughs.

"What, are you trying to seduce me?"

"Yes," Lily says, laughing back, though their laughter, his and hers, like old matching robes, deflates her. The fisherman wouldn't laugh, she thinks. Hal wouldn't doubt. He wouldn't even eat. He would push back his chair, carry her to their bedroom, and screw her whether she thought she wanted it or not. Ugh. Apparently it's a bodice-ripper she wants, a man who will lay claim to her, do to her as she will one day warn her daughters not to let men do to them.

They eat. Lily works to regain her optimism. Adam's beard is already thick from that morning's shave, and she thinks about how she will enjoy that, and how, tomorrow, she'll carry his roughness around with her, a raw cheek, a scrape down her stomach, and enjoy the charge she gets, not only from the lust-memory but from the secret—it's the secret that will arouse her, the secret of the beard burn her husband gave her. Her husband's secret danger. He might look gentle and sensitive, he might be a nonprofit guy who can't say the word *seduction* without laughing, but he leaves a beard burn that lasts for days.

Between bites, Adam asks, "Did you forget I don't like olives?"

Lily looks at him, thinking this is a joke. But what would the joke be? "Since when do you not like olives?"

"These kinds of olives. These wrinkly ones."

"They're cured."

"They're wrinkly."

"Okay."

"I thought you knew. I've said so."

"You mean you've looked at me and said, *I don't like these wrinkly olives*? I don't think I've cooked with them in over a year."

"At restaurants. Wherever. I never order cured olives."

"And I should have noticed that?"

Adam's expression, as he looks at her, is not that of an asshole. He is not patronizing or even bemused. He is hurt, she realizes. And somehow this, the profound need in his eyes for her attention, for her to attend him, like a mother, enrages her far more than if he were simply acting like a jerk. And her anger is big and quickly blossoming; it extends beyond him to his mother, and to all the mothers of sons.

"I'm sorry," she says. "I did leave out the anchovies, Adam. It's not as if I don't think of you. But I'll add olives to my list. I'll develop a new system. I'll make a note in my phone whenever you express a preference for one thing or another—or when I observe a pattern of distaste, as with the olives. Maybe I can set up a reminder, so that if my phone ever senses me going for a jar of olives, Siri will stop me with her sultry robot voice: *Wait. Adam does not like olives. Put those olives back!* I like olives, Adam, and I thought you did, too. I'm sorry. I will never cook with them again."

Adam shakes his head. "It's okay. I can pick them out." And he does. Then he wipes his fingers on the cloth napkin, as Lily, thinking, *That's more laundry*, thinking, *Quell your anger, woman; calm this shit down*, asks about his day, and Adam tells her about a contentious meeting he ran about a new aquaculture initiative he's trying to spearhead in a Rwandan refugee camp. Camps in Zambia have built fish ponds, he says; he sees no reason refugees in Rwanda shouldn't benefit, too. They're from Congo and, more recently, Burundi. They eat fish. And the camp has been consistently short on food, underfunded since the media stopped paying attention. Fish ponds, Adam explains, not only produce food; they produce fertilizer for fields, which then produce more food, and he thinks the novelty of it could draw attention from new funders. But his colleagues are pushing back. Aquaculture in camps isn't common enough yet, they worry. There are too many technical challenges; health concerns; questions of ownership, training, oversight, etc. He's been hearing it from his own organization and from partner groups, too, from NGOs and usually supportive UN staff alike. They still won't accept that the camp situation has become protracted, he says, that the refugees there will not be repatriated in the next twenty-four months or even in the next decade. Adam tells Lily that he's managed to push a demonstration pond through, for training and breeding, but they've run into logistical problems—boys from outside the camp stealing fish out of the pools before they can reach full size. A fight broke out between the local boys and refugee boys, and one kid had to be driven to Kigali to have his eye socket reset.

Lily's brain hurts when she hears this, it's so terrible. And yet it's so far away, too, and she realizes, as she's listening, that she forgot the laundry again, when she and the girls got home. She wails inside but waits for Adam to finish talking, because she doesn't need to tell him about her failure and because how can she be thinking of laundry as he talks about kids who might die of hunger, or malaria? Why doesn't it make her heart clang and break? Why doesn't she ever do more than donate money? Vira did more than donate money. My heart isn't hard, Lily thinks. It's only stretched, and a little faded—often there is only enough space for her own kids' shit and string beans.

By the time Adam is done talking it's 10:04 and the laundry room has been locked—the super will have tossed their wet clothes into a wire basket. He'll have recognized the girls' Wonder Woman briefs, purchased by Lily's mother in an attempt to bring "*some* representation of female strength, and even then . . ." into their underwear collection, which until her intervention consisted of princesses from Target because, face it, princesses from Target were convenient. He will have ticked off another tick on his mental checklist of all Lily has gotten wrong. Lily fears that one day, if Adam and she can finally afford to buy in their building, it will be the super who stops them. She keeps meaning to Google whether this is possible—*superintendent influence co-op board*—but then, as with the laundry, she forgets.

She says none of this to Adam. She restrains herself from nagging him about his not asking about her day; she does not insist on telling him the storyless story of the sewing party; she turns off that self and brings up another. This is what men hate about women, she thinks, that we are actors, that between our urges and our actions there are these layers, this angling and scrim. Yet aren't they, almost always, the beneficiaries? She guides him to the bedroom and strips to the red lace underwear-and-bra set she managed to put on while cooking dinner and not doing laundry. She zips on high-heeled boots, knowing, as she does so, that her order is off—she should have gone to the bedroom first and stripped and zipped before letting him in. But it works out. Adam smiles, not in a nervous way but in a sexy way, and says, "Oh," and takes off his own clothes. The sex is good. Lily comes without a great deal of effort. No one told her in her twenties that although she was having sex in fair quantity, her orgasms were like sad nubs compared to what she experiences now. No one told her that the homestretch could be unvaried, even mechanical, and totally transporting. She is transported. She is wrung. Adam has had something to do with it. Lily didn't think once of the fisherman. Does she really need anything more than this?

But Lily's awareness, mid-postcoital embrace, that she didn't think of the fisherman reminds her of the fisherman, specifically of the fisherman's hands, which might after all do something differently than Adam's hands, something astonishing, something that would transport her further, or more completely, or maybe even transform her, into . . . ? And then into her mind drifts the moment Adam first got home and sniffed the air, and she realizes that in that instant he smelled the olives and she is angry again, though at what she isn't sure. Is she secretly angry at herself, for not taking note of her husband's aversion, and angrier still that a little part of her cares? Vira wouldn't have cared, she thinks. Vira was a killjoy feminist, the kind of ragey, righteous woman Lily's mother became for a while around the time that Lily's father had his affairs and left, presumably in part because his wife had become a killjoy feminist. (*A Well-Kept House . . .*) Vira was worse, maybe, coming a generation later and marrying in the awkward '00s, when feminism was uncool. She had an idea about "natural states," according to Adam. Lily's red lace getup would make Vira smirk. But Lily likes it. Adam liked it. He likes it when she takes control and dominates him. This is empirically true. Yet it's also true that he wants her to know, as if by osmosis, that he doesn't like olives.

Is it possible that Lily should try harder? She did not take the tenure-track job, after all. She took this. Is it possible that the line she seems to have drawn—lingerie, yes; utter attentiveness to Adam's palate, no—should go? Vira, and perhaps Lily's mother, would say no. Vira would say Adam wants Lily to fulfill some dream he has of being a man coming home to a wife and family—a dream a man like Adam is not allowed to talk about in 2016—but that he also wants Lily to resist his wanting this. He wants her to go further than sneering, as she did about the olives; he wants her to take a stand, say *No, go screw yourself, and while you're at it, uncure this!* That's what Vira would do. Based on what went unsaid in Adam's stories—back when he used to talk about Vira—resistance was his first wife's main mode of turning him on. And she did turn him on, Lily thinks, in a way Lily never has. There was an energy to that marriage, an electric fence between them, charged by their fights.

Between Adam and Lily, there is something else.

And no, not just the children.

Another kind of fence shared, this one around them. A determination to be people who stay.

Also, and related: comfort.

Maybe Adam wants everything. Maybe there's nothing wrong with this. He wants Lily to behave like she's married to a deputy director and he wants her to skewer him for his shriveled idealism.

He wants her to tidy herself with a razor and he wants a full bush. He wants her to be Lily and Vira at once.

Asleep now, on his back, lit by the city's perpetual glow, he appears peaceful. With each breath, his nostrils whistle; the shock of hair at his brow quivers. An old scar on his cheek glistens. It's from his childhood, obtained during a sandbox altercation with a shovel, and usually it's invisible, or at least blends in with other wear, but from where Lily lies at this moment it appears as if still wet. She nudges him, so that he rolls away from her, and wraps her arm around him. She noses his smooth back, digs her feet under his warm calves. She is glad that they are hairy and that his back is not, and glad that he is always willing in the morning to stay a few minutes late while she runs down to get the laundry. She won't have to haul the girls down with her, fighting about who gets to clean the lint screens. Her toes are warm, and deep within she is warm, and Adam's back is smooth and smells good and she is glad for all of this, and grateful. She can continue living the life she already has. Second wife. Mother. Seamstress in training. Esther.

As her eyes close, Lily does not think about the fact that Esther is an orphan. She hasn't once thought of it—there are too many orphaned heroines for their orphanness to be notable—let alone wondered what it might mean for her. When her phone rings in the kitchen, she decides to wait it out, then, thinking of the shrill, penetrating beep that will follow once whoever is calling her at 11:30 has left a message, she scuffs down the hall and grabs her phone to switch it to vibrate. But it's her brother Lionel calling, her oldest brother, who almost never calls and always texts beforehand when he does. "Li?" she says, instantly understanding, so that when he says, "Sorry to wake you, I just got a call from Mom," she is already thinking about driving north tomorrow, to her mother, who must be dying. Never mind that their mother lives in Lily's city now, a twenty-minute walk away, in Prospect Heights. Years ago, when Ruth still lived in Massachusetts and Lily told her she hadn't gotten the job and was quitting academia, her mother had hung up, driven the five hours down without stopping, and burst into the apartment warning of regret. *And boredom!* she cried. *Children are more boring than you can imagine, even ones you love!* Lily had been caught wearing a robe and flipping through wallpaper samples for the kids' room—now that they were having a second and she was not going to be a professor, she had decided wallpaper was called for. It was 2:00 p.m. on a weekday. *It's 2:00 p.m. on a weekday!* her mother had pointed out. But this was when Lily was fully absorbed in the new pleasure of flipping through wallpaper samples and not looking for jobs or writing unctuous emails to former advisors. More than pleasure, she felt relief, a relief so vast it seemed to alter the color of things in her path: the begonias halfway up Montgomery Place turned a hot, saturated pink; a cup of coffee swimming with cream was almost perverse in its beauty. It was the no longer trying so hard that drove her in those early days to near ecstasy; it was the decision to simply be a very pregnant woman that gave her the confidence that afternoon to answer her mother with a blasé shrug and offer her a sandwich of meats and condiments that Lily had procured earlier from three different shops on a long, slow, beautiful walk past signs promising *designed + crafted objects*, as if there were another possibility, even as her mother was frantically driving south. Now, as she leans into her kitchen counter and waits for her brother's next words, thinking of that dismissive shrug makes Lily want to fall at her mother's feet.

Lionel says, "It's not an emergency, but things can go bad quickly . . ." and the tenderness of his parsing—for her sake, she knows, smoothing the way for his baby sister—deepens Lily's despair. "I know," she says, trying to stop him, but he goes on, "All those cigarettes she smoked, after Dad left . . ." so that Lily has to say it again: "I know. I remember. She smokes now, you know. Two a day. First thing in the morning and after dinner each night. She never stopped." Her voice is sharp. Lionel stops talking. Lily is seized by a vertiginous swaying. Lowering herself to sit against the dishwasher, she squeezes her eyes shut until she can speak. "I'm sorry," she whispers. A teary inhale comes from Lionel and without effort Lily matches it. For a while they breathe their ragged breaths together. Then they begin to make their plans.

SUSA

ESTHER

Her Stunning Marriage

A smaller room. A bedchamber, dripping with silks, dim, the drapes drawn. A bed. Esther wakes here, unsure whether she has fainted or been drugged. She touches herself. Everything is where it was, sash tied, robe closed, string tied around her hair. She rolls to sitting and a mirror confirms: nothing has been done to her. There is a door. She moves toward it.

"Esther."

She turns, wishing she had not sat up. She should have feigned sleep, meditated until she had a plan, a map in her mind: escape. The man is sitting in the room's far corner, on a stool—a very short stool. His voice is not what she would have expected. It's a soft voice, for a man, and produces, in concert with the tiny stool, a disorienting impression. Esther wonders—hopefully, desperately—if she was right when she first saw him, on the stage, if maybe this man is not the king but some kind of performer. However insane this line of thinking may be, it's hardly more insane than the reality she's being asked to believe: that the king of Persia has just spoken her name. That he has chosen her to be his queen.

The man, still watching her, rests his head on the wall behind him. The wall is covered in reeds, Esther sees, reeds like the ones in the river by the camp, except these have been dipped in gold, so that the whole wall appears like the side of a glintfish the moment it's hit by the sun. If he were a performer, she thinks, he would not rest his head on such a wall. He wouldn't allow his head to rock slightly, as he does now, as if giving himself a scratch.

And so her insane hope falls out her feet, replaced by a surge of fear and heat that rises through her so forcefully she begins to shiver. The king's hand is reaching for the wine bottle. The king's voice is saying, "Come." Esther is walking as slowly as possible, drawing out her chance to think. There must be a solution. But what? She thinks of stories she knows in which impossible things take place. Sarah. Eve. Isaac. Dinah. Her father told her these and all the other stories until she could tell them back to him. They had to be told to be remembered, he said. They had to be remembered so you knew how to live. But Esther, beholding the dwindling distance between her and the king, doesn't see how they can help her now. The story she is living is nothing she has heard. In this story, the king of Persia is carefully, perhaps ceremoniously, filling two goblets: one for him, one for her. In this story, she takes one and realizes that it, too, like the stool and the throne, is undersized, meant to make him appear larger than he is. She wonders if he will stand now, to welcome her, and then, when he does not stand, she wonders if this peculiarity could work to her advantage—if the king is so determined to maintain the aggrandizing artifice of his set pieces that she could run now and he would not leap up to catch her.

The king lifts his glass to her and waits. What would he do if she turned and fled? His voice is soft, she thinks, but he banished his queen. He banished his queen, but he is very short. All she can read in his face as he looks up at her is waiting. No clear pleasure or displeasure in his eyes. No ripple in those lines between his brow. Even his mouth appears oddly neutral, neither open nor fully closed. He is not a man primed for a chase. Yet even as she calculates, Esther knows she is fooling herself again. She knows there must be guards on the other side of that door, with sharpened lances taller than their heads.

The end of another idea feels like a death; her shivering grows more pronounced. Gripping the goblet to steady herself, she begins to drink. She drinks as she walked, letting a trickle drop back into the cup with each sip, trying to prolong the activity, to think. But her thoughts are scraps that go nowhere: an awareness that the glass she's holding is pressing ornate shapes into her palms, a vision of her mother threading a needle, an image of Nadav's mouth, his brown, unbearded face. Soon Esther is drinking quickly—she drains the rest of the wine in two gulps.

The king, his eyes on the empty goblet, smiles. "I shouldn't be surprised," he says. "You were the only one who didn't try to hide yourself."

Esther watches as he fills the glass again. Her throat stings. Her trembling limbs are very warm.

"Do you come with a voice?" he asks.

She lifts the glass to cover her mouth. I shouldn't drink any more, she thinks. Then she drinks, quickly, beckoning courage, and soon her stinging throat begins to hurt less, to open, and the king is still smiling up at her, without cruelty, she thinks, and without falseness, and she thinks, wildly, I will ask for what I want.

"May I go home?" she says, holding out the empty goblet.

The king laughs. But when she doesn't laugh back, the king blinks, a long, slow-motion blink, so that for an extended moment, she is examining the purple veins on the backs of his eyelids, and praying, not the prayers of her parents, only *Please, please*. When his eyes open, they fix on the glass. His fingers brush hers as he takes it—they are dry and cool. *Please.* He raises the goblet. He raises it higher than she expects, his arm stretched toward the ceiling as if he is about to make a speech. Then the goblet drops to the floor, where it cracks with unnerving precision into two equal halves.

As Esther steps away, her blood knocking in her throat, the king releases a quiet chuckle. "You've just arrived," he says mildly. Then he fills another goblet and places it, presses it, back into her hands.

What option does she have? She takes it, and drinks, and knows what she must do, or try to do. She will transform. Until now she has held this possibility at a distance, fearing the risk, knowing what she has in mind is not the kind of transformation she was taught. The lesson she was given in the magicians' tent the night before Marduk brought her to the palace was focused on turning one object into another, or making something larger or more abundant or of a different quality. It was a beginner's course, meant to tie her to her mother and her mother's mother, to give her some sliver of their power to possess. Until this moment, she hasn't known if she would ever try to use it. But now she knows. As the king refills her glass again and guides her by the elbow to the bed, she is so intent on recalling how to do the magic she barely registers that he has finally stood up. She is only a thumb's width taller than he, it turns out. "Sit," he says, and she does, obeying so she can travel in her mind to the tent.

"You are a beauty," he says.

Esther, thinking, I will make it not so, lifts her glass once more to her mouth, and rewinds in her mind to her final night in the camp. Not a sound came from the Gadol family's tent, but when

Esther crawled in, their matriarch was awake, sitting over a brown flame that stank of goat. Above her, hanging from the tent's smoke hole, dangled a piece of wood in the shape of a hand. A hand was a symbol of peace in the camp, but the stink worried Esther. Why would the woman be reusing cooking oil? The camp required this now—the Persians had begun stealing first oil during their raids—but wouldn't a magician, if she were a decent magician, simply make her own fire? Esther wasn't given a chance to ask. The woman's eyes were bright, her cheeks as dry and red as the riverbank. She smiled as if she'd been expecting Esther and began interrogating her at once. What was she here for? What did she want? What happened to her hair? When Esther glanced with apprehension at the horizontal forms of the Gadol family, the woman sniffed. *They're out!* she declared, leaving Esther no choice but to ignore or trust the dozen or so strangers in her midst. She began to explain her situation. *Ridiculous!* spat the woman at the idea of Esther being put up for queen. *Moronic!* that Marduk could think his plan might actually work. Could he be so dumb, the woman asked—or this was the gist of what she asked; she spoke in an old accent and with a lisp, from missing front teeth—could he be so stupid that he actually thought a man like the king would notice the difference between those figs and these, let alone call off the Persian brigands on Marduk's behalf? *Cruel!* she cried, that he should make Esther go. If Esther had become a burden, he could marry her off; even without a dowry she was pretty enough that some boy would have her. Esther shook her head at this. She knew better than to talk about Nadav, but the woman's outrage had begun to pass in her mind as a kind of sympathy, softening her, and so she talked about Nadav, and once she was talking it seemed to her she should keep talking, that the more she told, the more sympathetic the woman would become. Esther was wrong about this. *Frivolous!* cried the woman. *Trifling!*

She knew, as everyone did, of Nadav and his family, knew he was basically betrothed to another girl and that Esther was no one to stop him. Esther should let him marry the other girl and choose her own, more realistic match. At this Esther felt a roil in her glands, the bitter flare that came just before she acted rashly. "I didn't come for matchmaking," she said. "And it won't help me now anyway. Can't you teach me something?" The woman slitted her eyes and sniffed. For a second, Esther thought she was about to be slapped for her rudeness. But the woman sat calmly, her hands in her lap. She held them in a way that caused Esther to look up and see that the hand shape she'd thought was made of wood—a common enough sight, though usually hanging outside a tent—was in fact a human hand, shriveled to hardness from smoke and decay. She felt a surge of hope; this woman did have power. Esther grew aware that the bodies around her seemed to be not merely asleep but in a deeper state; their forms were not rising and falling with breath.

"How do I know you're teachable?" the woman crowed. "Most aren't. Especially trifling, swoony girls."

"My mother was from magic." Esther reddened as soon as the words were out. Her mother was a quarter-breed, at most. She would have hated Esther using her in this way. She hated anything that reeked of boasting.

"What was her name?"

"Rut. Daughter of Hanya."

The woman's dry face did not move.

"Did you know her?"

The woman rubbed her hands together. Esther, wanting to shake her, said, "What do you know about her?"

"They were at the top once," was all the woman said.

And then what?

The king is walking toward her. He retreated briefly, to retrieve the bottle, but now he is back. He is down to only his black robe now, and the robe is open—is she imagining this?—to an extent that it wasn't before. Esther closes her eyes and hunts for the place the Gadol woman showed her. A dark, cold enclosure. It was meant to be a space outside her body, meant to be deposited into an egg, or a seed, whatever object she was working to alter. But Esther brings it inside herself. Then she brings herself inside of it, lowering herself down until a vibration finds her. At first it's almost like a humming, and then, without warning, it's nothing like that, it's a school of fish pulsing at the bottom of the ocean, hundreds of thousands of fish in a resplendent eddy contained within her. But they won't be contained for long. They resist her boundary, pressing outward as they flash and pulse, forcing her to enlarge. The dangling hand breaks in, not as spell or tincture but goading, meant to propel. There was power in Esther, the woman said, more than she would have guessed, but it was old and lazy and had to be whipped into action, and it was fragile and had to be handled with care . . . so Esther lets the hand hang in the room with her, a calm, terrifying stillness in the center of the pulsing eddy. Catastrophe is what she's going for, a full vortex, but to get there, she cannot self-destruct. She must become the eddy, the fish, the infinite flashing, without inhale or exhale, no longer breathing but existing, not waiting but allowing, not wanting but receiving.

It is exhausting, this work, far harder than digging or chopping or squatting. She is very cold, then very hot. As the pressure builds, she feels as if each of her digits, each limb and nerve, is being squeezed in its own vise.

A pressure from without. Esther opens one eye. The king, seemingly oblivious to her efforts, is tilting the wine bottle into her goblet, and for a moment, relieved of the pressure and the flashing, she lets herself rest. She waits for the wine to flow;

when it flows, she will force herself in again. Here, you may be thinking, she will lose her courage. She'll drink more wine, she'll start enjoying it, this will go back to the story it is supposed to be, where the maiden wants her beauty, wants to be queen. But Esther is very stubborn. And her stubbornness is aided by the fact that nothing flows. The bottle is empty. The king calls out, "Another!" and Esther, wanting to stay ahead of whoever will be sent in with the wine, dives back in again. Down, she tells herself, and the heat flips back to cold. She is distracted briefly, pulled from the vibration by a recognition, obvious yet fresh: the king has people; she has none. Don't be distracted, she tells herself. Don't be afraid, go in again. She urges herself lower but the pain is shocking now, the dark hole grips, the lights begin to flash fitfully and with menace, no longer the pulsing school of fish but a storm. She gasps but keeps her eyes closed, refuses even to peek. She is aware of the king on the other side but wills herself further in, downward, and noise recedes. The vortex holds her. She has never felt cold like this.

Years pass, or twenty seconds. When she is loosed from the place, dropped from the swirling, the king is still alone and staring at her. He drops the empty wine bottle, but without force, and the bottle doesn't break as the goblet did—instead it rolls in Esther's direction, arcing and wobbling until it reaches her foot. She looks down. Her sandals are in tatters; her toes have grown talons. "Your wine," a voice calls, and the king rushes to slam a door, blocking a passage Esther didn't see before. He throws his back against it and calls back, in a singsong to hide his quavering, "Wait! Not now!" Sweat rolls down his face. Esther turns to the mirror. She is larger in every direction, taller, wider, longer. Her face is made of her features but they have taken on new proportions and aligned themselves at new distances from one another. Her eyes are weirdly far apart and her nose and mouth unnervingly close. Her stomach has swelled, forcing open her robe, revealing breasts as small as kumquats. She pulls the robe closed, but not before she's sure he's seen. Her thorny feet are obscenely long, her skin mottled and rashy, her hands so fat they look like paddles. She holds them up for closer inspection and flexes them, then rises on her toes and finds that she can do this, too, and at these assurances that she is still in basic command, the blood hammering in her ears calms a bit. Still, she is shivering as she turns to face the king, who is flat against the door, his eyes huge and desperate. "What is this?" he shout-whispers.

Esther arranges her throat. "This is me," she answers. Her voice is her own. A minor comfort. "Here I am."

WASHINGTON, DC

VEE

Banished

The instant she spun away, Vee knew what she had done could not be undone. She fled, taking the back stairs to avoid the women's party, running until she reached the guest room on the top floor, locking herself in. She shivered uncontrollably. She could not make thoughts. She heard the sound of the house emptying, heard shouting, Alex and Hump, then silence, and time.

A knock, later. Late. She may have slept. Hump's voice on the other side. "Mrs. Kent?" She opens the door, but he is not the same man. His white-blond hair is damp and pulled into a point between his eyes. His eyes are eerily bright, the blue a marble's blue. He strides past her into the room, plants his feet, folds his arms, and says, "What will we do with you?"

Vee doesn't answer. It's clear from his crooked smile he already knows the answer to his own question, clear that the smile is not flirtatious or even pitying but cruel. Vee holds the doorknob and looks at the floor. She is no longer drunk; her head hurts. She is very thirsty.

"You had to understand it was necessary," says Hump. "You've always been a fun girl, Mrs. Kent. We didn't imagine you making a fuss. Then boom. Frigid as an iceberg. Shipwreck . . ."

Hump's voice is the kind of wave that smashes you to the sand. It recedes, leaves a ringing in her ears, smashes again.

"All it was was a little bit of payback. *I got a slice of your wife, you—*"

"I understand," Vee says, wanting it to stop.

"You understand. Oh. Because the senator, he wasn't sure you did. But look, you're a smart girl. You figured it out on your own. So what's your problem?"

The doorknob is wet against Vee's palm. "Where is Alex?" she asks.

"Crying his eyes out."

Vee looks up. Hump flashes her a grin that's gone the next second, a snake behind a rock. "Mrs. Kent. Would you like to tell me about your little ladies' lib group?"

She stares at him.

"Your husband is not exactly a man of principle, Mrs. Kent. He's full of information. And you know, that Fiorelli woman was not unhelpful, either. I caught her on her way out. It sounds like there was some tantalizing *behavior* going on at your party, too."

"Get out," Vee said.

"We've had a nice thing, you and I."

She works not to breathe.

"This won't be permanent," he says.

"Where is Alex?"

"But it won't be fun. You were such a fun girl."

"Where is he?"

"A car will be here at six."

There are questions she should ask. Where am I going, what is *this*. Instead she envisions herself disappearing. Not going anywhere, not running away—Hump wouldn't let that happen—but simply fading. Ceasing to be.

"Hey." Hump, on his way out, sets a finger under her chin. He makes her look at him. He has never touched her before. "Get some sleep," he says, and flips the finger and slides it down to the hollow in her throat, then out the ridge of her collarbone. He presses the finger into her shoulder, hard, and Vee realizes, an agony falling through her, that her shoulder is bare, her dress still half-unzipped.

AND SO

It Was Recorded:

THE NATIONAL ENQUIRER

NOVEMBER 4, 1973

EXCLUSIVE: The wife of Senator Alexander Kent has been admitted to Fainwright Hospital, the renowned psychiatric institution outside Boston, Massachusetts, the ENQUIRER has learned.

According to the senator's chief of staff, Humphrey Sumner III, the senator's wife, Vivian, 28, a petite, attractive redhead who hails from a long line of New England statesmen, suffered "a psychotic break following a party [last Friday night] that grew quite out of hand. We're still trying to determine whether she may have been under the influence of a narcotic. She has a delicate constitution, and the senator is comforted that she is now receiving the best care possible."

Although Senator Kent was not available for comment, Barbara Haskell, the wife of Congressman Haskell of Illinois, told the ENQUIRER that the Kents' party was "a terrific time, with women and men on separate floors; I've never seen anything like it. There was wonderful music and lots of dancing. Vivian is wonderfully pretty, a fun-loving hostess. I guess you could say it got a little wild."

Asked what "wild" looked like at a ladies-only event, another guest, Diane Fiorelli, who traveled all the way from Rhode Island to attend the Kents' party, reported that she was "concerned from the beginning about how things might develop, and my concerns were shown to be legitimate."

When asked to elaborate, Mrs. Fiorelli declined. But Mr. Sumner shared context that might help fill in the gaps, saying that Mrs. Kent had recently attended meetings of a Women's Liberation group in Washington, DC.

Susan Silver, a former classmate of Mrs. Kent's who joined her at these meetings, encapsulated their feisty libber spirit, saying: "This group is only radical if you believe that equal rights for women is radical. It's only radical if you think women should stay at home serving their husbands and looking pretty. It's only radical if you fear women using their full intellectual capacity."

According to Dr. Matthew Pickles, consultant psychiatrist at Horizon Psychiatric Hospital in Los Angeles, who has not treated Senator Kent's wife, the anger often on display at such gatherings should not be confused with Angry Woman Syndrome, a condition he has studied for over 35 years, though he acknowledges there may be overlap. Moreover, he said, "These Consciousness Raising groups are known to be havens for ladies seeking an alternative lifestyle."

Mrs. Kent and Miss Silver were classmates at Wellesley College, an all-girls school in Massachusetts. Both graduated magna cum laude; only Mrs. Kent is married, and both women are childless.

Apart from Senator Kent, Mrs. Kent has no surviving family. Fainwright Hospital, which has treated luminaries such as the poet Evelyn George and the musician Sid Healey, refused to comment. Asked when Mrs. Kent might return to Washington, DC, Mr. Sumner said, "I would be remiss to make any promises with regard to that."

SUSA

ESTHER

Of Course She Will Not Return

She looks again in the mirror. The taloned toes are still there, the kumquat breasts, the misaligned face. The only thing that appears unchanged is her hair, which looks out of place now, its black lushness like a plant springing from stone. She can't find the strip of leather she tied it back with before the pageant. Before the pageant is another life—her fingers tying the simple knot.

"What have you done?"

The king peers at her from behind his fingers, clearly terrified, and Esther shrugs in his direction, as if to say, *You can see what I've done*. It's not only her body that's been transformed, she realizes. A strength has oozed into her, like the tar that bubbles up sometimes into the sands near the river. A slick of dominance. She thinks of her uncle. He wasn't smarter than her aunt. He was just in charge. Esther picks up the wine bottle, still lying at her remarkable feet. It feels small in her enlarged hands—small and light, as if she could throw it a great distance. A thrill washes over her, awe and shock at what she's done, and is still doing.

"Please." The king begins to whimper. "What do you want?"

Esther sets her paddle hands on her wide hips. "To be let go."

If a hero in this moment would add, *And my people—I want them protected. Stop the cleanse*, then our Esther does not behave heroically. She is too intent on freeing herself for selflessness, too desperate to dare ask for more. To the extent that she thinks of her "people," she thinks of Itz and Nadav and her aunt, the ones she most wants to see when she is returned. Mostly she worries about the trick of turning back into herself. She decides she will have to visit the Gadol tent first, for help. But before that can happen, she must be released, and before that happens the door the king is pressed against is shoved open, sliding the king forward and revealing a man carrying a tray.

Here is the bottle of wine the king called for. But the man is no eunuch. On his substantial frame he wears a high man's robes, on his face the particular blankness of a man unwilling to appear shocked. He was on the stage, Esther remembers, a member of one wall. He sets the tray down now with an elegant swish, then faces her, his chest no more than an arm's distance from hers, his gaze piercing. For a moment, she is daunted. The king himself seems to be afraid of this man—he has already leaped up from the floor, wiped his face, straightened his robe. Esther squeezes the wine bottle, draws the beast's strength into her throat, and says, "Let me go."

The man narrows his eyes. He is taller than she is, even in her current form. His mouth curls into a smile that can only—and will only—be described as evil. In a calm voice, he says, "The king chose a beautiful virgin."

"She isn't here anymore."

His entire face slides upward, a sleeve of composure tightening over his rage. He goes to the king and begins whispering in his ear, his mouth twitching like a rodent's, his words inaudible but audibly venomous. The king takes a breath so deep Esther can see his robe strain. Esther can imagine what the man is saying. Some part of her thinks: I am standing too close. But another part is determined to show no fear, and this part is more persuasive. The king's nature is gentle, she thinks—she is almost sure of it. He isn't capable of attacking her. And she turns out to be right, because in the next moment it's the tall man who is pouncing, who pushes her to the floor and presses a knee between her legs, hard enough she feels her flesh open. She hears herself shriek as he pins her hands; the wine bottle slips from her grasp. He is stronger than she thought possible; even in her augmented form, she has to use all her might to flip him onto his back, and once she has him there, he pushes her off, flips her, and pins her again. She has never fought anyone, she realizes, and a bolt of fear gets in, slicing through her skin. Above her, his eyes are full of hatred. He yanks her hands, positioning her arms above her head and jamming both her wrists beneath his forearm. This, she thinks, is where he grabs the bottle and rapes her with it. He will cut her throat and burn her body; he will find a way to hide her. Her mother's voice comes to her, a thing she used to tell Esther to do if she ever met a boar in the hills: *Play dead or run*. Trapped under the man, Esther sees no way to do either. Mother! But the man doesn't go for the bottle. Instead, with his free hand he begins to scratch at her face. No matter how fast she tosses her head, his nails find her. He moves to her chest, clawing. She smells blood.

"It doesn't scratch off!" she cries.

The man snarls. "But of course it does," he says, and his sneering reinvigorates her—she kicks him away and rises to her knees. He will give up, she thinks. I am terrifying and repulsive. But as she pushes herself up to stand, she sees that her hands are getting smaller. This is what he meant. "It's working," he says to the king, and before she can breathe again he's pushed her back onto the floor. Esther tries to fend him off with her elbows but she is distracted by what's happening in her body—it's not the scratching causing it, she knows, but her fear. But this thought delivers more fear, and now she can feel the reversal happening, she feels herself sinking again into the vortex but there is no violence now, only a peaceful cycling, neither hot nor cold, a terrain so familiar she starts to weep, for she is turning into a girl as they watch. The king looks as shocked as he did when she became the beast. But the man—he is the king's highest minister, Esther will soon learn—lowers himself to straddle her and clamps her head between his forearms. "You will not mock the king," he says, raining spittle across her face. Esther closes her eyes and he uses his thumbs to pry them open. "Do you understand?"

She can't nod. He grips her head too tightly.

"His entire court was present on that stage. It was you they saw him choose, and it will be you who is his queen."

He releases her for an instant then grabs her again by her hair and with his free hand shows her a knife, which she feels a second later at her throat.

"What we do," he says, speaking softly now, enunciating with exaggerated care, "we do for the people."

The blade presses. Esther works not to swallow.

"If we falter, who can they trust? If we fail to rule, how will they live? Queen Vashti disobeyed. If she wasn't punished, think what would happen. Imagine, across Persia: In the houses. In the beds . . ." The minister's eyes close. His face twists. At first Esther thinks he is merely demonstrating his instructions, but as the moment stretches, she sees that he is fulfilling them, and imagining, and that his fury is genuine. A string of saliva hangs from his lips. A scream forms in her gut. Then the minister sucks back his spit, opens his eyes, and says, without a hint of emotion: "The queen is dead. You are queen now. Do you understand?"

His face begins to melt. In the night station one morning, Esther heard a girl from somewhere else talking about how in death, in order to give birth to yourself again, for the next life, you become a man for a short while, until you're through to the other side. This is nothing Esther is meant to believe. It's nothing she has wished for. But as she passes out, the new queen, her exile complete, it's what enters her vision. The chest that could have been hers, the jaw, the hands that might have killed. Better than becoming a beast would have been to become a man.

Part Two

Wandering

MANHATTAN

LILY

A Clean, Blank Room

"Go home."

"I want to stay."

"Sweetheart. I'm fine."

"You're not."

"Tonight I am."

"I want to stay."

A machine by her mother's bed issues forth a string of beeps. The machine has been beeping all day without apparent pattern or consequence, but still Lily jumps each time she hears it, shooting forward in her chair. Earlier she asked a nurse, *What does the machine mean?* only to be given an answer at once so basic yet unintelligible she became worried that the nurse didn't understand either. Since then—many ages seem to have passed since this morning, when Ruth was admitted to what is unhelpfully called "the step-down unit"—nothing any nurse or doctor has done or said has reassured her. She knows this is "the best cancer place" in the city, and that their survival rate for stage IV non–small cell lung cancer—Ruth's kind—is better than anyone else's. But it's still devastatingly low. And somehow the staff's certainty, the speed with which they've decided what must be done with her mother and the efficacy with which they carry it out, upsets her even more. Can there be nothing mysterious or new or unique about Ruth's cancer, nothing in her character—her sharp, dry, critical, forceful, optimistic, loving self—that prophesies a different ending?

"Relax, Lil," says Ruth. "It's like a fart. The machine just farts now and then."

"At some point it has to mean something."

"Lovie. You're so tired."

"I'm not."

Ruth sighs and closes her eyes. Lily's brothers have gone home, Ian back to California, Lionel to Connecticut. The diagnosis was four days ago; the initial shock has passed. Lily's hurt at the fact that Ruth called Lionel first has been buried. Ruth will stay in the hospital for a couple more days, then, it's likely, go home. *She's in good hands*, Lionel keeps telling Lily. *Don't burn out too quickly*, Adam says. She has extended June to full days Monday, Wednesday, and Friday, all the school had space for, and employed one of their occasional sitters to cover for pickup, etc., when needed. Adam supports all this—emotionally, financially, though the latter will be a stretch—but reminds her: *The woman drives you crazy*. Lily would tell herself the same thing, if she were the old Lily, of four days ago. But this Lily can barely take her eyes off Ruth for long enough to go find a sandwich. Something has cracked in her, a pocket of fear she didn't know existed has burst its seams and it turns out to be infinite, an infinitely renewable resource that rages through her like fire; if in one moment it calms to coal, the next a wind comes through, reigniting the flames. She has not taken a true breath in days.

What is she scared of? Adam wants to know. Other than death, of course. Her mother has had a long life. There is that. He is trying to pull her out just enough so she can see: the whole world isn't burning. He has rubbed her shoulders and brought her tea and taken her on a long walk in Prospect Park and shown her a map in the latest *National Geographic* depicting the earth in 250 million years, the continents merged into one mass. He reminds her that he and the girls love her, they are here for her, they will be here for her. Gratitude cools her, then slides away, feeble compared to her fear. She is interested only in her mother's aliveness; she wants only confirmation of it, again and again and again. She watches Ruth now, surprised once again at how undiminished she appears, despite the tube under her nose, the saline needle in her arm. Her mother's ferning eyebrows are still dark, a hint of glamour marking an otherwise earthy face. Her gray hair is not thin; she went to Lily's stylist recently and had it cut short. Her ears look almost elfin with the oxygen tube curled around them, her hands atop the blanket well veined and capable. She wears her own robe, of navy silk, brought by Lionel, who thinks of such things. Normally, Ruth wears some combination of jeans and a plain top, a turtleneck or pocket tee or crew-neck sweater, paired with hiking-style shoes or boots, all of it well fitting, even youthful, but still stolid, restrained. Stripped down like this, Lily thinks, to nothing but her robe and her beautiful eyebrows, she looks like a Ruth Lily has not really known. The navy sets off her tawny skin. Lily has always envied her mother's skin color—her own she finds pasty, a mix of pallor and freckles inherited from her father—and now she finds herself willing its loveliness to be their salvation, to somehow overrule the invisible but apparently inarguable facts: that inside her mother a lung has collapsed; that cancer cells are spreading, and not slowly.

Ruth opens her eyes.

"Are you having an affair, sweetheart?"

"What?" Lily's voice cracks. "What are you talking about?"

"I'm thinking maybe you're sitting here because you're having an affair and you're waiting for the right moment to talk to me about it." Ruth looks into her eyes as she learned to do decades ago, at a HinJewBu retreat center set into the folds of a valley in the Berkshires, so that—to Lily, at least—it seems she is silently shouting: *I am looking into your eyes!*

"I'm not having an affair," Lily says.

"Okay."

"I'm not going to have an affair." Though it's impossible to say this without thinking of Hal. Last night, at theater class pickup, which Lily's sitter couldn't do, Jace was nowhere to be seen. But Hal was there, apologizing for her. She wanted to do the pizza plan, he said, but a work thing . . . and Lily nodded, forcing herself not to look at his hands, or even at his wrists, which she had also noticed, because they were covered in ginger hairs and very appealing. *Let's do it anyway?* Hal said, in the kind of helplessly flirtatious way that helplessly flirtatious people have, people who may mean nothing by anything, who simply exude sex by standing there. Flustered, Lily declined, telling him about her mother's diagnosis by way of explanation, though nothing about the diagnosis explained why she and the girls couldn't join him for pizza and though as soon as she told him she was flooded with guilt at the intimacy she had shared, for there were people she knew far better whom she had not yet told. Like that, she had crossed a line. And now, as Ruth spears her with that dogged gaze, Lily feels as though her mother can see the thoughts she has provoked, Lily's fantasy: those hands, on her hips; a gruff altercation nowhere near a bed.

"Okee doke," Ruth says, doubtfully.

"Aren't you going to ask me if maybe Adam is having an affair?"

"I know Adam's not having an affair."

"Why?"

"I know. Your father had affairs."

"Yet you're asking me."

"You're not entirely unlike your father."

"What are you talking about?"

"Hard to satisfy. There's a kind of engine built into your brain, always churning. Your nature is to be angry."

"It sounds like you've thought about this. But I'm not angry."

Ruth smiles. Her teeth are small and straight and pearly—another thing Lily did not inherit. "You're not staying tonight," she says. "I'll call the nurses and tell them to put the cot away."

"Mom!"

"Go home. Bring the kids tomorrow. I want to see the kids."

"They'll be too loud."

"That's life."

Her mother flings an arm in the air, a flamboyant gesture that takes Lily's breath away for a second. She places her hands atop the blanketed mound of her mother's feet and squeezes.

"Are you hiding from them?"

"What?"

"You know what I mean."

"No. I don't." Lily removes her hands from her mother's feet.

"I don't mind it here, is the truth," her mother says. "At home there's so much—so many things I need to do, and want to do, and so many, just, *things*. It's peaceful—this clean, blank room."

Lily nods before she can stop herself. Of course she knew what her mother meant. It's impossible not to recognize that the hospital has its appeal, despite the noises and the lights and the reason they are here. Here, you can be nowhere. A kind of free. But she does not want to admit this to her mother, let alone hear her mother essentially speak her own thoughts. Her mother has always done this, and always it makes Lily feel as if she's been pickpocketed. She knows this is unfair, that they are both allowed to have the same common human thoughts. Still, she feels an urge to slap her mother away. She felt this when her mother asked for her hair stylist's number, too; she wanted to say, *No! Not yours!* Instead she said nothing, because she is middle-aged and semireasonable and should be able to share a hair stylist with her mother. Still, she was peeved.

In the hospital, stricken with fear, it's a bit of a consolation, to feel peeved.

Her mother reaches for the wand that calls the nurse. "I'm going to push this button now, and you're going to come back tomorrow with the girls."

"Please don't! They have school."

"If you can skip three days of home, they can skip a day of school."

"Mom."

"Bring books. I'll read to them."

Any further argument Lily might have made is deflated now, because the book the girls would most want to bring is the very same one her mother would most want to read to them: *Esther*. Besides, what kind of person wanted to keep her mother from her children? "I'm staying over," she says, "but I'll go home early and get them. Maybe you can talk June out of being Vashti, because that's her current plan."

Ruth's right eyebrow rises. "There's no shame in Vashti, Lily. Didn't I teach you that? It's all the same costume anyway, some old scarves, a little thrift-store jewelry."

"I'm making them dresses this year. And no one wants to be Vashti."

Her mother smiles, though it's not quite a smile. "Since when do you sew?"

"A friend is teaching me."

Her mother nods, then lets out a long sigh. "You've made a place for yourself, my Lily."

"What is that supposed to mean?"

"It means what it means. Nothing more, nothing less. It means I love you."

Ruth thinks she has insulted Lily; she is trying to smooth it over. But Lily genuinely wants to know. What is the place she has made for herself?

Ruth is waving the wand. "You have to go home," she says.

"No. Please. Look," Lily says, sliding in her socks over to the duffel she's been stowing beneath the hospital cot and digging through until she finds the piece of paper. She returns with it to Ruth, who squints at it, asks Lily to turn on the light, then squints again. This, too, Lily wants to keep forever—her mother's far-sighted squint.

"What is this?"

"A flyer from the management company that runs our building."

"I see that. But what are these pictures of?"

"Laundry! Laundry that sat in the washers for three days. They posted these all over the basement. Adam brought one when he came to see you yesterday."

"Okay . . ."

"It's my laundry! I messed up. Yesterday morning, the super's wife knocked on our door and gave Adam two basketfuls of our clean laundry, all dried and folded—she'd done it herself."

"That's very kind of her."

"She wasn't happy."

"Ah well," Ruth says.

"Ah well?"

"This sounds ridiculous."

"But now they've told our landlord."

"Well, that's ridiculous, too."

"It doesn't matter! We could still get kicked out."

"Over laundry?"

"Yes! I don't know. I just don't want . . ."

"So I'm right." Ruth hands Lily the flyer. "You want to stay here so you don't have to go home."

"Mom!"

"Would you turn the light off, honey bun? And this laundry thing. You're showing it to me at this particular moment—why? You think it will make me happy that you're sometimes negligent. That you're not a perfect little housewife. And I'll let you stay."

Lily sees that Ruth is exhausted—and that Lily is the thing exhausting her.

Ruth brandishes the wand and presses a thumb firmly to the red NURSE button. "So you'll bring the girls, and you'll bring books."

"Mom." But Lily knows she has lost. Sorrow washes through her. So what if she can't tell the difference between fear and avoidance? Does it matter? Both are real. Both would be solved by the same thing—her staying. As it is, she hears the clopping of the nurse.

"Can you do me a favor, sweetie?"

Lily nods.

"Be kind to yourself."

Lily nods again, though she wants to weep. If she were any kinder to herself, she wouldn't do laundry at all. Her children would go to school with their underwear turned inside out. This has happened, but only once.

"Being kind isn't the same as letting yourself off the hook," her mother says. Again with the mind reading. "Remember that column I used to like? The one the sampler came from—*A Well-Kept House Is a Sign of an Ill-Spent Life*? That same columnist—Letty Loveless, she was called—once wrote something like, *Take care of yourself. No one else will*. And it sounded so harsh, and like it couldn't possibly be true, like if you believed it were true you would just give up. But I don't feel that way about it now. Now I think it's meant to be hopeful. Lily. Are you listening?"

The nurse knocks and immediately enters, as nurses do. She doesn't seem to notice that Lily's face is streaming with tears. Instead she listens without facial expression to Ruth's instructions. Then she is folding up the cot, handing Lily her duffel, and guiding both cot and Lily out of Ruth's room, into the glare.

GLOUCESTER, MA

VEE

Early Exile

Lighter. Bourbon. Virginia Slims. Vee has arranged everything on a tray and set the tray on the rug in Rosemary's upstairs hallway, where she sits, feet on the first stair, waiting for Rosemary to emerge from the bathroom. This is their ritual, six days into Vee's "visit," i.e., banishment: the three children in their bath, the women at the top of the stairs, drinking and smoking. Also part of the ritual, at least for Vee: until the bathroom door opens, she can hardly breathe. Rosemary reassures her endlessly that she likes Vee being here; Vee won't stay as long as she needs but as long as she can! Still Vee can't shake a fear that at any moment she'll be kicked out, that tonight the bathroom door won't open and tomorrow—when she returns from one of her walks—the front door won't either. Coming here has saved her. Vee is certain this is true. To Rosemary, to Annisquam, this place where their families spent summers. Where else could she have gone? Not to the mental hospital, as the tabloids claim she has done. Her nerves are tight as wires but she's not crazy, or sick; she can get through a day. She gets through by smoking and taking long walks: around the point, then off the point, up roads that lead into the woods and down other roads that bring her to water and rocks. She walks past her parents' old house, owned by another family for nearly a decade but still preserved, as the houses here are, with its white paint and black shutters. It's been kept as a summer house and is empty now, a couple weeks before Thanksgiving, but when Vee walks past it she imagines the door to the screened porch opening. She can see her mother walking out in her barn coat and duck boots and pearls to check the work of the fall cleanup crew. Vee is glad her mother can't see her. Of all her mother's humiliations, and her grandmother's—the affairs, the talking over, the taking for granted their endless work making her father's and grandfather's world—none of that was close to this.

When she isn't walking, Vee reads. She forgets herself. She is fine.

So it's not as if she needs Rosemary with her constantly. It's only when Rosemary is due to return from somewhere—school drop-off, or the hair salon—that Vee's lungs stop working properly. Her palms sweat, her mind rakes, a frantic speculation as to what is happening and when it will end. She feels wild with helplessness, and this helplessness and the helplessness she felt that night a week ago, after Hump came upstairs and told her a car was coming, get some rest, pack your things—can it possibly be that only one week has passed?—are so similar, as sensations, that each time she waits for Rosemary, she is pulled into the spiraling. She shouldn't have made him angry. She should have buttoned her collar. She should have let him undress her. She shouldn't have resisted. She should have known what to expect. She should have made a speech. She should have spit in his face, should have danced naked, shouldn't have drunk so much, should have buttoned her collar. She keeps thinking back to the Jefferson Airplane concert where she was dancing with her friends when three boys moved on them, threading arms between their legs and up their skirts and trying to push fingers inside them. No one paid attention to the girls' shouts; they had to flee, run back to their motel, lock the door. They kept laughing, until one of them cried. They should have worn jeans, not skirts. They should have kept their arms down and their legs closed as they danced. She should have buttoned her collar; she should have slapped him. In the upstairs hallway now, she hears the crunch of her zipper breaking. Should have obeyed. Should have known. Should have done better with the Suitcase Wife, to placate and persuade, save Alex's career before he had to resort to—

"Vivian Kent! What did I ever do without you?"

Rosemary, opening the door, is drenched from the waist down, a waist she insists is already thickening by the day. Her doctor has confirmed that she is pregnant, and though it's early still, seven weeks, according to Rosemary the swelling happens earlier with each baby. She plops down next to Vee, dries her hands on Vee's skirt, picks up a glass from the tray, and holds it out.

"No ice tonight?" she asks.

"I forgot the ice." Vee pours. "Sorry."

Rosemary shrugs and sips. Her face is flushed from work and steam. The first night, Vee asked if she worried about the kids alone in the bath—there are two boys and a girl, ranging from eight to nearly four—and Rosemary shrugged then, too, and said they were good at looking out for each other. She has always been like this, Vee thinks—steady, calm, difficult to fluster. Her face is broad, her eyebrows notably darker than her sandy hair, her legs and arms strong for a woman, maybe a little thicker than ideal, but in a way that fits the rest of her, so that she never appears large, only grounded, impossible to tip over. Not that she's masculine or hard. She's just Rosemary, unfailingly matter-of-fact. Even her nails she now wears unpolished, not unmanicured like the women's-group women's but neither lacquered like Vee's, whose own scarlet preparty polish is starting to chip. *Buffed*, Rosemary calls what she's done. She is self-assured enough to go with buffed.

Vee lights two cigarettes and hands one to Rosemary, who doesn't smoke on her own but is game with Vee. She smoked two last night, a personal record, but still nothing close to Vee's five. Vee has been smoking while she walks, while she reads, while she panics.

"That's getting infected," Rosemary says, taking Vee's left hand in her own and laying it palm up in her lap. They look: the tip of Vee's ring finger is hot pink and inflamed. A few nights ago Rosemary removed a splinter from this spot, but Vee has not been keeping it covered as Rosemary instructed. When she returns half a minute later with antibiotic ointment and a Band-Aid, Vee feels a pang of embarrassment. She is not a child. And the splinter itself was a humiliation—she got it from the bottom of her dresser drawer as she was pawing for her sew-on-the-go box. She hasn't told Rosemary this. What would she say? *I got this splinter while desperately trying to snip off some buttons my husband told me to button*? Who fought that fight? Even worse, who lost it as dramatically and pathetically as Vee has?

Rosemary dresses the wound and returns the Band-Aids and ointment to the hallway medicine closet. Vee finishes her friend's cigarette for her, then lights two more and holds one out for Rosemary as she plops back down. Vee pulls hard on her own, fighting off the homesickness that hit her when she glimpsed the inside of the medicine closet. Rosemary's boxes and bins and canisters and sewing baskets, her *belongings*, where they belong. Vee has so little of what is hers now: a few outfits; her essential toiletries, including the Pill; four pairs of shoes; and—as ever—her sew-on-the-go box.

She packed only what she could carry by herself so that she could refuse Hump's offer to haul her bags out to the car. She knew he would offer, just as she knew he would open the car door for her, and wait until she was situated, and ask if she was comfortable. It was a Town Car. Of course she was comfortable. *This car is officially taking you to a place called Fainwright,* he said. *But you have it take you where you want, so long as it's out of the way. No one sees you.* He winked. *This'll blow over soon enough, Mrs. Kent. We'll get you back.* He slammed the door.

He missed the point, of course. How could she possibly go back? She had been debased in her own home, put to a test she would have to be whorish to willfully pass, then treated like a whore for failing. A psychotic, possibly lesbian, drug-doing whore, no less. It was a level of abuse she had not been raised to endure, no more than she was raised to travel for more than a few days without a trunk.

Rosemary has been generous, of course, telling Vee to use anything, wear her clothes, go into Rosemary's bedroom and help herself to the books she keeps in a long, low case by the window. Rosemary must have at least a couple hundred, and Vee has been making her way through the shelves—from *Jane Eyre* to a half dozen Agatha Christies to *Lolita* to *Portnoy's Complaint*—without discrimination or pause. Today she devoured one, called *Surfacing*, in which the woman—never named—might or might not be going insane and her boyfriend reminds her of "the buffalo on the U.S. nickel, shaggy and blunt-snouted, with small clenched eyes and the defiant but insane look of a species once dominant, now threatened with extinction." Vee laughed and gasped as she turned the pages. Still, it makes a difference that the book is not her own—that her books and Band-Aids sit in a house now locked to her.

Rosemary takes a long drag on her cigarette and stubs it

out. "I should get the kids out," she says, without moving from the floor. She tilts the rest of her bourbon into her mouth. "But I do like when they're in the bath. It's like the car. They're contained."

Vee nods, though she can only guess. From what she's seen of Rosemary's life, mothering looks mostly like a lot of work. Rosemary loves her children, clearly. They are beautiful and funny. But they also never stop moving, and they touch everything they pass, lamps and walls and the artifacts that Rosemary's husband has collected, and seem to have only three modes of activity, one in which they eat, one in which they bounce around the house and yard, and one in which they cry and whine until they fall asleep. And there's this other one on the way. Vee hasn't mentioned to Rosemary her fear that she, too, might be pregnant. For all the time they've spent together in the past week, she hasn't told Rosemary much at all, only the merest outline of what Alex asked her to do in front of the men and what she did in return. And Rosemary hasn't pressed her. This is part of what has saved Vee. She plans to talk, at some point, and she plans to ask about the cross; she brought Rosemary's letters with her, too. But for now, ordinary chitchat is preferable. Vee hasn't forgotten that as she took her bath and did her makeup before the party, she longed to be here, with Rosemary, steeped in what she understood to be domestic bliss. This is where she longed to be, and now this is where she is. She listens to splashing, a yelp, laughter.

"Hello?"

Philip calls out before he has fully entered the house, then his lower half appears at the bottom of the stairs. Decent black oxfords, well-fitted wool trousers, wool overcoat in the process of being removed. The ceilings in the old house are low, so that only if Philip climbs the first couple steps will his upper body and face become visible. So far, six nights in, he has not done that.

"Up here. Down in a few," Rosemary calls back, and her husband disappears. "I should get them out," she says again.

"Want help?" Vee asks, but Rosemary shakes her head, as always. "I've got it," she says. But she does not get up. "Just a tiny bit more," she says, holding out her glass, and Vee obliges and lights herself a fresh cigarette.

"What's with these clothes?"

Philip's shoes have appeared again.

Rosemary swivels to look at Vee. "Did you change the laundry?"

"Shit," Vee says. She put in a load before her afternoon walk today, then forgot it.

"Don't worry about it."

But laundry is the only task Rosemary has asked her to help with, and Vee heads down the stairs before her friend can finish her sentence. In the laundry room, she finds Philip, strain on his face, expecting Rosemary.

"Oh," he says.

"Sorry."

"For what?"

Philip is not bearded, as Vee remembered him being—or did she make that up, unconsciously casting him as the fiddler? She isn't sure she would even know he was a Jew if she were to spot him on the street. He looks like something, to be sure—his hair is wiry and dark, his mouth full for a man's, for the men of a place like Annisquam at least. He is brusque, but also transparent, unable to hide his reactions. Or maybe he is uninterested in hiding them—Vee can't yet tell. She also can't tell if, for him, checking on the laundry is a way to boss Rosemary or an effort to be ahead of the times, an early adopter of what the women's-group women called "home-front equity." He looks at Vee now with visible mistrust. What does he want her to say? She is sorry about the laundry. Sorry for surprising him here. Sorry for being in his house. Surely he doesn't expect her to say all this.

She slides past him and begins to load wet clothes into the dryer.

"Did you get any calls today?"

Each night he asks this. He wants to know if any of the papers have tracked her down. As if they would doubt the tabloid story that she is rehabilitating at Fainwright. In an effort to reassure him Vee made a call to the hospital and was promised that they wouldn't tell anyone whether Vivian Kent is there or not—not because she is who she is, the woman was quick to add, but because of policy. And Vee understood. Half their patients, famously, were famous, most far more so than Vee.

She told Philip about the woman's promise. She reminded him that she has no family for people to badger, no aunts or uncles, no parents, no siblings, and that the only people who know where she is are Alex and Hump, who have no interest in sharing that information. She explained that no one recognizes her, that even on her trip northward, the driver, an Albanian man who was silent for 99 percent of the ten-hour drive, did not insist on any kind of costume when she got out at rest stops.

But Philip is not assuaged by any of this. He insists she wear a hat on her walks. When she tells him now, "No calls," he stays in the doorway, silent, until she twists around to face him. Philip is shorter than Alex but broader in the shoulders and meatier in the arms, like he might have been a wrestler once upon a time and has the potential to grow a little fat as he ages. He stands tilted against the jamb, arms folded, frowning, and for the first time it strikes Vee that he may be afraid not only of attention but of her.

"I'll leave as soon as I can," she says.

"Good," says Philip.

Vee nods.

"This is a quiet house," he adds. "Rosemary and I would like to keep it that way."

A flush of anger moves through her and as she turns away, and sinks her hands into the cool, wet clothes, she begins to hum, pretending great concern about locating care labels, until, finally, she hears Philip's footsteps in retreat.

SUSA

ESTHER

The Queen, Nine Months Pregnant

You had to understand it couldn't be prevented. She is eighteen, ripe as a rabbit. Her stomach sits in her lap. Her feet are being rubbed. The midwife doing the rubbing discreetly avoids the bulging knuckles on Esther's big toes, remnants of her beastly transformation, but that does not mean she—or any of the midwives—trusts her. They have been too close to her for too long. They know the other changes, as well: the slight deformation of her ears, pointed where they used to be round; the permanent rash that runs along the tops of her thighs; the way her nipples have turned from pink to purple. Granted, this last problem could also be linked to her condition. Either way, they will never go back to pink, just as her ears and skin and toes will never return to their original forms.

You had to know she didn't escape. Smart girl, very brave, became a beast. But this is not fantasy.

Esther's face is altered, too, though this has nothing to do with accidents of amateur magic or ravage by hormones. The minister's scratching did it, striped her cheeks with vertical paths slightly lighter in color than her skin.

She lives well, Esther. Like a queen! She is a queen. There are jewels and silks and velvet pheasant dinners and rare wines. Yet none of this has dulcified her. Last week, when she was invited to dine with the king, the king's minister—the one who scratched her and held the knife to her throat and who has turned out to be the only minister who matters—informed her that the wine in her glass cost more than the diadem on her head, but to Esther it tasted like overdried fig. She knows her chambers are basically another harem, if the upstairs version. There are plenty of windows, and she is allowed outside, but only in the courtyards, and only within the boundaries of the palace walls. The king and his minister mistrust her, for obvious reasons.

The walls of her chambers are so soft you could sleep on them if the world fell over, which it might have as far as Esther is concerned.

Another girl would have relented by now. But Esther, possessed of an extraordinary self-regard that pitches her alternately toward survival or doom, is still at war. If she cannot save herself, she has determined, she will make good on Marduk's ludicrous boast and save her people. They are still out there, she has learned, still being attacked, still leaving themselves attackable. It doesn't matter what makes them stay, she has decided, whether it's inertia, or stupidity, or some delusion Marduk managed to make them believe about Esther's powers of persuasion. All that matters is that they go. All Esther does now is to make sure that happens.

She tried Lara first, some weeks after the choosing, found her lying on her bed, as hairy as she was born to be, eyes closed. Esther's old bed was empty, and in the light then streaming down from the slit of a window Esther could suddenly see the ghosts of the tally marks she'd once made. How long ago was that now? Something about the way Lara had arranged herself, her legs spread comfortably like a man's, her palms resting on her breasts, gave Esther an understanding. "You were the one who erased them," she said.

Lara startled like a deer hit with a bow, opening her eyes and leaping up in one swift movement. She had grown fat, Esther saw. It suited her. Her sickly, stubbled skin was gone. Her eyebrows had grown together into one line that dipped slightly in the middle, like a great, gliding bird. Quickly, she took an inventory of Esther's queenness, from her jewel-heavy diadem past her layers of silk to the gold fringe that swept the floor wherever she went. Then Lara smiled, her thin but glittering smile, full of mischief and warmth, and Esther's throat went hot. She waited for Lara to embrace her. They were alone—the other girls had bowed absurdly low and fled when they'd seen Esther enter. She was not pregnant yet that day. She had known the king twice only, both times in blackness, encounters so brief and seemingly independent somehow of Esther herself that they made less of an impression on her than her first kiss with Nadav. She still felt at that time that she belonged more to the night station than she did to the royal chambers.

But Lara stayed where she was. "It was so hopeless making," she said. "One day, fifty days. What difference would it have made?"

Esther fought off tears. Why had she started with an accusation? She did not want Lara to hate her. She didn't want to go back to her chambers, alone, to sit upright through dinner, playing queen. What she wanted, she realized, what she wanted almost as much as she wanted Lara to help her bring a message to the camp, was for Lara to lie down with her like they used to, when they were still waiting. Lara's smell was as it had been, eucalyptus and salt. Esther would lie behind Lara and scratch her back, and then Lara would lie behind Esther and do the same, and all the while they would trade stories, until one of them fell asleep or got called off to some useless task. Esther's longing for this closeness was almost embarrassing in its intensity, as bodily as thirst or hunger. But what could she do? It was Lara who had spurned her, not the other way around. It would have to be Lara who came forward. In the absence of that, Esther would have to act as if she didn't care.

"So you tricked me twice," she said.

"Tricked you?"

"My tally marks. Our plan, to go as ourselves."

"I meant to do it."

"Really."

"I did. I meant everything."

"So?"

"I couldn't."

"Couldn't what? What we were doing wasn't hard. It was the opposite of hard."

Lara looked away. She shrugged. "I must not be as brave as your majesty."

"Don't call me that."

"But you are. That."

Esther emitted an involuntary groan. Apart from her robes, there was nothing queenly about her. There had been no training. There had been a ritual with the crown, but the priest spoke in an ancient language no one but he seemed to understand; nothing about it resembled any marriage Esther had ever seen, and afterward the king's minister breathed in her ear: *Try a fleck of sorcery and I'll have you impaled. Right here.* He'd shoved her with genius stealth into a pillar, then called the king off to some business of some sort. Since then, Esther had been attended constantly. She had been fed like a queen, and bathed like a queen, which was to say she had been fed and bathed like a night station girl was fed and bathed, yet more indulgently and with more ceremony, no longer part of a herd but elevated, alone. She had been praised. But she did not feel like a queen. It was all a costume. Couldn't Lara see that? She was squinting at Esther. She drew closer, examining, until her breath landed on Esther's skin. "What happened to your face?"

It was an opening. Esther felt an anticipatory unclenching, the confessional equivalent of salivating before a meal. She almost told. Later, she would return to the moment and wonder, if she had sat down in her queen's robes and told Lara everything—the cold, pulsing vortex, the beast, the near-escape, the knife—might it have made the difference? How, since then, she had tested herself, in secret, and found her powers so sapped it took her three hours to move a ring an inch? Would Lara, allowed in, have taken pity on her and gone to the camp? But that day in the night station she was so hurt still by Lara's defection, and so hungry for Lara's touch, and so angry that she was being denied it, and so disgusted by herself that she needed it, and so determined to protect herself against any of these feelings, that she gave back to Lara what Lara had given her and asked, coolly, "What difference does it make?"

Lara backed away. And that was how they stood for the rest of the negotiation, which is what it became, irrevocably, the second Esther said, "I came to ask a favor," and began to try to sell Lara on privileges like access to the wives' swimming pool and invites to an upper-tier banquet in exchange for Lara going to the camp. "And you'd get out of here for a while," Esther added. "I'll tell whichever eunuch brings you to take his time."

She was still innocent then—both of how a queen was supposed to talk to people and of how the people could just say no. Lara didn't even apologize. She said, "I can't."

"Why not?"

Lara, after a pause, said, "No one's told you what's happened with the camp."

"You mean the bandits?" Esther's voice dove deep, mocking: "*The king's cleanse*? They've been doing that for a long time."

"No. There's a new edict. Any non-Hebrew communing with a Hebrew will be put to death."

Esther laughed. "That's not possible. How would they buy or sell anything? How would they live?"

"I don't know."

"So the Persians must have stopped, then. Smashing the tents?"

"No. That's allowed."

"When was this?"

"Right after you were chosen. What's he like?"

"Who?" But Esther was distracted. *After you were chosen.*

"The king," said Lara.

"I hardly know him."

"But haven't you *known* him?"

"He's harmless."

"Clearly he's not."

Esther could have explained how the dangerous one wasn't the king, but said instead, "I have to go."

And Lara didn't protest. She said, to Esther's back, as nonchalantly as if they would see each other again in a couple hours: "Those things you offered me? The pool, the banquets? Do you really think it's up to you, to let me do those things?"

Esther went straight to the king. His guards scoffed—they had not been told of any permission granting the queen entry today. And the minister was away, in Persepolis.

"I have no permission," she said. She was shaking. "I won't go away."

Time passed. Esther had to sit down on the floor with her head between her hands; she could hear her teeth rattling. At some point, her arms were grabbed; someone hoisted her onto a chair. The queen must not sit on the floor. By the time she was led into the chambers, her shaking had given way to a dense pain that circled her head as if tracing the line of her crown.

The room where the king waited for her was not a room she had seen before. It was darker than his other rooms, without windows, lit only by torches and crude ones at that, the kind used in the palace's passages and storage closets. Dominating the space was a large table strewn with tools and what looked like tiny stones, along with shelves—these, too, strewn with objects—that filled an entire wall, from floor to ceiling. The table was the only bright surface, its length lined with torches.

Esther blinked, trying to bring something into focus. Even the king, seated at the table, appeared blurred at his edges. Without looking her in the eyes, he pointed at a long, low cushion.

She sat.

When he didn't speak, she began, "I'm here—"

"You're bold."

"I—"

He lifted a hand. "I understand."

Esther waited. Her head hurt. It took all her strength to hold it upright—her crown felt heavier than water. The king picked up a tool. It was made for him, clearly—small, for his hands. He looked at the tool, then he picked up one of the stones in his other hand and began to scrape the stone with the tool. Then he stopped.

"You want something."

Esther nodded, though he wasn't looking at her. She was struck by how tenderly he handled the tool and the stone. This moved her to speak more freely than she might have, to use the voice she had not dared use since she had told him she wanted to go home. "What have you done to my people?" she asked.

"You'll have to be more specific," the king said. He brought the stone to eye level, lowered it, and began scraping again.

"The edict. Why?"

The king bent lower over his table. "There are differences," he said, in a strange, singsong way, as if repeating something someone else had told him. "There are differences, and there are times when people must be reminded of these differences."

"I'm one of them. You know this."

He looked up and gave her a woeful smile. "I don't know what you are."

"I'm a Hebrew."

"You were."

"I still am."

"You're queen."

A fresh sharpness joined the pain encircling Esther's head. "You're punishing them because you despise me," she said.

The king set down his tool and stone and stood up from the table. Then he crossed the room to Esther and knelt in front of her. The torches sputtered behind him, throwing his beard and nose into shadow and making his eyes appear abnormally bright. He was quiet, examining her face. His eyes trying to get inside her eyes. This felt more threatening somehow than what he'd done with his sex the times he'd climbed atop her. Esther remembered his calm before he smashed the goblet. She worked not to flinch.

"I don't despise you," he said finally. "I mistrust you. I always will."

Esther felt tears coming, but she did not cry. If she had not asked to go home, she thought, if she had not become the beast . . . the camp would likely have been forgotten, left alone. *Right after you were chosen*, Lara had said, and now Esther knew with certainty: what she had done was worse than merely failing to save them. She was driving them more quickly to destruction. She began again to shake.

"Esther. Beautiful Esther." The king ran a finger down her left cheek, then another down her right. He touched her with the same tenderness and deliberation with which he handled his tools. Esther could see that he wanted to love her. She had sensed this before, in the dark, as he found his position above her, as he moved, and then stopped moving. But now she knew. He ran his fingers across her brow, pushing hair out of her eyes, and she could see that he was desperate to go back to before the beast yet couldn't, not fully, not just because of her changed toes and ears but because the beast had left an after shape, like the way the sun left imprints on your vision even after you'd closed your eyes. He could not unbeast her. He could not unshame himself. Knowing this made her feel weaker—a softness for him knotted in her breastbone—and also more powerful, because she understood that he was weak, too.

She did not love him. But she touched his hand that was in her hair. "I want you to undo what you've done," she said. "And I want to know things before the girls in the night station know them."

The king said nothing. He took off her crown—sweet relief—and laid her down. The cushion was long enough to be a bed. It was a bed, she realized. He took her breasts out of her robes and sucked them, and Esther, despite herself, or to save herself, allowed herself to feel a jolt of pleasure. But mostly she made herself like the ground. She closed her eyes. She endured.

Robes are timeless, convenient, easily opened, easily closed. When the king was done Esther closed hers and, without asking, went closer to his table. The objects weren't stones, she saw, but bones. Tiny bones.

"Birds," she said.

"How do you know that?"

Behind her, on the cushion, the king lay atop his own robes, unclothed. She did not look at him.

"I know a woman—" Esther stopped. It struck her that these bones were those bones, that the reason the palace kept commissioning more necklaces from Nadav's mother was not to adorn the wives' necks—Esther had never seen any of them wearing one, now that she thought of it—but to supply the king.

"She's very gifted," the king said.

"Why have her go to the trouble of separating all the pieces and making necklaces, only for you to take them apart again?"

"It's a puzzle. I like the puzzle."

On the shelves, Esther saw, the bones had been put back together again to form birds, or skeletons of birds. Some were complete, others partial. Some bones that could not take a wire through them, foot bones for instance, the king had fashioned out of silver. Esther lifted one skeleton to see how it could stand and was impressed by the intricate joints and loops, the melding of wire and bone. The thing weighed so close to nothing she had an urge to crush it in her palm. She picked up another, larger one—not a bird.

"Fox," the king said. "Be careful."

She touched a few more, letting him worry, feeling the beast's hardness climb up her back. Then she picked up the largest one and set it on the flat underside of her forearm, as if it were running toward her hand. "So how do you get the bones now?" she asked, without looking at him.

"What do you mean? Birds are always dying."

"I mean with the edict. She's a Hebrew. No buying, no selling . . ."

"I make an exception."

Esther set the fox skeleton back on its shelf. Then she picked it up again, twisted off its front feet, and returned it to the shelf on its back. She let the feet drop to the floor.

"Esther!" The king heaved himself off the cushion, tying on his underrobe as he went. He gathered the foot bones in his palm and held them under a torch.

"I'm not done," Esther said. "I want my people left alone. Send them into the desert if you want. But let them be."

He placed the bones on his table, out of her reach. "They can go into the desert whenever they want."

"But they won't."

He began putting on his other robes.

"Expel them," Esther said.

He worked slowly, meticulously. Black, purple, blue, red. He tied the knot as if constructing one of his skeletons, and she thought of Vashti. How could this man have been able to bear killing her?

"It's not up to you, is it," she said. Lara's words to her. "Expelling them, ending the cleanse. You're not the one in control."

The king did not react.

Esther picked up a bird skeleton. With her other hand she loosened her belt and formed a cradle of fabric in her robe, into which she tucked the bird. She moved slowly, in plain sight. But the king said nothing. He put on his crown, turned back to his table, and began to work.

That was the day the baby had been laid inside her. The following week, she found Baraz, to see if he would help her. He had been missing more often, others serving in his place. She had to search the palace twice before coming upon him in his room—lying on his long bed, eyes closed, as if asleep. She took off her robes. She was ready to let him rub his face all over her, to let him lick her and put his fingers inside her. It would not make her feel foul now, she thought. She was already fouled. It would be a mere transaction—this for that, her body in exchange for his body going to the camp. She laid out her terms. She assumed he would find the risk worth taking.

But Baraz, like the king, like Lara, said no. *No, I would not defile you in such a way. I'm sorry.*

That had been the worst. After Baraz, no one's refusal surprised her. Not the cook's or the chambermaid's or the gardener's. Yet she couldn't stop asking. She wandered the palace, the passages, the kitchens, looking for someone, anyone, who might yield, offering not her body but whatever she thought a given individual might want. When her belly started to grow, the midwives tried pushing her back to bed. *What's your itch?* they wanted to know. *What's your complaint?*

She ignores them whenever she can. She continues to find new targets. A stable boy. A wet nurse. It is such a simple message she wants them to convey: *Go now. Go far.* But no one even hesitates. *No, no, no, no.* They profess pity. She sees them looking at the lines on her face. From any distance her scars are unnoticeable—if only she kept her distance, like most queens—but up close they look like golden creek beds running through brown sand and provoke a range of reactions. Maybe they are chronic tear stains—the king has caught a miserable for a queen! Or the queen is part divine, sent rays by the sun. Or maybe she is a warrior, from one of the tribes that stripes its young. Only a few, the shrewdest of the ones she presses about the camp, suspect she may be a Hebrew. The king and his minister have told no one this small and large fact.

No, no. Not a single one even asks what message she wants delivered. Yet Esther tries. Her trying is like a disease. Even now, with her feet going numb under this midwife's rubbing, she is wondering what she might be able to say to entice the woman. Esther hasn't noticed before how blue her eyes are, so light a blue they appear almost colorless. One doesn't often see blue eyes in Susa in 462 BCE. Maybe it means she is weaker than the others, more apt to submit?

Then two other midwives walk in, slapping their hands together, putting an end to what has not begun. The blue-eyed midwife leaves silently.

"Time for a rest," the thin one says, as if Esther has not been resting.

They are affable, the midwives. They smile and speak kindly and sometimes it seems that they actually like Esther—that they are not simply doing their job. She likes them, despite their pushiness. They move with purpose, their sleeves double-backed onto their shoulders to keep their forearms free, their hands always doing something, or more than one thing, washing while they fold, or stuffing pillows with feathers while they stir a poultice with a foot. Their efficacy is extreme, almost to the point of strangeness, as if—Esther sometimes thinks—they might be sorceresses in disguise. Even their skin color—there are perhaps a half-dozen of them, their skin running from clay-dark to tusk-white—seems designed for her, as if visual harmony will be of help. It is. They are a comfort.

A hand moves across her stomach, pauses, moves again. "Good," says the fat midwife.

"Why?" Often, the creature inside Esther bucks or flutters. But now she feels only her feet, returning from numbness.

"Three hands," the midwife says. "You are perfect."

Esther returns her smile. It fills her, this praise—she can't help the flush that crawls up her neck as the midwives lead her back toward her chambers. The midwife is telling her that she will give birth to the king's child; she is also telling her, in not so many words, that the child will be a boy. The king's first. Vashti was barren, and his other wives have only borne girls—or at least girls are the only infants born to his wives that the king has claimed as his own. He wants his heir to be born to his queen. And so he will be. To Esther.

She crosses the threshold and goes cold. The silked walls, the tall bed, the cool silence, the boy in the corner already flush in the face from fanning her air, all of it wakes her from her moment of indulgence. As she climbs the steps to her bed, she feels small, and stupid. How could she forget, even for a moment, the camp? And why did she imagine the blue-eyed midwife might have been the one to obey her? She shouldn't be surprised anymore by the power she lost when she went from being a night-station girl to being queen. Esther has been low, too. She knows being low can make a person righteous, and if righteousness isn't power exactly, it's power's kin. Now she has only this: cool silence, ease, these bedclothes, this sensation of sinking. It is all, inarguably, exquisite. The boy inside her stirs. The boy in the corner fans. The door will be guarded. They tell her to sleep. But she is never tired.

BROOKLYN

LILY

Another Chamber

"Tennis balls?"

"Tennis balls."

"Okay . . ." She is listening to Ruth's story, or trying to listen, but her mind keeps catching on potential dangers in her mother's bedroom: the four-poster bed that must be climbed into, the rugs her mother has never bothered to stabilize with rug pads, the jagged rock her mother uses as a door stop, the piles of books strewn across the floor. Ruth has grown weaker in the three weeks since her diagnosis, though she won't admit it. The fact that her doctor has yet to deliver a solid opinion on whether her decline is largely a side effect of the chemo and radiation or a result of the treatments' failure makes it easier for Ruth to pretend she's fine. But Lily knows, or believes she knows, that her mother is dying. She sees that Ruth does not lift her feet enough when she walks, so that even if she hasn't tripped yet, she is perpetually almost tripping. Her mother's beautiful skin has turned pale. Apart from her appointments, she chooses to stay home. Her friends come in the evenings and Lily during the day, by herself Monday, Wednesday, and Friday and with June on the between days like this one, plopping June in front of *Super Why!* in the living room before making tea. Each morning she pauses at the bedroom door and exhales before entering. It is unnatural to see a person every day and be able to see them changing. Even her daughters, who are growing at alarming rates, look the same on a given morning as they looked the day before. But Ruth, each time Lily arrives, appears to have passed through years of life since Lily last left.

"So I sewed them into the back of his shirt," Ruth says.

"Did what?" Lily is noticing how thickly her mother's ceiling fan is coated in dust.

"The tennis balls. I'd read a column, 'How to Stop Your Husband from Snoring and Save Your Marriage.' This was in *McCall's*, before I knew there were other magazines. Or I guess I knew, but I didn't dare. In any case. It said the trick was keeping him off his back, and the trick to keeping him off his back was tennis balls."

"Ouch."

"He didn't try to stop me."

Lily tries to imagine this encounter. She comes up blank. She knew her father, both before he left, when she was almost eight, and after; until he died of a heart attack when she was nineteen, she and her brothers visited him in California once every year. So it's not as if she can't picture his face or hear his voice. Still, he is most real to her as a presence more than a person, a solidity who never took off his shoes except to bathe, sleep, or swim. She cannot remember him talking to her mother, even to argue. Instead she remembers the sensation of being with him; she remembers feeling when she was with him that authority existed, that whether she liked it or agreed with it it would continue to exert and produce itself. She remembers feeling comforted by this. She can see now that this feeling was a delusion, an internalization of the patriarchy, or perhaps the patriarchy itself, but that doesn't change the fact that she still thinks of her philandering father, dead for a quarter of a century, as a comfort. Whereas her mother, her mother who is here with her, who has always been here, who she wishes could stay here forever—with her mother it is not as simple.

"So did it work?" she asks.

"No. He just went on sleeping on his back and snoring. It was like he couldn't feel the balls at all. I was devastated."

"That sounds a little dramatic."

"Does it, Lily?" Ruth takes a long sip of tea. Her swallow is audible, and painful sounding, and Lily is sorry. Her mother rarely talks about her own feelings, she mostly pushes other people to reveal theirs, but she just confessed to Lily *devastation*, and Lily shot her down. "How did you even manage that?" she asks, trying to rewind. "How do you get tennis balls into a shirt?"

"You need two shirts. One larger than the other, and you sew . . . it's almost like a duvet? But instead of down, you're sewing in tennis balls." Ruth stops, seeing Lily's confusion, then says: "I was a very good seamstress once."

How Lily did not until this moment register that her mother has been talking about sewing, she doesn't know. Ruth's face is blank, her lips in the thin line she used to make when she was teasing the children, not letting a smile show. But Lily can't tell if she's teasing now, or if she's oblivious, if her sickness is starting to blunt her. She knows that Lily has been struggling to make the girls dresses, or rather struggling with the fact that she's not making them. Lily has told her how a week after her first lesson, she missed her second date with Kyla. Lily was in the hospital with Ruth, in fact, when she was supposed to be ringing Kyla's bell.

Kyla understood, of course. Kyla was sympathetic and concerned and asked how she could help and then, when Lily, overwhelmed, failed to respond, Kyla simply delivered a meal to Lily's building. She didn't buzz the apartment, didn't even demand that interaction, just left it with the doorman and disappeared. And each week she has checked in. *No pressure, just want to remind you I'm here whenever you're ready . . .*

But Lily is not ready. And Ruth knows this. She knows—Lily believes she must know—that Lily cannot go more than an hour without thinking of Ruth, that to go to Kyla's would seem a betrayal. Ruth has to know this. She has told Lily the dresses are a torture device she's invented for herself, that she should give up, use scarves, buy something online. And yet, without a hint of apology, she casually mentions she can sew? Not only that, she called herself a seamstress. Lily is mortified. How could Ruth have let her go on about the dresses—at one point Lily even described the machine parts to her, as if describing a new planet to the earthbound!—and said nothing?

"Lily," her mother says.

"Yes?"

"Do you want my help?"

"With what?"

"The dresses you want to make. You could buy a used machine, set it up on my desk. Or we could do it by hand . . . I could teach you some simple stitches—"

"No!" Lily smiles wildly, trying to soften her response, which feels less like a word than a flailing. She cannot imagine accepting help from Ruth, who has seemed all along to disapprove of Lily's sewing idea, and every other domestic effort she's made, however poor the result. Besides, her mother isn't well. "Thank you," she says. "You don't have to do that. But thank you." She takes Ruth's cold mug of tea. It's a gag mug her mother got at some

Purim celebration, with a knockoff Starbucks logo that says *Ohel Coffee, Product de Persia, Certified for the Court of Ahasuerus, 14 Adar 5773* and features a mermaidish queen in the middle of the ubiquitous green circle—Esther, presumably. Why did Lily pour her mother's tea into this if not to torture herself further? "I'll go make you some more?"

"All right." Ruth's voice is hoarse. "Whatever you like, Lily-pie."

Ruth is asleep when Lily returns with more tea, so Lily goes back out and sits on the couch next to June. She snuggles up to her daughter, nosing her cheek and trying, as she blocks out *Super-Why!*, to remember her mother sewing. Even once. Even if she was making that *A Well-Kept House . . .* sampler, which was technically embroidery and which maybe she didn't even make. But the image that comes to Lily instead is of her mother smoking. She is on the sun porch. She half sits, half leans, her buttocks perched on the bay-window sill while her feet press the floor, her bare legs a sunned hypotenuse. It must be the summer after Lily's father left, because that was the summer her mother made the leap to shorter shorts but hadn't yet moved on to the long, gauzy skirts she would wear in summers to come. (Did her mother sew those skirts?) They are shapely legs, with muscular calves and well-defined thighs, and her quadriceps do a little dance as she smokes, climbing up on the inhale and sliding back down on the release, and Lily, transfixed, then and now, watches the knot of muscle as if it might tell her something her mother won't.

When, after a couple episodes, Lily goes back into Ruth's bedroom, the blankets have been smoothed and the blinds raised, the room swept in light. Ruth emerges from the bathroom, wiping her hands on a towel with an officious, energetic air, and Lily lets herself feel a spasm of hope. Her hope surges when Ruth looks her in the eye and says, "How is Adam?" because of course *How is Adam?* means *How is your marriage?* and *Are you having an affair now?* and all this is Ruth's way of being her truest self. Never mind that Lily's blood pounds at the question because if she were to answer honestly, she would have to say, *I'm having one in my mind*. Which is true. The Thursday after she virtuously declined Hal's pizza-date invitation, he asked again, and she accepted, and since then he has occupied an unreasonably large and torrid portion of her thoughts. Nothing happened, to be clear. The place was a hole in the wall Lily had never even noticed before, called only PIZZA, it seemed, which of course made Jace, who had discovered and recommended it, a kind of urban pioneer. That this was in addition to her being a lawyer with nonexistent thighs only made the "date" feel more acceptable—what interest could Hal possibly have in Lily? They ate at a Formica table with the kids, and drank wine out of paper cups, and Hal asked the obligatory question about how Lily's mother was doing, though not in an obligatory way—he had a way of crinkling his lovely crow's-feet wrinkles in a way that reminded you of sun and also of storms he might have weathered and suggested that he was ready to empathize with your storms, too. All that was cheesy, and platonic enough. But then he looked at Lily's plate and said, "I see you really like hot pepper," and that was all it took—she was wet. It was mortifying, she would tell Ruth, if she were to tell her any of this, which she will not. And then, well, what happened next was maybe kind of mortifying, too, in its predictability. That night she seduced Adam, and the next night, too, and the night after that, and what has happened since is one of the stranger things that has happened in the past month but also, inarguably, the best: almost every night, after the girls are asleep, Lily leads Adam to the bedroom, or the bathroom, or once the kitchen, and they take off their clothes and do it. It's not something they talk about. There's no foreplay, no planning or premeditation. Even for Lily, who started it, it feels less like something she does than something she is led to, like a fucker's version of sleepwalking. She just keeps finding herself in the middle of it. Almost everything else that brings her pleasure she has put on hold since Ruth's diagnosis, things like dessert, or the Sudoku puzzles she likes, or Kyla's lessons. But sex? The more it happens, the more Lily makes it happen. She does not dwell on its relationship to Hal nor on the pitifully easy Psych 101 analysis of her behavior: compulsive sex as an attempt to defy death. Instead she orders new underthings, a French negligee, a pair of crotchless underwear, a garter belt—they both love the garter belt. So maybe there is some premeditation now. At a minimum, there is commitment.

Which makes it true when Lily answers her mother: "He's fine."

Ruth settles herself onto a loveseat that once belonged to her own mother. "Any progress toward a promotion?"

"Do you want more tea?"

"Sit."

Lily sits on Ruth's bed.

"Tell me," Ruth says. "I'm stuck here. Tell me something."

So Lily tells her mother about Adam's fish-farm endeavor, which is finally looking like it might happen. She sets the scene: a refugee camp west of Kigali. She describes the challenges, the skeptics. Then she explains the role she played in the turnaround, how after the pizza date it struck her that Hal—"this dad of a kid in Rosie's theater class?"—might be able to help Adam. Adam needed a fish expert who wasn't already opposed to his project, and Hal was a fisherman. He'd even worked with aquaculture pools, Lily happened to know, because he'd mentioned this, at the pizza place, because he was the kind of man who did not need to be prompted to talk about himself. Other things he'd mentioned: he was involved in some kind of artisanal kelp locavore start-up on Long Island Sound, and he knew just about everyone. Which could not hurt, Lily thought. She set up a date for Adam and Hal, and that was that: since then Adam has brought Hal on as a consultant and they meet for regular drinking/planning sessions in the neighborhood. *Are you sure it's okay?* Adam keeps asking, because his meeting Hal means Lily putting the girls to sleep on her own, and while at some point Lily might have said no, this particular scenario she supports entirely, for it relieves her of guilt *and* furthers Adam's cause. He still hasn't gotten a full go-ahead, she tells Ruth, but last week, thanks to a funder Hal brought in, they received a sizable grant, the kind of money they've been waiting for, which will help to draw other money and quiet the doubters.

"What's this Hal like?" her mother asks, as if that is the point.

"He's fine." It is good to have given Hal to Adam. He served his purpose, she has decided. Which sounds mercenary, she realizes, but isn't mercenary better than gaga? The women she knows whose husbands have cheated insist that it's impossible for the cheating to have nothing to do with their marriage, but Lily is starting to think they're wrong—you *can* want something and still fully want another thing. That they conflict does not mean you are conflicted.

"It's important for men to have friends," Ruth says. "Your father never had friends."

"Mm," Lily answers.

"Adam is a good father."

"Yes." Lily is noticing how Ruth keeps tilting on the loveseat, righting herself, then tilting again. She is clearly uncomfortable, maybe in pain. She looks embarrassed. Lily has not often known her mother to be embarrassed, and it is hard not to feel embarrassed for her. Lily looks away, to give her privacy.

"When he came by last weekend with Rosie?" Ruth is saying. "The way he looks at her—it took my breath away. Same way I felt when I saw him hold her after she was born. Do you remember?"

"Of course." But Lily doesn't know if she remembers. They have photographs, which serve as memory. Her mother's sappiness is grating and worrisome—since when does Ruth use phrases like *took my breath away*? Since when does she reminisce in plaintive tones? Lily is certain now that her mother is dying. "You do realize that's setting the bar pretty low," she says. "No one has ever looked at a woman holding her baby in a loving way and said, *What a good mother!* You never said to me, *The way you look at your daughters just takes my breath away.*"

Ruth, who has tilted again, gives Lily a long look. "I'm sorry."

"I'm not asking you to be sorry."

"Okay."

"Okay."

They are silent for a moment, Lily holding tears in her mouth.

"I wouldn't mind some more tea, lovie."

"Of course."

"And can you take this? On your way? Hang it up for me?"

Lily didn't realize her mother was still holding the towel she'd used to dry her hands, but she sees that Ruth's arm is shaking now, as if the towel she's proffering were a dumbbell. She sees that Ruth inches her bottom to the very edge of the seat before pushing herself to stand, and that she climbs onto her bed with difficulty. "Oh Lily, I'm tired. I had a little burst there, but I'm zonked."

Lily watches out the corner of her eye, making sure her mother is settled before going to hang the towel in the bathroom.

Her Post-its are still attached to the wall, warning of the step down from the riser on which the toilet sits. *Step down! Be careful! We love you!* The ones she put up when her mother first came home Ruth removed immediately, but these—stuck up nearly a week ago—her mother has not touched.

"I regret it," her mother says when Lily comes out of the bathroom.

Lily, not sure what she's talking about, picks up her mother's mug. Ruth is working to get underneath her blankets. "With those tennis balls," she says. "I should never have done that. It was cruel of me. He was right to be angry."

"But you said he didn't try to stop you."

"That wasn't how a man like your father got angry."

"How did he get angry?"

"He slept with other women."

Lily waits for more. But Ruth is quiet.

"You're saying you blame the tennis balls for his affairs?"

Ruth pulls her blanket up to her chin. She looks small. "That does sound dumb," she says. "Doesn't it."

"Not dumb—wrong. Are you cold?"

Ruth nods.

"I'll go make more tea."

"Lily?"

"Yes."

"You should know that your father didn't leave. I kicked him out."

"Okay," Lily says automatically.

"Okay," says her mother.

Lily thinks of Adam and Vira, and the fact that they fought not only about whatever they fought about but also about whether she left or he kicked her out. Does it matter? The result is the same. Lily's father is gone. Vira is gone. She wonders if her mother is trying to assure her in some way, or to warn her. Or maybe it's not about Lily at all. Maybe she just wants her to know. *This was something I did.*

Lily speaks softly; Ruth's eyes are fluttering. "So why has the story always been that he left?"

"It was the only acceptable thing to tell my parents."

Lily watches her mother for another minute, then opens the door to go make more tea. But June is standing on the other side, looking tired and happy. "I'm done," she says, heaving herself up onto Ruth's bed and sliding under the blankets next to her grandmother. She lays an arm across Ruth and looks up at Lily. "I stay here. You get Rosie and come back."

"She's not out for another hour," Lily says. "We'll go together."

"I stay here."

"Enjoy this time. Then grandma has to rest."

"She can stay," says Ruth. She pats the bed on the other side of her. "Come on, Lily-pie. Lie down with us."

"I was going to make your tea."

"The tea can wait. I'm not cold anymore."

Lily sets down the mug and stretches out next to her mother.

"Come under the covers."

"I'm fine."

"I know. Come under the covers."

It is warm under her mother's blankets. Lily's toes have been cold for hours, she realizes, maybe all winter. On her back, close enough to feel Ruth's heat, she looks at the stamped-tin ceiling, at two paintings her mother bought from artist friends, at her mother's bookshelves. On a high shelf is a collection of Ruth's favorite ashtrays, which she asked Lily to put away after her diagnosis. It strikes Lily that apart from the ashtrays and the loveseat and Ruth's books, there is almost nothing in this apartment that was also in the old house, and that in the old house, there was almost nothing that was Ruth's alone. She lived there for years by herself, of course, but you could always feel Lily's father there, in the rugs and furniture. Her father had traveled, and many of the objects in the house had been chosen by him, and carried long distances by him, and seemed to represent—to Lily, at least—his worldliness. There was an antique Japanese teapot with a built-in strainer, an abstract sculpture, a custom-built turntable and speakers that cost more than his car. Lily's mother had little: a Childe Hassam etching of the harbor, which she hung above the fireplace, and mementos from her childhood, which she stored in several hatboxes in her closet. Even her books she kept in her bedroom, so that Lily, when she was very young, wondered if books were something private, and maybe a little shameful, like underwear. The ashtrays eventually showed up in so many corners of the house it seemed they'd been sprinkled there by fairies. But mostly she continued ceding the house to Lily's father.

Why should it surprise her, Lily thinks, that Ruth used to sew? She lived in that house for decades; she'd lived there before Lily was even born. The woman Lily has imagined to be her mother is the one who came after her father: the woman smoking in those short shorts, and then in her long skirts; the woman who pushed her way into the inner circles of the local synagogue until she'd forced a shift toward egalitarian language in the prayers; the woman who for a time brought a book called *Let's Talk!* to the breakfast table and tried to engage her children in frank discussion about their bodies; the woman who drove south to beg Lily not to give up her work. Yet even that woman was in the kitchen each day when her kids got home from school. She never worked a paying job. She was a woman who could not tell her parents that she was the one who had chosen divorce.

Lily can hear Ruth breathing next to her now. Both she and June seem to be dozing—June punctuates her grandmother's labored inhales with short, quick sighs, as if she's excited even in sleep. Yesterday afternoon, Lily walked into the girls' room to find that they had rolled out between them a six-foot-long stretch of IKEA paper and were scribbling madly, and not only scribbling but painting—they had taken out the bin of paints that they were not supposed to use without Lily's help. But before she could scold them, she saw what they were making. Two dresses. June's of black circles, strung like a garland in the shape of a dress, made with Sharpie—another thing they are not allowed to play with; permanence, fumes, etc., . . . *But look!* they cried. Lily looked. It's coal! June cried, and it took Lily a moment to realize: her daughter got *coal* from the kohl in the Esther book, the stuff the maidens, all except for Esther, used to darken their eyes. The circles saturated the paper to the point of dampness. They shone. It was a dress for a queen, or a funeral. And Rosie's. Lily stepped farther into the room. She could feel the girls watching her, afraid she was going to make them start cleaning up. But she was only getting a better view. Rosie's dress was like a muumuu that had been dipped in a tropical rave, densely patterned with green diamonds, pink spirals, purple lightning bolts, orange tongues. Were they tongues? It didn't matter. Rosie looked up at her—into her—with tensed brows, as dark and luxuriant as her grandmother's before the chemo started to thin them. Lily got it, in a way she had not before—their desire for the dresses was not about having something but being it.

She turns onto her side. Her mother and her younger daughter look nothing alike, but they nap identically: noses up, mouths open. June smiles at something, goes slack again. Lily's heart squeezes. It amazes her that the girls believe she is doing it, making those dresses. Where and when they think this is happening, she does not know—perhaps they have in their mind a kind of Rumpelstiltskin cellar where she works through the night—but of course that's not the point, is it? The point is that they trust her. Even when she doesn't trust herself.

"Mom?"

Nothing. Then a drowsy "Mm . . . ?"

"I'll find a machine," Lily says. "I do want you to teach me. To make the dresses. Okay?"

Nothing. A clanging comes from Vanderbilt Avenue. They are building wooden crates to protect the trees before laying down new cable, but it sounds as if someone is hitting metal against metal.

Silence again.

Then a rustling. Ruth's hair rubbing her pillow as she nods.

GLOUCESTER, MA

VEE

A Sublime Representative of Self-Centered Womanhood

The road up through the woods is narrow enough that Vee can walk in one of the tracks while smacking, with a long stick, the saplings that grow along the side. She has not walked this road before, though it looks similar enough to others that she loses herself for a time, walking slowly, enjoying the solid thwack as her stick hits the trees. She jumps, in fact leaves the ground, when she hears an engine approaching from below. The road turned to gravel a good half mile back, which she took to mean—as it had for other roads—that no more houses lay ahead, and that the gravel, when it petered out, would turn into a footpath into the rocky moors the locals call Dogtown, at which point Vee would turn around. She is not naïve enough to wander alone into that place—she knows of a violent history, though she has never bothered studying it; she senses, correctly, that there is more to come. The one time she did dare venture in, pushing past the ragged boundary and following a path through briars and blueberry bushes and poison ivy and stunted trees, she came to a massive rock, more than twice her height and the width of two cars, into which was carved, in foot-tall letters: HELP MOTHER. She turned and marched back as quickly as she could without running, her blood pounding, her eyes trying to search the trees on either side of her without appearing afraid. Now, at the sound of the engine, her instinct is the same. She resumes walking so as not to appear rattled, hitting the trees in a steady rhythm even as her cigarette hand quickly adjusts her hat a bit lower over the side of her face. She inhales deeply, trying to calm herself; she blows smoke toward the trees. She is not calm. Puff thwack puff thwack puff, until a man's voice husks at her: "What'd they do to you?" Then Vee is staring at the back of a red pickup truck and smelling the pipe smoke that's trailing out from the cab. Quickly, the truck is gone around the bend.

She should turn around. But she can't. It's the pipe smoke, she tells herself, as she continues up the road in the dust the truck has left behind. She loves the smell with an almost scary intensity; she feels, when she smells it, as if she might fall down. Her father and grandfather were pipe smokers of the kind that set their pipes down only for photographs, though there is one black-and-white of senator and governor together—it hangs still in the yacht club's billiard room—in which both men, son- and father-in-law, blow smoke at the camera. Vee's father was smoking a pipe when he had the stroke that killed him—his coffin smelled of it, if you leaned close enough.

Vee did not adore her father or her grandfather. Neither man allowed that. Even in their slippers or swimming trunks they appeared monumental. They could not comfort Vee, like her mother or her grandmother, but neither did they become real to her in the way her mother and grandmother did. The women's realness came with a cost; it made them impossible not to hate, in a way—their comforting and combing and correcting, their bodies and hands and hair always near. The men never got close enough to ruin the illusion of their omnipotence—they were immortal, somehow, even in death. So what the smell gives her now is a feeling of safety. If she falls down, the smell tells her, she will be picked up. It makes her feel warm, though the day is cold.

It is mid-December already. She has been at Rosemary's more than a month, and though she still has no idea what she will do next, her initial panic has for the most part ebbed. She no longer fears at any given moment that Rosemary or Philip will kick her out, and the tabloids rarely mention her now. Also, she got her period. She was about to send off for a kit from a laboratory in North Carolina—she'd asked Rosemary to drop her off at the library, where they had a new book called *Our Bodies, Ourselves* that provided instructions and an address—but then she bled, and another layer of fear fell away. She almost shouted from the bathroom. She felt like celebrating. But what would Rosemary, at twelve weeks now, her waist thickened even to Vee's eye, make of that? And Vee hadn't even shared her fear that she might be pregnant. The lightness the friends established early in Vee's "visit" has somehow persisted, so that Vee has still not asked Rosemary about the cross that was burned on her lawn, and Rosemary hasn't pressed Vee for any details beyond the basics of what happened in her town house the night before she tripped up Rosemary's steps with nothing but a bag and her hat. They talk about memories, and their parents, and what they will drink, and Rosemary's pregnancy, and whether the laundry—still Vee's job—needs doing. At Thanksgiving, they debated stuffing recipes, then cooked together, and Philip, though he still asks when Vee plans to leave, allowed Vee to be at the dinner since Vee had no family and Rosemary's parents, who knew and loved

Vee—though they rigorously avoided any discussion of what she was doing there, alone—were the only guests.

Beyond Rosemary, Vee has found a doctor willing to keep her name to himself and refill her prescription for the Pill, which seems to her now, though she is not currently having sex, as critical as food and water—like her own private armor. The library book agrees. The library book—which she couldn't check out; it was reference, and besides, she wouldn't dare be seen reading it; even in the library she had read it tucked inside a large dictionary—quotes a handbook that calls the Pill "the first drug to weaken male society's control over women."

Vee is confused about sex. She wakes sometimes from dreams pinned by an arousal so intense it's more like pain, a certainty that a body has been on hers, a desperation to call it back. But it's not sex, per se, that she misses—she doesn't think so. She has enjoyed not putting on a girdle, not shaving her armpits every day. It's not sex—she tells herself—but it is something. Rosemary hugs her. Rosemary is a generous hugger. But that's not it, quite, either. Rosemary's friendship, as much as Vee loves her, cannot be enough. A man is required—she knows this even as it shames her. She has not been unattached from a man since she and Rosemary, at thirteen, went on a double date with two boys named John and John.

The smoke is still in her nostrils when she reaches a driveway, at the end of which stands a small house of unfinished wood, newly built—she can smell that, too. Enough trees have been cleared around the house that she can see it, but not so many that she feels exposed as she stands looking at it. She wonders if anyone else knows that the house is here, if the man who drove by is a kind of hermit, or outlaw. She hears the clicking of his cooling truck. She sees a row of tools leaned against the house, shovels and hoes and axes and a machete. She wonders if he is planning to build a shed—if his wife, if there is a wife, will insist on a shed. She would, she thinks. But why? Her walk has left her confused. Would she want the shed to protect the tools, or to hide them for appearance's sake, or to make him build it? Vee knows she often can't tell the difference between what she wants and what she thinks she should want, but knowing this doesn't make it any easier to tell the difference.

"You here to beat down my trees?"

Vee hadn't noticed the man walking toward her, carrying a leash. She backs away.

The man stops. He surveys her. He wears blue jeans, a hunting jacket, and—the only incongruity—a clean shave. "My dog jumped out of the truck," he says. "Want a ride down the hill?"

Vee shakes her head.

"Okee doke." The man heads for his truck, then shouts before closing the door: "If you'll be so kind as to get out of my way?"

Vee moves to the edge of the driveway. She would like a ride. But a dog, she thinks, doesn't just jump out of a truck. Does it? Not if its owner is kind?

The truck reverses to where Vee stands. The man rolls down his window, a wary look on his face. "Sure you don't want a ride?"

She shakes her head.

"Where'd you come from?"

Is this fear? Vee wonders. Or is it shame? Her body feels heavy, her thigh muscles on the verge of collapse. The truck's running board is oddly clean, as if he leaps into his seat instead of climbing, and she rests her gaze there, listening to the blood in her ears.

"You mute?"

"You alright?"

When she doesn't answer, the man climbs down from the truck. "Oh god," he says. "Don't cry." And Vee, who didn't know she was crying, starts to cry harder. She feels insane suddenly, standing in a strange man's driveway, letting him take her by the shoulders, falling into him. She has fallen into him. "Oh god," he says again—she hears it, muffled, through her hair. "Oh no," as his arms wrap around her. Then: "Goodness, you didn't look this small."

Vee has never slept with a man whose family she didn't know. She has only slept with Alex and two boyfriends before him. He could be diseased; he could be a murderer. She leads him toward his house. She doesn't smell pipe smoke on him, doesn't smell it inside. She wonders if she dreamed it, if she is dreaming this, too, hallucinating the lumberjack in the woods and her hands on his neck—could it possibly be real? But if she were hallucinating, she would hallucinate a mattress on the floor and there is a bed—a simple one, built of the same wood as the house, but still a bed. If she were hallucinating, it would be a collision so hasty they would simply unbuckle and pull aside, but beneath him she is naked. The man's eyes are open and looking into her eyes, though she can't tell if he sees her. She barely sees him. She sees Alex pushing her to the floor, sees Suitcase Wife up in the ceiling, sees Alex pushing his hand up Suitcase Wife's skirt, working his whole hand up inside her, then Vee feels it inside herself and Suitcase Wife has disappeared into Vee, their backs hitting the floor with a terrible sound, though that might be the thwack of Vee's stick hitting the trees. Smack. She slams her hands against the man's chest. She feels a rush of power. Then she sees the dog leash hanging on the bedroom doorknob, within his reach, and hears herself say in a squirrelish voice, "What about your dog?" and as the man laughs, and comes, fear grips her again, and now this is all she feels, bright, blinding fear, until he is off her. He says something but she can't hear; she is underwater in the tub again while Alex talks at her. She finds her clothes. Her hat. Where is her stick? When did she let go of her stick? She hears his footsteps behind her and decides she'll turn down the ride again—even if he insists, she'll say no. She needs a cigarette. She needs to walk.

But it turns out he doesn't offer her a ride because when Vee opens the door a dog is there, its tongue out, its tail wagging, waiting to be let in. "Good girl," the man says, kneeling down to hug her, and Vee runs until she is out of sight.

The house is empty when she returns, Rosemary out picking up the older kids from school, and Vee goes straight into the shower. When she hears the children's voices she doesn't bother getting dressed, just wraps her robe around her and heads downstairs. She is ready to talk now. Something has been knocked loose and she needs to talk, to tell Rosemary what just happened and everything else that has happened and how terrified she is not to know what will happen next.

"Oh."

It's not Rosemary who has brought the children home. Philip stands at the kitchen counter, slicing an apple. Without looking at her, he says, "Doctor's appointment," and Vee, clutching her robe, turns to go back upstairs.

"Where were you?" Philip asks in his odd, blunt way, sounding neither angry nor kind.

"Walking."

"We need to talk."

"Let me change."

"It won't take long. Kids!"

The kids gather quickly, as they never do for Rosemary, and Philip, handing out the apple slices, says, "Go outside."

The children look at their father, then at Vee, and go. Only the girl hesitates for a few seconds, peeking back at Vee through a frizzy shock of bangs, then putting an apple slice in her mouth and following her brothers out the sliding door. At four o'clock, it is already dusk outside. Philip offers Vee an apple slice. She declines. She wants him to release her before Rosemary gets home, not because Rosemary mistrusts her—Vee has to believe that Rosemary does not mistrust her—but because a woman in a robe with a husband is not something any woman, let alone a pregnant woman, needs to see.

Philip takes his time washing the paring knife and the cutting board, then drying both. Vee has never seen Alex wash anything, so though she's impatient for Philip to speak, she is also fascinated. Philip swings the dish towel over his shoulder and it's as if he has performed a kind of dance—that's how impressed Vee is, despite herself. He puts each item away, opens the refrigerator, and, with his back to her, says, "You should go home."

"I'm sorry?"

"It's time. I got a call today, at the office."

"From?" She wonders if the reporters have at last tracked her down, wonders why they continue to bother—are the *Enquirer* and its lookalikes really so short on copy?

"Your husband," he says.

Vee waits.

"He wants you back."

Vee's elbows sink to the counter. She is shocked by the relief that floods her.

"He says to tell you his chief of staff . . . Harold? Humbert? . . . doesn't want him calling. He doesn't want you to go back yet, he thinks it will make him appear weak. These people." He shakes his head. "You people."

Vee could be insulted but focuses on her relief. Why not? this relieved part of her asks. Why not go back? Why not shrug it all off, as she might have done in the first place, go along with his request and get back to her life? This would be in keeping with a string of things she has argued to herself before: If she had stripped that night, it would not have killed her. She would still be in her marriage. She would not be so confused. Maybe they assumed she would do it because it was what she should have done. Etc.

She thinks of the house in the woods, the man above her, their urgent coupling. A thrill pulses in her wrists, and she imagines going back to Alex with her knowledge of this thrill, the secret of this afternoon. She imagines it would help, getting to have that and keep it. She used to be above him, at least in the ways a woman could be above a man. She was the one with the money, the one with the background. Then he flipped it all inside out. He doesn't need her background anymore; he is in the house they bought with her money; even if she goes back, she will have been a nutty, drug-addicted probable lesbian. But to have made him a cuckold . . . it would be something.

"You should go back."

Philip can't know that Vee has been thinking the same thing, or that his saying it out loud, commanding her, has the opposite of his desired effect. She feels herself harden, feels her back rise into a line. *Why should I listen to you?* She does not say this, of course. He can still kick her out; she must not make him mad. Instead she picks the one remaining slice of apple off the counter, puts it in her mouth, and chews. She can't go back, she knows. She couldn't go along and she can't go back. Yet she wants to be able to. This is the problem. It's as if Vee herself—who Vee is, at her core, what her father and grandfather would have called her *character*, if she had been male—has not caught up with the life she's meant to live. She has always had questions, granted, niggles of ambivalence that kept her from being as good as Rosemary or her mother: her little secret with the Pill, her women's-group habit. But she never wanted to cause trouble. She wanted to go along—certainly it's true that she wanted to want to go along. That night at the women's party, remember? She decided she was ready to give up the women's group, decided they were ugly hippies and that she was done with them and ready to claim her place, her power, as one of the wives. But then, well, she had not gone along. She had not stripped. She had caused a great deal of trouble. And now, it seems, she is a woman who causes trouble.

She swallows what's left of the apple's pulp, looking not at Philip but out the sliding glass door to the yard, where the boys are running and throwing leaves in the near dark. Where is the girl?

"It's getting cold out there," she says.

Philip sets a pot on the stove.

"I need a little more time," she says.

"We've given you time."

"I have to figure some things out."

"It's not good for Rosemary." Philip is doing nothing now but looking at her. "Having you here. She's got the pregnancy. The kids." *Me*, he adds with his eyes.

"Did you tell her about the call?"

"Not yet."

Vee watches him. Her robe has loosened slightly, but she doesn't clutch at it now. She simply stands there, looking at him as he looks at her, watching as his eyes drop, knowing what she's doing even as she didn't intend it. Half a minute passes. Then the door slides open and the kitchen fills with cold and shouts, the kids throwing off their hats, Philip ordering them to pick them up, and Vee slips out. Her robe is tightly wrapped again by the time she reaches the stairs. But Rosemary, who is sitting on the third step to take off her shoes, notices the fact of it—she scans Vee from top to bottom before returning her gaze to her shoes. Vee could explain. But to explain would sound like a defense, which would suggest she's done something that needs defending. So she kisses the top of Rosemary's head, says, "Welcome home," and goes around her and up the stairs, to change.

Later that evening, after the children are in bed and Philip is in his office at the back of the house, Vee and Rosemary sit on the living room couch. Vee drinks bourbon. Rosemary drinks wine. She says the doctor told her no hard alcohol. And no more cigarettes.

"Why?"

Rosemary shrugs. Her feet are pulled up under her, swallowed by a flannel nightgown that makes her appear at once like a little girl and a much older woman. She looks very tired.

"Was it just a routine visit?"

"I think so."

"You don't know?"

"I've been spotting a little."

"Like, getting your period?"

"No. Just a little spotting. It comes and goes," Rosemary says again, with maybe a hint of impatience, and for a moment Vee wonders if what Philip said to her in the kitchen, about how Vee isn't good for Rosemary, is something Rosemary said, to Philip. She wonders if Rosemary is thinking about the robe. But then Rosemary takes a long sip of wine and says, pointing at Vee's pack of Raleighs on the coffee table, "You can smoke. I don't mind. I like the smell," and Vee relaxes.

She drags the pack toward herself with a socked foot. "Are you worried?" she asks.

"There's not much use in worrying. Right? He said bed rest might help. But I'm not doing that."

"Are you going to tell Philip?"

"What."

"What the doctor said."

"No."

Vee lights a cigarette.

"But I can't be intimate," Rosemary says. "And I have to tell him that. According to the doctor."

"Which part is according to the doctor?"

"Both. I mean, he hasn't come near me in a month. So it may not be necessary to tell him."

Vee nods. She waits. Maybe this is when Rosemary begins to talk. Certainly it's not turning out to be the night for Vee to tell Rosemary about the lumberjack man, as she'd planned to. But Rosemary can tell Vee about her marriage. And maybe tomorrow, or the next day, Vee can tell.

But Rosemary is quiet, sipping her wine. Vee pours herself more bourbon. She is drinking quickly tonight; she can't help it sometimes, this urge toward oblivion. She is frightened by Rosemary's spotting. She feels guilty about the robe and the kitchen encounter with Philip, though nothing happened but a bared sternum, a hint of bone. She drinks for a little while, then ventures, "So . . . it sounds like the doctor's a little worried. Even if you're not?"

Rosemary groans. "Have you ever been able to tell what a doctor thinks?" She finishes off her wine, sets the glass on the coffee table, then leans her head back into the couch so that she's staring at the fireplace across from them. Vee looks at it, too: a classic colonial fireplace lined with black bricks, big enough to cook in and to heat the whole house. The house is chilly. Philip keeps the thermostat at 67.

"Should I build a fire?" Vee asks.

Rosemary says, "Nah. It's too late."

"Good. I don't know if I could even do it anymore."

They laugh. But Rosemary still seems sad. She seems unlike Rosemary.

"Do you hang stockings?" Vee asks, waving her cigarette at the mantelpiece. "Do you put up a tree?"

Rosemary shakes her head.

Vee grabs a throw off an armchair and spreads it across her friend, and Rosemary sinks further into the cushions. "Thank you," she says. Then: "I want to lie down."

"It's fine. I'll just finish this cigarette and head up myself."

"No, I mean on this couch. Right here. I'm too tired to sit up."

Vee stands up so Rosemary can stretch out, then, when Rosemary pats the space next to her, she lies down, too, with her head on the armrest and her glass on her chest. They look at the ceiling together.

"Will he not allow it?" Vee asks after a while. "The tree?"

"He hasn't said that."

"I thought it was the mother. If the mother's Jewish, then the kids are Jewish, and if she's not, then . . . ?"

"I'm converting."

"Are you serious?"

Vee turns to look at Rosemary, but she's too close to see her clearly. What she notices are Rosemary's hands cupping her belly.

"Did he ask you to?" she asks.

"No. He's not religious. He doesn't care about any of it."

"So why?"

"We're a family. So we should be a family."

Vee, on her third bourbon, is finding the idea preposterous. "What about the cross?" she asks. "Aren't you scared?"

"The cross is even more reason. A unified front. I'm not going to hide."

"But you wouldn't be hiding. You'd just be being. Yourself."

Rosemary doesn't say anything for a minute. Vee slides her glass onto the coffee table, then maneuvers until she's on an elbow, looking at Rosemary's profile, which appears entirely unperturbed. She starts to wonder if Rosemary is asleep with her eyes open. If everything she's been saying is not quite what she means to say.

Then Rosemary says, "It's okay if you don't get it."

Vee stands and lights another cigarette. She walks to the mantel, then to the window, where she bumps into a little side table. A strange sculpture—is it made of pewter?—sits atop it, a thing she hasn't really looked at before, dismissed for its abstractness. She doesn't look at it now, only labels it in her mind—*Philip's*—and walks back to face Rosemary.

"Is it what you want?"

Rosemary sighs, drawing the throw up to her chin. "I find it fascinating, actually. It's very different. Nothing like Episcopal. Obviously. His mother—I really like her—she invited me to this CR thing in Cambridge. I think I'm going to go."

"CR?"

"Consciousness raising."

"Oh. I've been to one of those. Or something like it. In DC. I wrote you about it."

"But this is Jewish, too. I guess they talk about the stories, and how . . . She says it's really empowering."

"Rosemary. How can you go to this group and also convert *for* your husband? It sounds like a new height of hypocrisy. Is it even allowed?"

Rosemary turns to look at Vee. "Solidarity is always allowed."

"You can't be in solidarity with everyone at once," Vee says, even as she knows exactly what Rosemary means. Rosemary means you stand with your man; she means in the end it's all anyone cares about. How, Vee thinks, can she not be talking about Vee herself? Irritation flames in her gut, followed by longing. She longs to tell Rosemary everything, right now, not just the outline she offered her first night here—the part about Alex demanding she strip—but what happened in the town house kitchen before the party, and what he may have done to Suitcase Wife, and what Vee thought and felt.

But she is afraid, too. Isn't Rosemary saying that it makes no difference what Vee thought or felt? What's to stop Rosemary, when she hears that Alex called, from telling her to go back, as Philip did?

Rosemary sits up. She looks like herself again, friendly, open faced, optimistic, an optimistic pregnant woman heading to bed. "Do you want to come?" she asks. "To the meeting? Everyone is welcome."

"Maybe," Vee says. She is thinking of the women's-group women, and of the wives, and of how Rosemary has always belonged, with Vee, to the latter. Wasn't it all bullshit, though, if you could move around at will? Preppy to hippie, Episcopal to Jewish, polished to buffed and back again? She is also thinking that she does maybe want to go to the meeting, if only to do something, and spend a few hours in the city, and that she will have to convince Philip to let her go, and of how demeaning that will be, to ask another woman's husband for permission to go out. She is thinking that she cannot stay here forever. She is thinking of the argument she'll make to Philip: if Alex wants her back, he is going to want to protect her; Hump is not going to send the tabloids after her; no one is going to come beating down Philip's door. The more Vee thinks of the argument she'll make, the more she wants to go to the meeting. She'll tell him she won't talk, only listen; she'll act like a reporter, interested but not implicated.

She likes this idea. Interested but not implicated. As Rosemary says good night and heads upstairs, Vee thinks maybe, after what happened to her, she is not meant for solidarity. Maybe she was never meant for it—hence her ambivalence about babies, and her judgments of everyone: the wives, the women's-group women, Alex. Poor Alex. Maybe Vee has never been on the right path. She climbs the stairs, her legs woozy with bourbon, her mind suddenly, startlingly clear: a vision of the wooded road to the man's house; a recognition that she will walk it again tomorrow.

SUSA

ESTHER

Her New Scheme

The idea comes to her as she's walking in one of the far courtyards. It's almost dusk, the time in the camp when the fires are lit, and Esther sniffs the air, thinking she smells the tang of the first smoke, a hint of sumac and rice. She imagines the shout that might have a chance of reaching her aunt or Nadav, then feels its possibility trickling back down her throat. Her voice can't possibly be strong enough. Even if it were, by the time she got one word to them, the guards would haul her inside. She would not be let out again.

They stand in the corner now, tracking her. She still isn't sure who they work for exactly, whether they answer to the king himself or to the wicked minister who acts as the king's puppeteer. She used to think knowing this would help her somehow, but now she understands that it doesn't matter.

What she doesn't understand is keeping a thing that you know wants to escape. Keeping it, dressing it, feeding it, praising it, and all the while, you know it doesn't want you. It seems to her it would be a great humiliation. Yet no one appears humiliated except for her.

The child has made it better, and much worse. He came in the middle of the night, waking her like the river was inside her, needing to get out, and the midwives arrived instantly, though it was, oddly, Baraz she turned out to want. She called out for him, she cried for him. When someone told her they had looked but could not find him, the weight that howled into her back in that moment, a hot, massive fist that contained her mother and Lara and Itz and her aunt and Nadav and her father and Mother Mona and Esther's own birth, made her want to die. But she had no choice; the child's seizing was hers. And then he was born, a boy, his little wand swollen and waving, and she gave up a cry.

He looks unlike anyone she has known. Even the king admits this; he wonders aloud if his child is of another world, a god; his mistrust of Esther deepens. Once upon a time, she has learned, the king served as a steward in Vashti's father's palace; whichever girl in the night station said he himself was not of noble blood was correct. So even as he reigns he is displaced, and his son's entrance has displaced him further. The child is four months old now, with yellow hair the color of a grass that grew in the city where Esther was raised, along the washing creeks. His eyes are darker than brown. His name is Darius. The king's choice. Esther is grateful for it, though her gratitude stings: Darius is not a Hebrew—or won't have to live as one, at least. And he is, as the midwife knew, not a girl. He is the king's first son. He is in line to reign. Esther is glad for all these things, though her father would mourn the child not knowing the stories and prayers. Maybe she will tell him someday; or maybe, she sometimes thinks, he will discover them on his own, like Moses. She is glad for Darius's warmth, when he isn't being taken away to be nursed or put to sleep. But she is also aware that he has sealed her fate, because even if she were released now, she would never be able to leave.

She knows from Baraz that the attacks on the camp have grown more violent. He goes as close as he can, he tells her, he looks and listens. This must be what he was doing when Darius was born, Esther decides. He is sorry—his sorrow is visible—that he can't do more. He tells her everything he learns. He tells her children have died. He tells her women are raped.

But what do they gain now? Esther asks. If the camp is already in pieces, why do the Persians keep smashing it?

There are many poor among the Persians, too, says Baraz. It's a solace for them. Not to be the lowest.

Oh.

A bird lands on the palace wall, choosing the last bit of sun. It's the same type of bird Esther saw from her pallet in the night station one afternoon, black with yellow wings, and she slows her feet, not wanting to scare it off. Don't go, she thinks at the bird, even as she waits for it to lift. Don't fall any further, she thinks at the sun, though she looks forward to night, when Darius is brought to her. She stands, her back to the guards, waiting for the instant when the sun will abandon the bird to shadow and the bird will fly, and when it comes, and the bird wings away, Esther's blood beats with what she takes at first to be longing until she recognizes it for what it is: a new plan.

Late that night, from a chest in the corner of her chamber, she unearths the bird skeleton she took from the king's bones room. It's still intact, held together by the king's handiwork of guts and wire, as light as a reed in her cupped palm. Esther studies it, then turns it over into her other hand and studies it more. She has dismissed the boy with the fan to go stand outside with the guards. She is alone, except for Darius, asleep in his basket—she has an hour, maybe, before his cries will wake the nurse, who sleeps as lightly as a cat behind the closet door.

She stands the bird upon the chest, marveling at its silver feet. If this one works, she thinks, she won't have to sneak or cajole or seduce her way back to the bones room. She hasn't been allowed there since her first visit, when she broke the feet off the fox, and the minister has warned her that if she attempts to visit the king again without official invitation, he will have her locked in her chambers from one moon to the next. He traps her in corners. He pretends to whisper in her ear, then licks. Once, under the table at a banquet, he drew the king's golden scepter—a thing she had never seen the king so much as touch—up under her robes until its tip arrived at her entry point. After that he decided that anytime she was brought before the king, the king had to point the scepter at her before she could approach. And the king now does this. He appears even smaller since Darius was born, as if his son's strange beauty has diminished him further. He does whatever the minister suggests.

Esther touches a finger to the bird's beak. It looks oddly long, without eyes or feathers to accompany it. *You will talk*, she thinks, and almost instantly, she believes she can do it. Enough time has passed. Her magic must be accumulating again. *You will.*

She works each night, while Darius sleeps. She has no one to guide her now or provide instruction. She must make it up. She must be patient beyond her capacity for patience. She knows the beak must come last so starts with the feet, and one night, a few weeks in, the silver toes begin to quiver. She jumps, forgetting Darius, settles him before the nurse can hear—he likes his stomach patted—then mazes in her mind back to where she began, reconstructing the order of breath and mind that led to the quivering. She tries again. Nothing. But the next night, her energies renewed, the feet again quiver. The next, they turn from silver to bone. The next, a layer of skin grows upon them. In this way, she works her way up the bird. Each time she achieves a new turn, she panics—she will never be able to do it again. There is no formula, no incantation or trick. Only faith and focus. But every night—except when she is kept late at a banquet, or called to the king—she sits with the bird and brings another part of it closer to life.

The wings are not easy. The yellow doesn't want to come in. She almost gives up. Does it matter if they are yellow? Maybe this is a different kind of bird. But she's certain it's not. She keeps going. She must press the point of herself into the bird's wings with great force yet slowly; she can't leave a hole. She thinks of her mother whittling one of her needles, working until the tip was so fine she could push it through cloth and watch the cloth close up again behind it. Esther's task is similar now to the needle's: she has to enter and disrupt, while leaving the bird intact. She hums, to steady herself. She goes so slowly she isn't sure she's moving, and every time she is interrupted by Darius crying—forcing her to dive, eyes closed, onto her bed, the bird hidden inside her robe, readying herself for the nurse's entrance—she must begin all over again. Sometimes she is too tired. Sometimes she brings Darius into her bed, deciding that this bird business is a kind of madness, vowing to stop. She has this boy. It could be enough. But the next night, always, she begins again. And eventually, at a moment that does not announce itself as any different from the moments that have come before, the yellow blooms.

But the wings are not as difficult as life. She knows the bird contains it. She is more confident about the bird containing life than she was about its wings containing yellow. But how to make it breathe? She presses herself in, but that doesn't work, then she tries it as a kind of transformation, but that doesn't work, either. She puts her mouth to the beak and offers her own breath to the bird, but her breath comes back at her, smelling sour. It's only when she gives up one night, and in giving up loosens her hands around the bird, and in loosening her hands around the bird accidentally spurs it to open, that the bird exhales the breath it's been holding since it died so that it can receive another. It shivers. Then, without apparent shock or grogginess, it begins to fly. Esther cries out before she can stop herself, prompting the closet door to open so that she must call in her mind to the bird, *Stop come now at once*. And it obeys! I am its master, she thinks, lying with it beneath her cover linen, her heart pounding with the bird's as the nurse pads across the chamber to find Darius sound asleep.

Life, though, is not as difficult as the voice. And the voice is not as difficult as the words. Can a bird utter human words? It takes Esther two months to figure out a method. By the time she does, by the time she has filled the bird with sounds and pulled them out as forms—*Esther says, Go*—she knows she is carrying another child, but she is so elated by and focused on her work, she barely notices. If she has trained it correctly, the bird will fly directly to Nadav's mother, because she is the one it already knows and because Esther has deemed her, after Itz—who may be inaccessible, hiding in the tent—the one most likely to listen to a talking bird. Esther fine-tunes the bird's Hebrew until it cannot be misheard. *Esther says, Go. Esther says, Far.* All that's left is for her to teach it the smells that will lead it to the camp.

GLOUCESTER, MA

VEE

Other People's Husbands

Every afternoon for twenty-nine afternoons, Vee walks up the hill and sleeps with the man in the woods. He is not a lumberjack or quarryman, as his clothing and truck first suggested, but an architecture student at Harvard taking time off to "investigate" himself. His name is Benjamin, and Vee has fallen in love with his house. She loves the plain wood of the walls and the silence of the sunlight that falls through the large windows. She loves that they are new windows, not divided into panes like all the windows Vee has ever lived behind but plain faced and unfussy, and she loves that not everything here is new. Benjamin's family has owned the land for centuries; they claimed it when Dogtown was still an active settlement, after the Indians were pushed out and before the place was abandoned to witches and feral animals. There is history here and there are modern windows and all of it makes Vee feel as if she is at once regaining something from her own past while also wriggling loose from its hold. For the first time in her life she has experienced pangs of actual desire to make house, and because she and Benjamin are alone, unwatched, with no one to see or remark or expect, this desire does not seem suspect; it does not seem perhaps to be someone else's desire. With Alex, anything she did was not merely something she did but something she did to confirm or dispel an idea of herself. In Benjamin's house, she moves freely between activities without self-consciousness, chopping onions, or poring over his plans for a vegetable garden with genuine interest, or making love, or reading on the window seat or in his bed. Benjamin does not interrupt her, as Alex did, as if her reading were merely a placeholder as she awaited his next communication, and after she closes a book, Benjamin asks her to tell him about it. About herself, he asks little. Vee has told him only that she is recently divorced, which she considers a lie only in a technical sense, and living with a friend nearby. And Benjamin is fine with this; Benjamin calls himself a "counterstructural." God is he glad, he says, not to be in Cambridge now. Vee agrees. She went with Rosemary to the Jewish consciousness raising group in Cambridge and is glad not to be there now. She might be done with cities altogether, she sometimes thinks. Which is yet another reason to love Benjamin's house in the woods.

On the thirtieth day, Vee spends the night, and on the thirty-first, she does not go back to Rosemary's. Instead, she drives Benjamin's truck into town and returns with bread; cheese; two bottles of wine; a bone for Georgina, Benjamin's dog; and a palpitation beneath her sternum. She plans to stay the night again and, tomorrow, to ask Benjamin if she can move in with him.

The next afternoon, after a shower, together in their underwear—for Benjamin has overfed the woodstove—they set the kitchen table and sit down before their second picnic. A moment spreads out in which Vee cannot quite believe that this is real. To have lived that life on Dumbarton Street with her vanity and Senator Kent and now to be here, wearing almost nothing, her stomach folded in the open, across from this lanky, weathered-faced, pale-chested man who always waits for her to speak, in a house without a single window covering, is almost too great a transformation to bear. She is happy, however unknown the future might be. The palpitation begins again. She has dithered over the phrasing—*for a time?* or *for a while?* She knows she must not frame her question as a need, though it is in fact the case that she needs a place to live. The room she has been sleeping in is slated to become a nursery to Rosemary's new baby, and though Rosemary is too polite to say that she would like Vee out in advance of her due date, she has begun putting up wallpaper samples on the wall behind Vee's bed. Living in Benjamin's house would mean being close enough to Rosemary but not in her way, and away from Philip who, since the day in the kitchen when she stood with her robe a little too loose, has stopped hectoring Vee to leave but now regularly stares at her breasts. Rosemary, Vee believes, must see this. She is not stupid. But does she also see how Vee waits a beat, lets him get his look, before turning away? And if she does, does she trust that Vee does it not proudly but out of desperation, a desire not to be kicked out again? If Benjamin would take her, all this could end.

Vee waits until they have emptied their first glasses. She reaches across the table to wipe a bit of brie from his lip, then, catching his smile at being babied, she dives in. "I've been thinking . . . maybe I could move in?"

For a time, she tells herself. Don't scare him. But she can't add the words. Benjamin is looking at her with a new expression, his eyes tense at their corners, his mouth pitched at a hard angle.

She has prepared for him to hesitate, of course. He has come here to live alone, away from bricks and crits and people. And he won't want to ruin the charge between them, which relies at least in part on their strangeness to each other—they have yet to exchange even their last names. But Vee has an answer for both of these problems. For the first, she planned to inform him that even Thoreau depended on his mother and sister to do things like his laundry, and for the second to argue that they can have it both ways, that she, at least, does not need to know anything more about him. All she wants is to live forever in a new house on old land with a man named Benjamin and a dog named Georgina as a woman named Vee without any titles or papers marking them.

But this look he is giving her is not about living alone, or about sex.

"I'm married," he says quietly. "Back in Cambridge."

It takes Vee a full minute before she can talk. By then she is scavenging around the bed for her clothes as Benjamin follows and dodges her at once, apologizing and trying to convince her not to go.

"Get away," she says. "Please get away from me."

"I'm taking some time off," he says. "But I can't stay here forever. I have a son."

Vee would cover her ears if she could but she must pull on her dress, her coat, her hat. She stuffs her stockings into her bag and her bare feet into her boots. "Nothing has to change," Benjamin says, and she remembers him musing just yesterday about how this land wasn't his family's to claim, how it belonged to the Indians and how someday there would be proper reparations made, remembers how even as he said this he rested back in his bed, clearly unprepared to go anywhere or give anything up. She runs, for the second and last time, away from the beautiful house.

An hour or so later, Vee opens Rosemary's front door as silently as possible. She would prefer to stay outside forever, walk the miles to the nearest coffee shop, walk until she reaches another planet, but she is without scarf or gloves, both of which she left at Benjamin's in her rush to flee, and her bare feet feel close to frostbite inside her boots. She doesn't want to see Rosemary, not yet. She has told her about a man named Benjamin up in the woods, told her enough to make Rosemary smile, and though Rosemary has not asked for more—Rosemary has been distracted, Rosemary has seemed more and more often not quite herself—she knows enough that Vee cannot now tell her that Benjamin has a wife and child. Vee is not a woman who sleeps with married men.

Yet she is, apparently.

She hears the children playing outside, on the other side of the house.

She will slip upstairs, lie down, pull herself together.

"Vivian."

It's Philip calling her, as no one calls her.

"Just a minute," she calls, her voice shaking. She bends to untie her boots, a process mercifully slowed by her numb fingers, so that by the time she is following Philip's voice into the living room she has managed to take a deep breath. Her chest vibrates painfully, and she realizes, as she enters the room to find Philip lying on the couch with one forearm flung across his eyes, that what she is, more than angry, is hurt. She and Benjamin joked a few times about both being on the lam, but now it turns out he really is, of his own choosing—Vee is alone in having been sent away.

"Are you okay?" It's almost comical, hearing herself ask these words even as her body longs for a private place in which to cry. She tries not to look at him, in his wrinkled shirt, no tie, and gold-toe socks. She has never seen him without shoes on. Alarm sings in her ears, telling her there is danger here and her hurt must wait, though of course the danger is not unrelated to the hurt, the danger is the married man laid out before Vee, Vee who did not intend harm but harmed nevertheless. "You have to leave," Philip says, his eyes still covered by his arm.

"Where's Rosemary?"

"Not here."

"What's wrong?"

"This is my living room."

"Yes?"

"So why must I be talking to you right now? Why must you be here? You're not a good influence."

"I . . ." Vee flounders, bewildered. "Do you mean the cigarettes? She hasn't been smoking anymore. Hasn't been drinking, either."

"I mean you. Just you."

"What are y—"

"You're a slut. Where do you go, Mrs. Alexander Kent? When you leave here for hours at a time. For whole days now, apparently. Do you think I don't know?"

Vee didn't know that Philip knew, but now that she does, she thinks, Of course. "Do you think *I* don't know about the cross?" she says. It's the first insult she can think to hurl at him. Then, seeing his confusion: "They burned a cross on your lawn, Philip R. And apparently your wife didn't even tell you. She protects you, and what do you do apart from some dishes like you're the goddamned messiah incarnate and not just another jerk who stares at her friends' tits and—"

"You have a way with words."

"You think smut is hard to come by?"

"I mean," says Philip, in a calm, awful voice, "that you shouldn't have trouble finding somewhere to go. Rosemary told me the women at the group loved you."

"What does that have to do with anything?" Vee snaps. The women at the Jewish consciousness raising group—clearly Philip cannot say *consciousness raising*—loved Vee because Rosemary, without asking Vee's permission, told them Vee's story, the same story the two friends had still not discussed in any detail, and one of the women said, *My goodness, you're Vashti!* and all the others oohed and aahed. Apparently Vee was living the story of some queen banished a million years ago in ancient Persia. But Vee did not know or care about any of this and was peeved that Rosemary had offered up her story. She did not love the women back, as Philip clearly hopes she did. She starts to explain this, how she is not going to live with one of the Jewish libbers, when suddenly Philip bolts upright on the couch, looks at her, and hollers: "We were fine before you came! Everything was fine!"

Vee takes in the hatred in Philip's gaze. Something has slipped in him—he is nothing if not a contained man. "I don't understand," she says. "You're fine now."

Philip laughs, a whistling, scary laugh. Vee hears the children, somewhere outside. "Where is Rosemary?" she says, suddenly afraid, not for herself now but for her friend.

"Wouldn't you like to know." Philip covers his face with his hands. He stays like that as he takes a deep breath, then he rubs gruffly at himself and appears again, the skin under his eyes a startling, bruised blue. "You probably think she'll tell you not to listen to me," he says. "Tell you to stay. So stay right here. Wait. Hear it for yourself." His voice has dropped to a monotone. "She'll be home soon. She called a little while ago."

"From where?"

"The hospital."

"Why is she at the hospital?"

"She lost the baby."

"No." Vee drops to her knees.

"It started two nights ago."

"My god."

Silence. Then Philip says, "You're so upset. Yet you haven't even asked how she's getting home."

"I can go get her," offers Vee.

"You're too late. You weren't here. A friend is driving her."

"I could stay with the children, so you can go."

"I'll say it again. You weren't here. You're too late."

Vee's fingertips throb with returning heat. She lets out a wail. Then Philip is standing above her, snatching her up by the shoulders. "What gives you the right to cry," he says, his face inches from hers, his eyes, on her chest, devastated and dry. "Who do you think you are?" Vee steps backward, out of his reach, but he's on her again, his hands on her breasts this time, squeezing and pushing her away at once. "Get out," he says. "Get the hell out." She feels the shove coming. She understands that she will fly backward into the table behind her and that she and the weird sculpture will fall together into the wall. Then the door opens to Rosemary, and behind her the children, and behind them a white sky. The children have been running and are red-cheeked, gawking, the girl with a look in her eyes that sets Vee's blood pounding. But it's Rosemary whose face, pale as the sky, terrifies. "Lionel," she says, addressing her oldest in a voice like an empty tunnel, "take your brother and sister upstairs. I'll be right there." She does not look at Vee as she tells her to pack. Vee does not look at Rosemary's abdomen. Then Rosemary is walking up the stairs with excruciating care, matching her feet on each step, her hand white from its grip on the banister. And soon she's gone.

MANHATTAN

LILY

For She Had Neither Father Nor Mother

Ruth is gone. It was sepsis, finally, one of the words Lily learned to dread, though sitting now with her brothers, in a bar a few blocks from the hospital, she cannot seem to feel what she imagined she would feel. Lily's and Lionel's spouses have taken their children home and to a hotel, respectively. Ian has called his boyfriend in California. He was crying when he hung up but sits silently now, sliding his whiskey through closed lips, while Lionel, clearly in shock, keeps talking. He says words he has already said, things like *Four blocks from the hospital, three siblings, four hours dead* and *And then you called me and I still didn't get it, I didn't know how fast it would happen, I wouldn't have brought the kids, I would have just gotten in the car* . . . Ian was already in the city, visiting, but Lionel, who lives so much closer, missed Ruth's last cogent hour. Lily called as he was driving, so he knew, but you can't know such a thing until you know it. He talks. All three of them drink. And soon—Lionel announces—it has been not four but five hours since their mother died.

Lily finds herself thinking not of Ruth, or even of Ruth's body, but of the hospital room itself, its steady blankness, like a clean sheet, before and as and after Ruth died, and of how strange it is that she and her brothers will likely never return to it.

"What happens now?"

The room had been a different room from the one Ruth had been in during her first hospitalization, but it had also, of course, been the same room, the room Ruth had known Lily had not wanted to leave but had her thrown out of anyway. *Go home.* As if she was not home, with Ruth.

"Lily?"

Lily feels Lionel's glass nudging hers and looks up.

"What do we do now?" her brother says. "With her body, and her apartment, and her finances . . ."

His shock is in his eyes. It's bigger than Lily realized, and more encompassing; he is shocked, she sees, not only that Ruth is dead but that she has died without leaving him instructions. That his sister is now the one likely to know what he does not. He can't imagine all she knows—about cancer, yes, but also about cards for doctors and nurses, and cremation versus burial, etc. They have traveled a great distance since the night five weeks ago when he called her with the news, when Lionel was the one Ruth chose to tell first and Lily was naïve enough to think her mother might make it to Purim.

"The funeral home is coming for her," Lily says gently. "Tomorrow's the burial, then we'll sit shiva . . ."

Lionel groans. "The funeral the day after is ridiculous. It's not like we can reach all the people she knew in twenty-four hours."

"We'll have a memorial service in a couple weeks. She and I talked about—"

"I still don't get why she had to be so Jewish."

"I don't know, Li, but it's what—"

"Seriously, who does that? Who marries a Jewish guy who isn't even remotely observant, converts *just* as he's leaving you, then keeps going whole hog like you're actually the Jew?"

"I think you are," Ian offers. "If you convert. Also, *whole hog* . . ."

"But not really." Lionel scowls. "And why? What was her end game?"

Ian chuckles into his glass. "You're such an asshole. There was no end game. I think she liked the people."

"So hang out with them! It was all so embarrassing. *My mother is having a bat mitzvah*. Good god. And then when we had to do Shabbat on Fridays and she'd put her hand on our heads and say, *May you be Lionel, in all that you are?* The worst."

Ian signals for another round, and then they're quiet for a while, even Lionel. Lily remembers her mother doing that, though hanging from the memory there is no strong feeling. But it would have been different for Lionel, who was already twelve when Ruth converted. Even Ian, who had just turned eleven and had a bar mitzvah two years later, must have gotten used to life without Shabbat and general Jewishness. Whereas Lily had been seven, old enough to vaguely remember before but not old enough to be attached to it. For Lily, the divide has always seemed to be about her father leaving. Not that she was older when that happened; like Lionel, she is pretty sure the conversion and separation were concurrent events. Just that her father has figured in her mind as the bigger deal.

"You know what she told me?" she says. "He didn't leave. She threw him out."

"That's not true," Lionel says immediately.

"It's what she told me."

"I understand. But it's not true."

"Why would she say it, then?"

"For the same reason anyone says anything—because she wanted it to be true?"

"Is that why you say things, Lionel?"

Ian swivels on his stool. "Please stop. It could be true."

Lionel snorts. "Are you kidding me? There's no way."

"What do your kids know of your marriage?"

Lionel slits his eyes.

"Ahhh," Ian says with a note of triumph, and suddenly Lily is disgusted by them all. "Forget it," she says, slapping a hand on the bar. "Who cares? No one cares. Do you know what else she said to me? Just yesterday? This one will neither surprise nor offend."

Her brothers shake their heads.

"I brought the *Times*. And she saw me slide the book review under the stack. Which I always do. And she said, *You have no right to do that*. And I was like, *What are you talking about?* I thought she might be confused, like she didn't know who I was suddenly, or what was happening. Then she said, *You have no right to be jealous, Lily. You haven't written anything*."

Ian whistles softly. "That's harsh."

"But correct!" Lily says.

"Oh come on, Lil." Lionel's voice tilts into the one she guesses he must use with frustrated clients. "Couldn't you still maybe get some kind of—"

"Stop. I didn't tell you that so we could talk about me. I told you because it was just so Mom." This is true. Though it is also probably true that on some level Lily does want to talk about herself. She cannot pretend not to be aware that certain problems she has neglected await her once the immediate aftermath of Ruth's death is attended to. The Purim dresses, for one. The morning after she and Ruth agreed that Ruth would teach her to sew, Lily picked up a rental machine from a shop on Avenue N and set it up according to Ruth's instructions, but by the next day, Ruth was too tired to get out of bed. Now the machine is still sitting on her desk, unused, and the dresses are still not made. And then there is the problem of Adam. Or if not of Adam, then of Hal, who continues to invite Lily and the kids to the no-name pizza place each Thursday and hang out not quite in the background during her nightly trysts with Adam. Adam thinks it's nice that she and Hal take the kids out together. And Adam benefits—in bed, on the kitchen island, on the bathmat. So maybe it's not really a problem? Adam and Hal have their meetings—Hal has even started giving presentations to Adam's bosses; his *charisma*, as Adam calls it, is apparently a real asset—and Lily and Adam have theirs. And won't it all end now anyway, automatically? At this moment perched between her brothers in this bar, Lily can't imagine her body ever wanting anything like that again, not with Adam or Hal or anyone. She can't even imagine standing up.

You have no right to be jealous, said her mother.

But then what can she be?

This is the worst problem, of course, the one that hangs over everything else, like a silent, fiery planet on the verge of explosion, or maybe implosion—what Lily is going to do with herself. Beyond mothering. And being mothered. And screwing her husband and fantasizing about his friend/colleague. And trying to save Ruth. She'd been given someone to save after all. She'd been given a mission, albeit a twenty-first-century, American, self-involved mission. But unlike Esther, Lily failed. Now that Ruth is gone, what force will steer her? Beyond semiprofessionally screwing up laundry, which strikes her now as pitiful in the same way that hiding the *New York Times Book Review* from herself is pitiful: opposite ends of the same spectrum. To care or not to care. Even the spectrum is pitiful. As if all Lily boils down to—if one were to boil her, singe her shell off, pick out her meat—is a poster woman for a think piece on having or not having it all. But Lily's conundrum goes beyond whether or not to work. She will work again, if not at the work she already knows how to do, if only because they will eventually need and be able to afford—once both girls are in school—a second income. Her question is, Who will she be?

Lily sips her scotch and winces. Why is she drinking scotch? She doesn't like it. She is drinking it because it's what her brothers drink. She slides her glass toward Ian and waves for the bartender. "Do you know what Mom liked to drink when we were kids?"

"Bourbon on the rocks," Ian says.

Lily orders a bourbon. Six hours have passed, then seven. Out the bar's window they watch the last slash of light disappear from the narrow street. Ian lays his cheek down on the bar, and Lionel says to Lily: "You did good."

"What do you mean?"

"With Mom. This whole . . . all of it."

"Okay."

"Did you ever feel—did you ever want to just call the doctors and . . . ?"

"I did call the doctors. Often."

"But I mean just to—"

"Wait a second. Was that a backhanded compliment?" Lily's head is heavier than she realized. She is maybe drunk. "Are you accusing me of not seeing what was happening?"

"No!"

"What happened was entirely common in non–small cell lung cancer patients. The chemo weakens the immune system, and once infection sets in, sepsis—"

"Lily! That's not it. I promise. I was just saying, I don't know how . . . if I were in your place, I don't know if I could have . . ."

Ian slides his glass into Lionel's, shutting him up, then lifts his face off the bar and slides his glass into Lily's. Clink. Clink. "He's saying thank you," he says, and slides Lionel's glass into Lily's.

The clinks repeat themselves in her ears. Her brothers are quiet, watching her. For years she has thought of them as enlarged versions of their boy selves: Lionel the natural boss, interested in money, attentive to details; Ian the jock and peacemaker who tried his best to go along. She has sensed that they think in the same way about her: the smart but hapless baby, overly sensitive, thinks too much. But Lionel is anxious, even fearful, and Ian, if she bothers to think for even a minute about the basic facts of his life, has not been able to just go along.

Lily picks up her glass, empties it, then clinks it against her brothers' glasses. I'm the one doing it now, she thinks. *May you be Lily, in all that you are.* One of the glasses will topple off the bar in a minute, and then they will leave, and get in cabs, and go their separate ways, but until then she toasts with her brothers, clink, clink, and they nod together to the beat.

SUSA

ESTHER

Descent

The bird is perfect. She has taught it the scent of sumac, and cardamom and sesame, too. When she frees it in the courtyard, the bird flies without hesitation over the wall and away. She trusts it as she trusts herself. It is her, in a sense. When it reaches Nadav's mother, and speaks, it will speak Esther's words. The guards eye her but no more than usual. They do not ask questions. The triumph she feels with the bird safely over the wall is so replete she could lie down on the stones and sing; she feels as if the bird has been released from her own chest.

But that night, on her pillow, she finds the bird's bones, picked clean. She knows the bones as she knew her own hands; she knows they are not another bird's bones masquerading as her bird's. Next to them is a miniature scepter: an invitation to a banquet in the king's rooms.

She is not surprised, the following evening, to find herself seated next to the minister. He wastes no time. "Spices have been prohibited in the camp for months now," he says in greeting, swirling his finger in his wine. "Your poor bird didn't have a chance."

Esther stares at her plate, avoiding the minister's glinting ornaments and his toothless, fearsome smile.

"And your eunuch? He's a coward. Soft. Always has been. But you knew that, didn't you." The minister slows his words, as if talking to a child. "He didn't go close enough to the camp to have any idea."

Esther imagines strangling the minister with the gilded collar he wears. It might be doable, she thinks—if she could bring back the beast, she could do it. But she doubts she will ever again have enough power to become the beast. And even if she could, wouldn't Darius be harmed, seeing his mother like that? And the new child inside her—what would happen to it? Still, she can feel her giant paddle hands on the minister's neck. She sees vividly the color his skin would turn, a red as fierce as the sumac he's banned. She faces him. "How did you capture it?"

"Your Majesty. Did you really think they would listen to you? Are you so arrogant as that? Even now?" Spittle shines in the corners of his lips. "You must know they are cowards, too. Like you, trying to escape fate. Yours, theirs. Your poor bird was the only brave one. You should have seen it when it found me, my palm outstretched, full of spices. Oh, the fragrance of my skin!"

A hand arrives on her thigh. It rests for a moment, then the fingers begin to walk her robes aside. The king rises to say something and the minister's head follows but his fingers stay behind and keep walking. Esther clamps her legs together and watches the king's mouth move. When he is seated again, the minister grows bolder. He looks at her as he speaks; he speaks to her as he forces his fingers between her thighs; he forces his fingers between her thighs as he brings meat to his mouth with his other hand. "I twisted its neck," he says. "It was easy. Not so different, really, from ordering the killing of the queen." He leans closer. "The king regrets that, you know. You must—you are not stupid. You must know that Vashti is the one he wants."

Did she know that? Esther can't decide. And she can't see how it matters now. She presses her legs together more tightly, trying to squeeze the fingers into retreat, but it's difficult to clamp down one part of your body with all your might while keeping other parts—in particular the face—appearing jovial and relaxed. It is, in fact, as Esther is neither the first nor last to discover, pretty much impossible. And the face must take precedence—the face either masks or gives away. As the minister's fingers reach their intended goal, Esther shifts sideways but cannot escape.

"But as you also know," the minister continues, "one must not change direction. The queen had to be killed. The bird had to be killed. All this is clear. Less clear is how you brought the thing to life. Your people—" his breath in her nostrils, smelling of meat "—insist there is one God. They insist to the point of torture. To the point of death. It's their one bravery, I suppose. And perhaps it's why they stay. Perhaps they imagine from that quarter will come their relief." The fingers go slack for a moment, before coming alive again at his next thought. "But that's irrelevant to what I want to know, which is how you can be one of them, yet play God."

Esther struggles to speak. "I did no such thing."

"The bird," breathes the minister. "You created the bird."

"The bird was already a bird."

"Is that right. I want to know how you do it."

"That's not possible."

"But Darius is growing larger."

"What does that have to do with it?"

"He's walking. He might be sent to the training grounds.

They're far from here, you know. He'll make a fine warrior. One day a warrior king."

"I'll go with him."

The minister chuckles. "You'll go nowhere. Teach me."

"It can't be taught," says Esther, her voice hoarse with the effort of trying to ignore his hand. Where is the beast? The beast would not have to endure this. "You have to be born into it."

"Ahhh. But that's what everyone told me when I was a child. *Stop your airs. You're nothing but a butcher's son.* I was lower than the king, who was not high. But now look at me. I tell him what to do." The fingers wriggle. "Look at me."

Esther vomits onto her plate.

It is the only alternative to screaming. It is excused, her condition being what it is. It gets her out of the room. But it does not get her away from the minister more generally, neither his actual presence nearly everywhere she goes—pressing, rubbing, taunting—nor his questions, which torment her now as if he's grafted them into her mind. Had she tried to act as God? But what else would make them go at this point? If not pillage and rape, if not a ban on spices? Somehow the ban scares her the most—it seems the kind of silent loss that could finally tip a people out of existence.

She begins to walk the palace again, searching, though she does not know at first for what. She sees faces, Itz's and Nadav's and her aunt's and her aunt's washing partner's and Marduk's and faces of people whose names she never knew. But the faces are false, she knows. Even as they appear clearly in her mind she sees that they are facades of faces, molds, as if the real faces have been caught in sap. Who knows if these people are alive anymore? Even Marduk appears as an innocent, his long cheeks and hard eyes calling up a longing in her. She has been gone too long, she understands. The understanding makes her more frantic. She is looking, she realizes, for the bones room. She wants a fox, to replace the bird. If playing God is what she was doing, she will do it again. She has the energy for a fox. She is almost certain. She will teach the fox not scent but language, and the fox will dig until it hears her people talking up above, then it will deliver her message. At last. And then they'll leave, before they're all killed.

If the idea is impractical, so be it. Through portal and passage Esther searches, Darius on her back or running beside her, her stomach preceding them like a moon. The midwives don't stop her this time, maybe because she carried the first one well, or because he is the boy the king wanted; that need is sated. Or maybe they let her go because she moves so quickly, like a surging wave, that they are afraid of what she might do if they try to restrain her. This isn't the same as their fearing her, she knows—if they feared her, she would have power over them, and she doesn't. It's her lack of power that scares them— they know she is fully trapped; their fear is that she will blow.

A week after the dinner, her punishment arrives. Darius is taken from her rooms. He'll be raised at the training grounds, she is told by one of the midwives as she measures Esther's stomach. So matter-of-fact Esther almost misses it. *Just right. Not much longer now. Your son . . .*

She is allowed one visit each week.

When she sees him, she thinks she might bite into him. Take a doughy forearm into her mouth. Swallow an ear. When he is taken again, she cries until the midwives do something—she never knows—that makes her fall asleep, and when she wakes, and remembers, she begins again to cry. She would kill herself trying to get to him, if she did not have the other one inside her.

So she begins to teach the minister. He will not succeed. She comforts herself with this. Even if a shred of magic were buried somewhere in him, he would not be able to access it; to access it, you had to be receptive; to be receptive, you had to be capable of admitting all you did not know. But she can't let him fail outright, either. If he fails, he will blame her. He will take Darius to Persepolis the whole year round. She has to make the minister fail without realizing it; she must make him an eternal apprentice, so that he inches forward, or perceives himself inching forward, but never quite enough. This will be its own kind of sorcery. She will have to trick him into thinking he is learning until he dies.

It will be a kind of circling, she thinks, endless movement without actually going anywhere. Like the camp used to do before the attacks started, when all they were hiding from was the sun.

She teaches the minister. He does not touch her during their lessons, a pleasant fact she understands has nothing to do with humility; he is simply unexcited by the prospect of molesting her without the king present.

Darius is returned to her. Though he is walking now, often away from her, she does not let him out of her sight.

Her stomach begins, once or twice each day, to harden as if into rock. Her time to find the bones room is running out.

She searches. But the minister is probably right. Why would they leave now if they haven't already?

She searches. But what if they are already gone? Maybe they walked off a year ago, into the desert. How would Esther know? The only information she gets comes from within the palace. Everyone could be lying. Even Baraz. Maybe especially Baraz.

Baraz is nowhere to be found.

People stop looking her in the eye.

Only the midwives touch her. And Darius. Though he runs now, fast, laughing.

A midwife tells her that Darius was well cared for, by a woman who claims she knew Esther in the night station, a woman with one eyebrow. And Esther thinks of the last time she saw Lara, and wonders if it's too late, if Lara might yet be a friend, if she might help. Esther starts thinking she sees her, around corners and behind doors, but she can never move fast enough to reach her.

The minister tells her she is losing her mind.

She is the minister's teacher.

But the minister may be right.

She is dreaming when he wakes her, his voice a comfort she brings into the dream with her, a dream of childhood, a floor of papyrus reeds, yellow grass, Darius's hair, Darius a friend, Esther only as tall as the grown-ups' knees, Baraz's voice: "Shhhh, wake up," a tilting sky, a bowl of rice. It takes his hand on her shoulder to lift her out. At once, her blood begins to pound. Is the baby coming? Has Darius been taken? She rises onto her knees. Darius is there, his skin pink in the light thrown by Baraz's torch. Her inside is calm.

A whisper. "Come."

"Where have you been?" She hasn't seen him in weeks.

"I'll show you."

"You didn't tell me about the spices," she says.

"Shh."

"Why should I go with you?"

"I didn't know. I am only told what it is useful for me to know."

"You said you spoke—"

"Never with them. I never said I spoke with them directly."

"The bird—"

"I know." Baraz swallows visibly, his Adam's apple sliding in a way that reminds her that he is both a man and more than a man. "Please. I need you to come with me, without more words."

"I can't leave Darius."

"He'll cry."

"I won't leave him."

Baraz suffocates the torch before opening the door to the passage. They walk in darkness, Esther carrying Darius until Baraz, sensing her struggle, takes the boy into his arms. Esther is barefoot as Baraz ordered her; their soles purr across the stones. They walk through portal and passage, far enough that Esther, losing track of the turns, takes up a fringe of Baraz's robe between her fingers.

When they stop, Esther touches the wall nearest to her. It's smooth and solid—not a door. She feels Baraz at her feet, his hands working at something in the ground. She kneels and feels her son's feet tickle her neck; he is cocooned, she realizes, in the space between Baraz's legs and chest. Then a current of air rises and Baraz has her by the hand, leading her downward. Rungs in a wall. She has to lean back so that her stomach will clear them. Baraz is still above her, she can hear his almost soundless movements, his hands settling something back into place. She waits at the bottom, sand damp beneath her feet, her leg muscles quivering. The exertion has stirred up tears, and a fantasy: they are in the bones room. Baraz knew without her telling him what she wanted. Never mind that the bones room had not required a descent.

The torch flares. They are in not the bones room but a low-ceilinged cellar, empty of furniture. Three other eunuchs stand waiting near an opening in the wall. A tunnel, Esther sees.

Baraz says quietly, "It's not for you."

Her chest starts to ache. "This is what you were doing," she says, realizing. "When Darius was born."

Baraz nods. "This is where we've been anytime we weren't somewhere else."

Esther is gripped by a sudden, wild fear. They have made some kind of deal for Darius. She can't understand what; it makes no sense; when Baraz woke her, he didn't want Darius to come at all. But that could have been an act, too. They are going to send him out this tunnel, her boy who has only just learned to walk.

But when she reaches for him, Baraz lays the boy in her arms and smiles. Has she ever seen him smile? Then he gives his torch a shake, nudging the flame higher and illuminating more of the room, which is larger than it first appeared. As Baraz walks backward, it grows larger still, and for a few suspended moments Esther believes that it could prove infinite if only Baraz and his torch would keep pressing into its borders. All we have to do is walk, she thinks, until we've reached the camp.

Baraz stops. In a far corner, there is a bed. A rug. A tall drawer. A chair. In the chair, there is a woman. She appears older than Esther, though by how much is hard to tell. Her features are youthful but her skin hangs slightly, as if living within the earth has shrunk her, and she sits with an ambiguous stiffness, as a young person might do in fear or an old person in pain. Her eyes rest dully on a middle distance. Darius squeezes Esther's hand and Esther, squeezing back, wonders if the woman before them is dead. If her head is hanging from the ceiling by a rope Esther can't yet see.

"If it were only my life," Baraz says, "I would have . . ."

The woman turns. Her eyes fill with light. They are green eyes, set in a silt-brown face, surrounded by black hair that does not fall, like Esther's, but rises, wild, its own crown. She is different. But she is also, Esther sees, the same. Beautiful in the way that Esther is beautiful, a way that cannot be changed. She is the queen.

Part Three

Reinvention

BROOKLYN

LILY

Not a Good Influence

At the reception after the memorial service, Lily and her brothers let people squeeze their hands. A few come at them with hard embraces, undeterred by whether or not Ruth's children know who they are. There are many they don't know, more than they expected. People from Gloucester none of them remember. Women from Cambridge. Lily knows some of the local friends, especially those who belong to Ruth's synagogue on Garfield Place, where the event is held, but there are at least a dozen other Brooklynites she has never met. The social hall has been set up in a manner that surprises and moves her: not plastic sheets, as there were on the occasions when Ruth dragged her to something, but substantial white tablecloths; not supermarket platters but cheese and fruit plates put together by a group of women who, based on the dates and figs they've procured and the way they say her name, clearly knew and loved Ruth. There is decent wine, and two tall vases filled generously with flowers. When Ian gave his eulogy in the sanctuary across the street, Lily cried; she had declined giving one herself because she did not trust she would get through it. But here, there is not a lot of grief to be felt, rather, a low-grade numbness in hand after hand, words after words. Her friends talk in one corner—she hasn't seen them in a while, but they came with strong hugs and an unmistakable tenderness. In her peripheral vision she watches Rosie and June play dodge-the-mourners with their cousins as Adam and Lionel's wife work to corral them. Early this morning, as Adam was getting the girls dressed, Lily heard fighting and walked in to find June sobbing, *You said she was here!* and Rosie shouting back, *I said her ghost was here!* Adam waved his hand at Lily: *Get out of here, I've got this.* But how could she not wait to hear what came next? *What's a ghost?* June screamed. *It's dead! What's dead? Gone!* June stopped trying to take off the shirt Adam had just put on her. *Does she have a face? No. Does she have words? No. Does she show up? No.* June burst into tears. But now she races gleefully among the dark-clad grown people, who must seem to her like a woods, and what Lily wants more than anything is to walk the three blocks home and lie down with June, as she and June lay with Ruth, and watch her nap with her nose up and her mouth open.

An hour or so into the reception she and Lionel and Ian wind up in a corner, left to themselves. "An intermission," Lionel observes. "For the inner mourners." They stand silently for a while, drinking water handed to them by someone who somehow knows that this is the moment when inner mourners are struck by a terrible thirst. Their water is refilled and they drink more, and stand more, until Lionel says, "Oh god."

A few seconds pass. Then Ian says, "Oh my god. Is that?"

"What?" Lily, ever the shortest, can't see the room as they do.

"It's that woman," Lionel says. "The governor's wife."

"The senator," says Ian.

"She's a senator?" Lily asks.

"She was a senator's wife. She did something to get thrown out, Mom would never say what. They were friends as kids. She came to live with us for a while. You were like three. Maybe four?" Ian brings a hand to his mouth.

"What?" Lily asks. "What's the big deal?"

"She was Dad's first affair," Lionel announces.

Lily looks to Ian, who nods. "I'm about ninety-five percent sure that's what happened."

"That's awful," Lily says.

"He hated her, though," Lionel says.

"That's even worse. Why?"

"He blamed her."

"For what?"

"Everything!"

Lionel's voice has turned weirdly bright, and Lily sees that a nearby cluster of mourners has dispersed, making visible a petite, reddish-haired woman who stands more erectly than the other seventysomethings in the room. She wears a black collared dress, black tights, heeled boots in a navy suede. Lily is reminded of a photograph she once saw of Edna St. Vincent Millay. It's not just that both women are small, with fluffs of red hair. There is a frankness in this woman's expression as she scans the room, a quiet audacity as she spots Lily and her brothers and walks toward them, her boots clacking on the old parquet floor, her dress unbuttoned nearly to her breastbone so that her pale, narrow chest seems to glow.

A hand, outstretched, shows her age.

"I'm very sorry," she says.

Lionel offers his hand, then withdraws it as soon as they've touched. "Kent," he declares awkwardly, as if by naming her he might dispel her.

"Barr," the woman corrects. "Vivian Barr." Her voice is peculiar and somehow fitting, metallic yet also sonorous. "You knew me as Vee."

"We remember," Lionel says.

The woman nods. Lily sees that the skin on her chest—her *décolletage*, Lily thinks, this is a woman with a décolletage—is not milkily pure, as it appeared at a distance, but marred by moles and spots and fine vertical lines that meet between her almost nonexistent breasts and disappear into her dress. Lily's brothers wait for the woman to leave—even Ian, who used to bring injured mice into the house, offers nothing more than a cool nod. But Lily is transfixed. She understands that there may be reasons why Vivian Barr's name did not appear on Ruth's invite list. Even so, she finds herself gathering the woman's hands—they are small, and soft, the tiny bones and veins palpable under the skin—into her own. "Thank you for coming," she says.

"You're Lily," says Vivian Barr.

Lily nods.

"You were very small when I knew you."

"Yes."

"My condolences. I loved your mother very much."

Then the woman is walking away, and Lily's brothers are whispering before she has left the room about Vivian Barr's many crimes: how she not only slept with their father, and did whatever she did to get kicked out of DC, and took their mother to the Jewish group that converted her, but was also the one who started Ruth smoking—she was the one, if you thought about it, who killed her. And not only that: their father blamed Vivian Barr for their mother losing the baby.

"What baby?" Lily is pulled from watching the door Vivian Barr has disappeared through. She was thinking about how Vivian Barr must have learned about Ruth's death in the obits—*Ruth*

Rubenstein, born Rosemary Burnham, of Gloucester, Massachusetts—and how although there are others present today who knew Ruth as a young woman called Rosemary—including Lionel, Ian, and, just barely, Lily—no one else, to Lily's knowledge, knew her as a girl.

"You know about this," Lionel says.

"She might not," Ian says.

Does she?

"She was pregnant with a fourth," Ian says. "Like second-trimester pregnant."

"My god."

"I swear we've talked about this," Lionel says.

Lily searches her memory. Is it possible—it does not seem possible—that she knew this and somehow forgot? Ruth never told her, she's certain of that. Maybe she wanted to protect Lily, her one child bearer. But after she'd had Rosie and June? Why not then? Lily reaches for a glass of wine off a passing tray and gulps as she thinks back. She throws her mind at her childhood like a net. What she catches, though, is not her mother—it's Vivian Barr. Lily is certain. The villainess herself. Her hair is redder. She is standing in the kitchen in a robe. Lily's father is there but Lily's father is not what Lily sees; Lily's father is there in her memory only as a presence, as he was always there, even after he left. She sees only Vivian Barr, in her robe. Lily is outside, cold, looking in, the scene soundless. The scene is only a moment, held in the sliding glass door: Vivian Barr barefoot, though it is not summer, her belted waist pressing into the counter, her hair giving a little shiver, her hand placing a piece of apple into her mouth.

SUSA

THE QUEEN

Her Earlier Reentry

Once more, it's as you imagine. The exodus begins in the middle of the night. A heavy dark, the air sweet with the shybrush that grows along the creek.

So there must be a breeze. It might be strong enough to lift the cloth that covers her hair. She might faint. The air, the cloth, her skin, all of it fluttering, touching, touched.

She works to concentrate, to attend to what is happening: I am out, I am here, I must find the camp and take them far away by sunrise. She is dead, according to the public record. And she has to stay dead, to make her exodus before she is found alive. If she's found alive, she will be truly dead.

She looks to Baraz. Behind him, like another country, the palace looms, still innocent of their flight. Ahead, she sees a herd of broad, humped animals, and a vertigo rises through her. Where is she? What has happened to the outside world? Then Baraz nods and begins to walk, and she sees: the animals are the tents. The camp is ahead.

Yet as they walk, the tents appear to shift and sigh, to behave as the animals she first saw. This will happen often in her first days out: she will see a vision of a thing before the thing itself, and the vision will be hard to shake. A towering flame before a distant tree. A silver belt girdling the sand before a creek. She will recover; she will orient to the disorientation. For now she is in shock. Her eyes twitch at the vastness, strain to go everywhere. It's a physical effort to make them focus and look for what she's supposed to be looking for: the tent Esther described to her, with its asymmetrical roof, the odd angle to the back wall, the beautiful, bright fabric hung as a door—

You thought she *was* Esther?

You wanted her to be Esther.

Oh. But that's not possible. The queen and her child—soon to be children—can't leave the palace. Only in a fantasy, a farce, could they be allowed another fate: return heroic, save the people, destroy the villain, etc. Happy coincidence, vengeance, reversal, rejoicing. There will be a story like that, but this isn't the one.

She is Vashti. Thirty paces from the camp, Baraz stops, slips off his sandals, then kneels to remove hers. He hooks the straps onto one of his thick forefingers, lowers himself into a crouch, and begins to slide so silently toward the camp that if Vashti were to close her eyes she would not know he is there. She closes her eyes. She is overwhelmed again by the space around her, the sky, the air prickling her skin. You can't know when you're kept from night and day and fresh air for so long that when you finally get it, what you've been craving, it will be terrifying, almost painful. She can't hear Baraz. She startles. But there he is, looking back for her. And here she is, beginning again to follow him, to try to mimic his crablike dance. Do this, she tells herself. Only this. Tomorrow, or maybe by now it's today, later, there will be time . . . But she is distracted. A new sensation. It would not shock another—Esther, for instance. It's only sand, scraping the sides and bottoms of her feet. But not once in her twenty-eight years—it's easy to forget how young she is, this former queen—has Vashti walked barefoot, and the agitation brings her back to the baths of her youth. Eucalyptus branches, lashing and scratching. By the end of the old women's beating she would be pink and tingling and raw, and yet always, she wanted more. The Babylonian baths were training, in this way, for the erotic. But Ahasuerus did away with them anyway, just as he did away with any other of her people's customs that he could in his opinion easily replace with his own. Vashti was enraged at first. Who was he, a former steward, to make the rules? Later, after she grew inexplicably tender toward him, she forgave him. He was not a natural king, like her father and grandfather, with a face that never gave way. He was suggestible, and very short, and worshipped her so fully that she not infrequently saw a bit of drool fall from his mouth as she disrobed. She had the power, and he knew it, and so she let him choose his trappings the way he wanted them. But the baths she never stopped missing. The harshness against her skin now as she slides after Baraz.

Just slide, she tells herself. Focus. She has had nearly three years in a hole in the earth. You might think by now she would have used up all her thoughts, traveled to every splinter of her past ten million times. But you would not be accounting for madness. Early on, when she was first trapped, it was true that she thought nonstop. Her thoughts made a frantic loop of regret and fury as she flailed and scratched at the walls: *should have done what he wanted; should have spit in his face; should have killed herself; should have turned the guards on Ahasuerus; should have done what he wanted . . .* She knocked her head against her walls. Her thoughts would have destroyed her if she had not shut them down. She shut them down. Went numb. So what is happening now as she follows Baraz across the sand is not just shock but a coming alive, a rebirth that is not entirely within her control, and her mind as if to make up for its time of hibernation begins to move as fast as a splitting star. Her feet trying to mimic Baraz's remind her of her father criticizing her flat arches, which did not belong, he said, with her narrow heels and long toes; they were the arches of a peasant, they exposed something base in her; and the timbre of her father's voice calls to mind his death, midspeech, on his throne, when an improperly affixed candelabrum fell from the ceiling above him, splitting open his skull. How many ways she felt then, at fifteen, horrified and in awe and curious, so curious to see the contents of her father's head . . . but then she was swept up by her king's chief minister and pushed toward Ahasuerus, who was standing, as always, at the ready. Her father would have murdered this minister if he'd seen what the gesture was allowed to grow into, but Ahasuerus was teachable, at least, he was malleable. Vashti did not mind that, she thinks as she slides, remembering the first time they made the spring journey from Susa to Persepolis, how readily Ahasuerus tossed his chin away when they passed the Saka camps along the way, though his own family had been nomads not so many hundreds of years ago, and Baraz's back now, in front of her, the broad animal bulk of it, is so precisely the shadow to Ahasuerus's slight one that she is reminded of yet another reason she could not do as he asked: not because she had drunk less wine—she had drunk plenty—but because she was and had always been a queen and he was and had always been a steward in a king's robes. So she understood, when she was asked to appear before him and his men in only her crown, that he would regret it. She also understood that this did not mean that he did not think he wanted it. For a short while she had worked to decide which was more important, what he thought he wanted now or what he would want later, until she realized, or was it that she remembered, that she did not have a choice; she could not do it; she had been trained from birth to be a queen, the same training that makes it a struggle for her to squat now and copy Baraz's crab walk, for she was raised up with sticks and strings, like a wall plant, taught to walk with her clavicle to the sky and to keep her robes closed except in the baths, and except for her husband, and she had done all of this, and she had opened them for him, too; she had gotten over what would have been her father's disapproval and let him please her, and she had pleased him; he knew what he'd been given, so much so that even when she could not bear him a child he kept her and refused the children of his other wives as his heirs, and refused the shock in the court, and refused to believe it would not happen with her eventually, that her body that had been swaddled and shrouded and shod and finally crowned could possibly be a body that failed, and though she felt certain he was wrong she was grateful for his faith. So there was a certain rightness between them, until that night.

But now Baraz is slowing and pointing. Now Vashti is scanning for the tent with the bright, beautiful flaps; she is prodding herself, Stop thinking of that night, pay attention to this one, you are supposed to be dead, you will be dead, but this warning only reminds her of the second choice she had to make that night—would she play dead or would she run?—which just like the first choice quickly revealed itself not to be a choice at all because a queen could not run and so she said she was sick, too sick to stand, and as soon as the words left her mouth it was not untrue, there was the wine, after all, and his cracked demand, and the party all around her, swaying, and a necklace she wore that was heavier than her crown, which she also wore, so that she began to tip backward, and once she was down she could not get up. But now—

She sees it! The tent is as Esther said it would be, the door's fabric bright enough that it conquers the dark, so bright it seems to make sparks fly, and Vashti looks up, straight at the sky and its staggering sweep of light, and thinks, I am doing both now, I am playing dead *and* running, and she starts to laugh, and Baraz muzzles her, and then they wait until the noise has settled back into her bones before they pull open the tent's flap.

MANHATTAN

LILY

Out of Eden into History

After the memorial service, an emptiness opens up in Lily. It comes without words; it is sensation only, a physical presence distended with absence. When she wakes it is waiting for her, nestled in crevices like a dark moss, and it crouches there, almost politely, until she gets through lunches and shoes and hugs and sees the people out the door. But once she stops moving, to drink her tea or sit on the toilet or stand in the shower, the emptiness unfurls like a great, pungent fern, an elegant slayer of anything that is not it.

Adam tells her it will be okay. He tells her not to rush whatever she has to go through; he's here for her; what can he do for her? He says all the right things and even does a lot of the right things, like calling the preschool and saying they'd like one more month of three full days a week, and calling the sitter and asking her to cover the other two days. This even though she has seen him madly tallying on scrap paper while reading through their bank statement, and hears him working late each night, once talking with a colleague about the need to employ teenage girls at the camp's developing fish farm so as to reduce violence against them in their tents. Lily's need feels pathetic in comparison to these other needs, and this feeling, combined with the fern, drops her into a low-grade paranoia. When he says, *What can I do for you?* is he following some kind of manual? When he finds her in a listless moment and hugs her tightly, is he hugging her only because he fears what she will do if he doesn't?

On day four, she manages to sit at the computer and read the news. It is good to be made to think of the world, even if the world consists of crap. The goodness lasts for a couple minutes, then she opens up the online White Pages and types in *Vivian Barr*. Her brothers have built the woman up to such a degree—the exiled wife, the smoking seductress—that Lily has come to think of her as not only estranged from Ruth but in hiding, more generally, from the world. Yet here is her address and phone number, publicly displayed. When after four rings Vivian Barr answers, she does not seem surprised to hear from Lily, nor does she force Lily to stumble toward some kind of ask. "You'll come for tea," she says, and they make a date, for Friday. It is Wednesday. Lily goes back to bed.

The next day, day five, she tells their sitter not to come; she's going to spend the day with June. She thinks this will help fend off the fern but she is wrong. The day passes in a soup—they lie down together twice, but June never falls asleep, only Lily, who each time she wakes has an instant of forgetting her grief. Then she remembers. At two, in the shower, she is so overcome, nearly paralyzed, by the pore-opening steam that by the time she gets out, June has liberated an entire box of tampons from their wrappers. At six they go to pick up Rosie from theater and Hal, who has already said how sorry he is about Ruth, says it again, and does Lily want to come for chili? Jace made some last night. He is solid, standing there, his voice a cup of comfort. And Lily goes, because Adam has a late meeting and won't be home until nine and at home there are only noodles to eat and the empty soup to stand around in until the girls somehow go to sleep. Hal and Jace's place is close, on Seventh Street, a garden-/parlor-floor arrangement in a building they seem to own. But Jace is not there, only the chili. Jace has a late meeting, too. So after the chili has been eaten and the children dispatched somewhere downstairs to watch a show, Lily finds herself standing in Jace's kitchen with Hal, who has handed her a can of beer. The beer is cold. A long silence passes between them. Hal leans against the sink in his canvas pants and T-shirt while Lily stares into a middle distance so as not to look at the photos on the fridge. She tries to think. She gets as far as, Oh please, I am not going to be that woman; it's too predictable, too depressing in its predictability; hello midlife, hello grief, hello lust, hello there was not supposed to be this kind of wanting on the heels of death . . . but now a line is being drawn in her ear. A finger is following the curve there, slipping down the side of her neck, curling forward into the hollow, where it rests, on her pulse. Her hand stays on the beer, her other in her jeans pocket, but she waits for his mouth, opens to it, feels a silent, trembling wail fill her throat, falls in. Their kissing is a kind of kissing she once did with some regularity, sloppy and urgent and wet, a kind of dredging each other with their tongues and teeth. His hand is under her shirt. Her breast is out of her bra. Her hand is out of her pocket, feeling for him. And it keeps going like this, like they are teenagers in a field, pushing and pressing and pawing but with minimal contact so that the contact, where it is made, sears and enflames. There is no looking, it's always dark in the field, there is only touching, and there is no noise, there are children nearby, and then it's done, because the children are done, and clomping up the stairs, begging for dessert.

5B, the doorman tells her the next day. Then, *This way*. Then, *Ma'am?* Lily nods, and moves toward the elevator. She knows she wants to be here. She has made a great effort to be here. But the emptiness is bad today. It climbs into her sternum. It says, Retreat. Slump back down Vivian Barr's Upper West Side block with its cabbagelike plants blooming between the trees and their little fences. Get back on the train. Go back to bed.

Still, she pushes the buttons. She rises.

"Welcome."

To Lily's right, Vivian Barr stands in an open doorway, wearing a belted dress and a pair of orange-velvet pumps, and Lily feels immediate regret at her own choices: a wool skirt and cowlneck sweater, both nice, but still. One of her friends calls cowlnecks "the new aging woman's cardigan," and here Lily is wearing one to visit a woman decades her senior who is pulling off a V-neck dress and heels.

"Come, Georgie," says Vivian Barr, and for a moment Lily worries she is confused. Then a small dog trots out and begins to sniff at Lily's boots. "Shall we let her in?" Vivian Barr asks.

And the dog, though it seems impossible, nods.

The apartment is stately, as Lily expected, but not large. High ceilings, substantial moldings. A living room into which they do not go, a hall lined with art, a galley kitchen connected by an archway to a dining room painted in a dark hue that some decorator in Brooklyn would probably call *tarnished pewter*. Here it does not seem false, though. A mahogany table is set with two woven placemats, each laid with a dessert plate, saucer, and tea cup. A massive plant fills the window, catching what little light reaches a midfloor apartment at noon. Lily understands that it's a lovely scene, one that in another era of her life would make her feel serene, but in this era, today, she wishes Vivian Barr would turn on the chandelier. She wishes there were lunch instead of tea, music instead of silence. Vivian Barr has gone into the kitchen, where a kettle is boiling, leaving Lily to arrange herself awkwardly in the arch, neither in nor out of the space. She watches as the older woman attends to various tasks, moving with striking efficacy. She dons an apron, seizes tongs from a drawer, shuts the drawer, opens her oven. She is reaching for the lowest rack when she teeters and begins to tip forward.

It's possible that Lily is wrong about this, that the habit of bracing for Ruth to fall is distorting her perception. But her hand is on Vivian Barr's shoulder before she can stop herself, and even as she recants internally she continues to hold on, as if she might prevent Vivian Barr from falling headfirst into the oven and at the same time pretend she's not touching her.

Vivian Barr does not fall. She stands, removes her slight, sharp shoulder from beneath Lily's palm, and arranges two scones on a dish.

"I pick up Georgie's doo every day," she says, without looking at Lily.

"Of course. I'm sorry."

Vivian Barr hands the dish to Lily, fills a teapot with boiling water, takes a trivet from a drawer, and leaves the room. "It is possibly true that I should wear more sensible shoes," she says.

"Oh!" Lily cries, following. Her fear has woken her up, shaken the emptiness from her scales. "No! I love your shoes."

Vivian Barr pours tea. Everything matches, from the teapot to the sugar dish. "I hope you like Darjeeling," she says, and Lily, feeling certain that she has insulted the woman by seeming obsequious or condescending or both, says, "You know, I found a beautiful pair of heels in my mother's closet. Black. Gold heels. I had no idea."

"The Roger Viviers?" asks Vivian Barr, spreading her napkin across her lap.

"I don't know."

"I remember a pair of Roger Viviers. You can set the scones down."

Lily puts down the scones. "They smell delicious."

"Levain," says Vivian Barr. "The one I prefer you have to get there at seven if you don't want to wait, but that's not difficult for Georgie and me."

Lily lays her own napkin in her lap, then awaits further instruction. Can she take a scone now? Drink her tea? Vivian Barr is merely sitting, her gaze on the teapot, her hands in her lap. Is she saying grace? Lily doesn't think so. It is hard to imagine Ruth being drawn to someone so inscrutable, though of course this woman could have changed. Would have. From the few articles Lily was able to track down—using what she could not help but notice were her still excellent research skills—she learned that Vivian Barr may have experimented with drugs when she was younger, and possibly in lesbian sex. She had some kind of breakdown and was hospitalized at the famed Fainwright. Those stories, though, seem to bear no relation to the woman in front of her, who with smaller silver tongs is now transferring a scone from the dish to Lily's plate. In her formality, at least, she seems older than Ruth. She deposits the tongs onto a tong-shaped dish. Then she looks at Lily, the first time today she has looked at her directly, her irises at this particular angle in this particular, dark room a surprisingly bright green, and says, "I did not sleep with your father. I assume that's what you've come to find out."

Lily, who is unprepared for this, cannot find her voice to say no—though of course yes would be more honest; this is at least part of why she has come—and merely shake-nods her head like a toy as she butters her scone. Vivian Barr can't know that Lily would only hate her a tiny bit for having done such a thing, and that she wouldn't judge her, that some piece of her even wants it to have happened because Lily is now guilty, too. If Jace is not her friend, she is also not a stranger. If Lily did not sleep with Hal, she engaged with him in a kind of mutual molestation. As she left Jace's house last night with the girls, she looked only at her own feet.

"Rosemary was my closest friend," says Vivian Barr, as if in answer to Lily's thoughts. As if to say, *No. Really. I am not so bad as you.*

"Did you try to tell her—"

"Of course."

"She didn't believe you?"

"I don't know. She was angry. And she was grieving."

"A miscarriage. My brothers told me."

Vivian Barr nods. "I'd been absorbed. I wasn't able to see straight. But I saw she was suffering. I didn't think she owed me her belief."

"So you just left?"

"She threw me out."

"She threw my father out, too. A couple years later."

"I would believe that." Vivian Barr sips her tea. "With me, she was gentle, of course," she adds. "That was Rosemary."

Lily is bothered, suddenly, by Vivian Barr's flip tone about her father, and by the way she says *Rosemary* with a winking note in her voice. As if Lily must understand, as if she knew Rosemary, too. She has known *about* her, of course, known that she existed, but as with all the other befores—her mother before she was Jewish, before she was divorced, before she stopped sewing, before she smoked—Lily, last, remembers almost nothing. If she thought of Rosemary it was as a distant cousin, or a ghost. Mostly she didn't think of her. She didn't think of her to the point where she named Rosie Rosie! And apparently Ruth herself didn't think of Rosemary, or pretended not to, because she did not protest. It wasn't until the morning of the funeral, when Lily was walking the rabbi through the various family members' names, and the rabbi said in her peaceful way, *Rosie . . . That's interesting . . . Jews, as you may know, don't typically name our children after living people*, that Lily realized. And all Lily could think to say was, *Well, now she's dead*. But she couldn't say that. Just like she can't say now, to Vivian Barr, *Stop saying Rosemary*.

"What was she like?" she says instead. "When you first met her."

"We were four, dear. I can't remember."

"What's your first memory of her?"

Vivian Barr looks at the scone still lying on the serving dish. "Well—I remember the first time we ever took a sailing lesson. We were seven, maybe eight. And your mother—her mother had to drag her, literally drag her, onto the dock. She was screaming. She was so terrified that her mother had to hand her to the teacher, and the teacher had to hold her down, and then when we left the dock she grabbed one of the cleats and held on so tight she started to slip out of the boat. The teacher got her, of course. I remember him working her fingers loose; he was trying to be gentle but he was also shaken—you can imagine. He must have been a child himself, maybe sixteen."

"How terrible," Lily says.

"I don't know." Vivian Barr, who has not taken her eyes off the scone, grabs it now without the tongs, breaks off a chunk, and dangles it beside her chair until Georgie comes and snags it. "I think she forgot it, mostly. And you know what? By the next year she was the only one of us racing Beetle Cats. She wound up being the best sailor in our class, boys included. The most fearless of us all." She feeds Georgie another chunk of scone. "That's how your mother was."

"What do you mean?"

"I mean she didn't dwell. Later, for instance, when she was married? She was always writing me these glowing letters, even when someone else might have had a few complaints. Even when something scary happened—like once there was this cross burnt on your lawn because your father, you know—and she told me about it, but she didn't dwell. She didn't fret or want my pity."

"I never heard about that."

"No. Why would you have?"

"But then why—"

"Her conversion? I don't know. I think the cross strengthened her resolve. She took me to this consciousness raising group—"

"I thought you took her." Lily is thinking of her brothers, who told her this. Did they remember the cross burning? It seems like something both impossible and necessary to forget, something she cannot ask them.

"No. She took me. Your father's mother invited her, and she invited me. It was still new, then, to talk like that about things like sex and chauvinistic husbands and awful goings-on from your childhood. Your mother was in heaven—you could see that those women would become a kind of second home for her. She didn't say much, but she loved listening to everyone else talk." Vivian Barr pauses. "She was a private person, your mother. She was the kind of private person who wears a face that makes her seem like a public person."

Salt pools in Lily's throat. "That's true."

Vivian Barr watches Georgie lap up crumbs from the rug. When he is finished, she hands him another chunk of scone.

"So you really didn't take her?" says Lily.

"I didn't take her."

"Or have an affair with my father?"

"I didn't do that either."

"Did you teach her how to smoke?"

"I don't know if *teach* is the right word, but I encouraged her, yes. I got her drinking bourbon, too. Before that, she drank Tom Collinses." She looks pointedly at Lily, who has never heard of a Tom Collins and does not know what to say. "Girly drinks," continues Vivian Barr, and shakes her head. "But she did love cigarettes. I stopped soon after I got to New York. Anything that reminded me of that time, I stopped. But Rosemary was never a quitter."

Lily bristles at this attempt at praise. Is it fair that Ruth kept smoking while Vivian Barr quit? It is not fair.

"But I do want to add, about the affairs—I'm not saying he didn't have them."

Lily nods. She thinks of her mother telling her she is like her father, *hard to satisfy*, and wonders if last night's make-out session with Hal was somehow fated. Maybe there is something in her beyond her control. Maybe she will blow up her life.

"Try the scone, dear."

What can Lily do? She takes a bite of her scone as Vivian Barr and Georgie watch, then she watches Vivian Barr feed the rest of her own scone to Georgie and, when he's finished, bring her hand to his head. Her fingers are long and nimble. They work through the fur, untangling, caressing.

"Excuse me," Lily says. "Which way to the bathroom?"

"Just down the hall."

As soon as the door is closed, the tears Lily has been holding back spill out. From her mouth, from her eyes. She watches herself in the mirror, sitting on a tiny toilet, weeping, missing Ruth as she has not yet missed her.

Lily isn't sure how much time she spends in the bathroom. Ten minutes, maybe twenty. She rinses her face, pats at it with a hand towel, then abandons the effort and drifts back down the hallway, composing herself as best she can, checking her watch. It's nearly two. Their sitter will be unlocking her bike soon, jumping on in her sprightly twentysomething way and pedaling toward the girls' schools. Doing Lily's only job.

Lily slows. The art in the hall is not art after all but printed matter of some kind, news articles, or—she looks more closely. Clippings from a magazine, dated from the mid-1970s and '80s. They all share the same title: Ask Letty Loveless. Lily knows this name. *Dear Letty Loveless*, she reads. *Why is the Miss America Pageant still popular even after the protests?* To which Letty Loveless has written a response titled: "Why Do Birds Sing?" Next to that is, *Dear Letty Loveless, How should I groom between my legs?* and next to that, *Dear Letty Loveless, I believe Diane Fiorelli's story because I was attacked, too, but my husband won't believe me and I don't know what to do.* Lily skims enough to get the drift—Letty Loveless lacks love for all kinds of women in equal measure—then she falls into a kind of trance, unable to stop reading. There are stifled housewives who write in, and members of the Women's Liberation Party who confide in Letty Loveless their vision for an armed uprising. Women who've had abortions and regret it, women who haven't and regret it. Women whose faces are falling, women who lust after other women, women who believe makeup is a moral failing, women who've never touched their own genitalia, women who love their children but hate their husbands, women who love their husbands but hate marriage, women who hate all of it and want to run away. Spinsters and widows and the cheated upon and the cheaters. First and second and third wives.

They all write to Letty Loveless, and they are all abused by her. *Here is the flaw in your argument*, she writes. Or, *If you're asking me to determine whether or not you are fundamentally, irresolvably lazy, I offer this: Lie down for a day. Do nothing. See what happens.* Or, *You think you can be a wife without being a Wife. But it's not possible. You will have to give something up*.

Lily inches her way down the hall, oblivious to the dry tears stiffening her cheeks and the dog nosing around her knees, fully lost, until, deep in one of the letters responding to a woman called Poor Housekeeper in Walla Walla, she reads: *Perhaps you would like me to tell you that a well-kept house is a sign of an ill-spent life. Then you could go on and feel righteous in your mediocrity. This has fast become a stance adopted by Women's-Group Women toward Wives . . .*

And so on. Lily returns to the line she knows by heart. *A Well-Kept House Is a Sign of an Ill-Spent Life*. This is why she recognized the name Letty Loveless. These were her mother's favorite columns. But look at what Ruth did, how she twisted what Letty Loveless intended to say, took from it what she wanted.

"Everything all right?" asks Vivian Barr. She has followed Georgie into the hall. She arranges herself in her elegant dress.

"Is all this . . . yours?" Lily asks.

"Oh, yes." The older woman nods. "My life's work."

"Seriously?"

Vivian Barr gives a small, rueful smile. "Well, seriously in that I wrote them and that it was most of what I did for over a decade. But *life's work*, no, I do not mean that seriously. Most of it's trash. As I'm sure you can see. And yet, clearly not trash enough for me to trash it."

"My mother loved Letty Loveless."

Vivian Barr lets out a cross between a gasp and a gravelly chuckle. "Did she," she says.

"Didn't you imagine she might read them?"

"I didn't—"

"This one here? She put it . . ." Lily points to the passage about the well-kept house, then drops her hand. She feels suddenly protective of Ruth, both of the edit she made and of the fact that the words meant so much to her. "And there was another one she liked," she says. "About taking care of yourself."

Vivian Barr squints. "Well. Letty Loveless was not, shall we say, generous."

"No," Lily says. "I can see that." She sounds rude, perhaps, but she is thinking of the cumulative hours she spent looking at the *A Well-Kept House Is a Sign of an Ill-Spent Life* sampler, the way it became one with her mother's voice, the voice in Lily's head. That Ruth removed the quotation from its context, thereby altering its meaning, was neither here nor there. That she may eventually have arrived at the thought herself didn't matter. Here is where she found it: in a column written by her old friend.

Vivian Barr shifts her weight from one orange shoe to the other, clearly tired, wanting to sit back down.

"I wonder if she ever wrote to you," Lily says. "To Letty Loveless."

"Rosemary? I doubt it."

"Why?"

"She was too proud for that."

Vivian Barr rests a hand on the wall next to her. Her chin is soft in a way Lily didn't notice before. The lines that gather on her chest are deep. Lily knows she should release her from standing here, in the hallway. But she is thinking of Vira. Where is she standing? How has she aged? Is she married again? And she is thinking, too, that she doesn't actually want to know, and that there is probably someone else who feels this way about Vivian Barr, someone for whom Vivian Barr remains a kind of legend, occupies a Vivian Barr–sized hole they will never fill. Here she is. A woman with a dog in a dark hallway, wanting to sit down. A woman who loved Lily's mother once and knows the things in her that did not change. Because she is right, Lily knows. Her mother would never have written to Letty Loveless herself.

"Would you like more tea?"

Lily follows Vivian Barr back to the table, but she is still thinking about her mother's pride, and she is thinking about her mother being held down in a sailboat as she screamed. Can it be true, as Vivian Barr said, that her mother simply forgot her fear? It is true that she rarely seemed afraid, even when she was dying. If she feared anything, it seemed to be Lily winding up like Rosemary. But maybe that, too, was pride. And maybe the pride that kept her from being someone who would write to an advice columnist—or seek out at some later point her oldest, closest friend—was also fear.

Once Vivian Barr has poured them more tea, and they've gone through the rituals with the sugar bowl and cream, and Georgie has accepted sugared cream straight from Vivian Barr's spoon, Lily says, "Do you still give advice?"

Vivian Barr's smile is fuller than Lily has seen it. The skin around her eyes whiskers, the green of her irises seems to deepen. "Try me," she says, and Georgie perks his ears, eager for whatever Lily might say. She didn't plan on talking about the Esther dress saga. She's been making some progress at last, despite or maybe between the fern's reaches. The fabric arrived, then a book of patterns, then a book she realized she needed about how to read patterns. But last night, after cutting out the shapes and laying them on her bed, she realized she had bought nothing to sew them with, no thread, not even a needle, and it became clear to her again: even with a needle, even if she still had the machine she had to return to the rental shop, Lily cannot sew two dresses by herself. She explains all this to Vivian Barr, then tells her about Kyla. "So I'm trying to decide whether to ask for her help," she says. "I know she would, in a second. But I kept rejecting her offers before. It feels rude now to go back."

"I wouldn't bother," says Vivian Barr without hesitating. "Too complicated. Take the fabric to a dry cleaner, one of the ones that do alterations. If the dresses are as simple as they sound, they'll have them ready the next day. They'll charge you what, maybe twenty dollars?"

This is not something Lily has considered. It's a very practical idea.

"Your mother was quite skilled in the sewing department," adds Vivian Barr.

"I know. I didn't know, but then I found out."

"She didn't sew after she was Ruth?"

"No."

Vivian Barr nods. Her smile has disappeared.

"Did you ever think to reach out to her?" Lily asks. "Once enough time had passed?"

"I didn't think it was my place."

"You both lived alone."

"And?"

"And in New York—"

"Do I look like I need company?"

Lily flushes. Something has flared in Vivian Barr; Lily has offended her; it is time to go. She begins to push back her chair. But suddenly Vivian Barr has propped her elbows on the table—a move as surprising coming from her as a fart might be from someone else—and she is looking at Lily, really looking into her eyes, in a way that reminds her, yes, of Ruth. "When I lived at your house," she says, "you and your brothers were always racing around. Inside, outside, up the stairs, down the stairs. Sometimes it seemed . . . well. I was very fragile right then, very absorbed. I've said that, I realize. My mind is sound. But sometimes it seemed to me . . . With your brothers, I might have been a tree. But with you, there were these moments when I would see you looking at me, really looking, like you saw something. Something I didn't yet know about. This sounds ridiculous, I realize, because I was grown and you were a little girl. But I felt, always, a little afraid of you."

Lily thinks of her kitchen memory—Lily on one side of the glass, Vivian Barr on the other. Does Vivian Barr have the same one? Is she trying to apologize in some way? Lily cannot ask this. She cannot say to this woman, *I remember you in a robe, there is something desperate about you, in the robe, you are in a robe in my kitchen, maybe with my father* . . . They have already discussed Lily's father. That is done. If there is anything else to the story, if Lily is not the only one here who has grappled with another woman's husband in a kitchen, Vivian Barr is not telling. So Lily says—and it is true, and it was true last night when she said good-night to the girls, her blood still firing from her trespass: "I feel that way with my older daughter sometimes. Rosie. She looks at me, and I think she can see not just something but everything. It's very unnerving."

Vivian Barr looks at Lily for a long moment. Then she sits back from the table with a sigh. One of her hands drifts downward. Within a second, the dog is there, fitting himself to her fingers. "Girls are always unnerving," she says.

SUSA

VASHTI

Is Her Mind Sound?

For an instant, engulfed by the tent's blackness, Vashti fears she is in the earth again. The sky, the breeze, the sand, must all have been a hallucination. Fevered answers to questions she'd thought she'd stopped asking. Sour air fills her nostrils. A keen forms in her throat. I am entombed again.

Then a torch flares. An arm shimmies into view, a chest, a man—or not quite a man. A man-sized boy whose bones have stretched faster than they've been fed. He wears only a cloth at his hips; in one hand he holds the torch, in the other a knife. Vashti knows at once that he is Itz. The boy who lost his mother's spoon and accidentally stole another, the boy who started the war on the camp. He would be the first to wake. His head lifts the tent's ceiling; his jaw has the overshot squareness particular to pubescent boys; an Adam's apple slides in its slot. Vashti takes it all in. She will relay what she sees to Baraz—each hair, every angle, the kinds of details he will miss on his own—and instruct him to bring all of it back to Esther. Not the small number of tents remaining, nor the empty-stomach smell, but the beauty of her cousin as he brandishes that tiny blade. This will be Vashti's token of thanks, however small, for the hours Esther spent in her cave, telling Vashti what she needed to know.

"We won't hurt you," Baraz says. He lifts a hand, his gesture for peace, a gesture he used so often on Vashti in her first days in the hole that she began to think—because it worked on her—that he possessed hypnotic powers. But it doesn't work on Itz, who continues wagging his knife at them, and whose eyes, dark in their hollows, are impossible to read.

Vashti is sorry, to come upon them like this.

The others are stirring now, a collective rumbling like a caravan. They are more than one family—they are, she will learn, four families and assorted abandoneds—and Baraz, trying to preempt attack, says loudly: "Esther sent us." He says it again, making sure they hear the name, for though Esther insisted they speak basic Persian, and though Baraz loves Esther, he has the same view of her tribe as most, Vashti included, that they are an insular and stubborn people.

He says it a third time, and as their faces rise into the torchlight now, creased with sleep, blinking, they are silent, with the exception of one man who leaps up and says, "How can you prove it?"

This is Marduk, of course. Vashti recognizes him right away. *A bit like the king*, Esther said, and this is true: the uncle puffs his chest and steps in front of Itz. He looks from Vashti to Baraz and back with a practiced violence in his eyes, though it's easy to see, in his stooped form—his son, behind him, stands a full head taller—that his gaze is more forceful than any harm he can actually inflict.

She thinks of all the proof she can offer. All Esther told her to help her ingratiate herself with them. Vashti knows about the goblin. She knows about the rugs that rolled Itz back and forth from the river, and she knows how Marduk and his wife laughed, *like vultures*, before he slapped his niece. She knows more still: that Marduk was forever jealous of his brother Harun; that he lives in fear that he's a fool. A *blowhard*, Esther called him, perhaps not with that word but with another that meant the same in that time and place.

But not everything Esther told her will be of help. Much of it—most of it, probably—they do not want to hear. And some of it would only stretch their disbelief further. The malformed tips of Esther's ears, for instance, or the bird she brought to life. Even if her exertions might demonstrate her devotion to the people in this tent, they will not go down smoothly, for they are not tales of mere goblins or simple sorcery but—Esther's term—*perversion*. She had sat on Vashti's bed as she said this, her hands absentmindedly catching her son's hair as he toddled by to explore some other corner of the cave. Vashti watched the boy as he went, digging in the floor and poking his fingers into the walls as his mother told her story. She watched one thing and listened to another. The beast Esther had become. The nails the minister had dug into her face as Ahasuerus watched. (Poor man, Vashti thought, before thinking, Poor girl. He had never chosen before. He had only been chosen, and in a desperate moment.) The skeleton she had stolen from the bones room. The breath she had drawn from the bird as the boy slept.

What she had done was to pervert nature itself. *I didn't see it that way*, she said. *But the minister made me see it. I played God.* Vashti didn't understand at first. She didn't think Esther, or anyone, ought to listen to the minister. *But you said you had a lesson*, she said, *with a sorceress in the camp; you said your own mother came from a family with sorcery running through it. Not the same*, Esther said. What they did and what she had done. They turned grass into rope, lit fires out of rock. They did not turn a living being into another being or bring a dead thing to life. So even if Marduk and Itz and the others believed it, Vashti knows that they would not want to know. Neither would they want to know about the bare, almost vacant tone with which Esther had laid out her story before Vashti, like a servant laying a table of words. Vashti did not believe that Esther was in fact unharrowed by all that had happened—whenever she turned back from watching Darius, Vashti caught something, a twitch in her jaw, a darkness in her eyes—but she understood that Esther needed to pretend to be. And she knows that Marduk and Itz will need for her to have been that, too. Blasphemy, and suffering, will have to be excised. They need—look at them—something, one thing, that is not tragic.

"Your figs," Vashti says. "I know, Esther told me, that you have a secret method of splicing their seeds, and that this is what makes them the most delicious in Persia."

Marduk looks at her. There is pride in his eyes, wound with sorrow (his fig trees are no longer his) and warning (the secret still is), and Vashti nods, her promise not to tell.

"She sent us here to tell you. Tomorrow, there will be a massacre."

She lets the lie sink in. They'll all be dead within a year, that much she can see. She feels no regret, only a growing ease in her role. She is not in a hole and she is not in a palace; she is in a tent. A middle place, a moveable place. She will convince them.

"Esther says you have to go."

The man and boy stare at her. Marduk lifts his chin. "She could not come herself?"

"No. She could not come herself."

"She won't help us?"

Vashti can't speak for a moment. She nearly laughs, not

because she finds him funny but because his query, his angry hope that has somehow survived these years, strikes her as impossibly sad. What did he imagine his niece was waiting for? What kind of queen did he think he had created, that she might have the power to save them and also the cruelty to bide her time? "No," she says at last. "I wish I could tell you how she tried."

Itz steps out from his father's shadow. He has lowered the knife but his face contains its own sharpness. "What have they done to her?" he asks, and though his cracking voice betrays his youth, it is the only youthful thing about him. If there is a problem, Vashti thinks, it will be Itz. He and Vashti are not entirely unlike. They both know what it is to be hidden, trapped, for the sake of your own life. He sees through Vashti's hedging. He understands that she *could* tell them how Esther tried and that she chooses not to. Even if he does not know the details, how she went to the king unbidden, brought to life a bird, offered her sex, he knows: Esther was never in a position to save them. He does not believe, as Vashti counted on everyone believing, that a queen is a queen is a queen.

"She is treated well," Vashti announces, avoiding Itz's eyes. "She has one child, a boy, and another soon to be born. She sleeps on a bed of silks . . ." As Vashti describes Esther's days, the shaded courtyards she walks in, the robes she is wrapped in, the banquets she attends, she includes every sumptuous detail she can think of, colors and textures and scents, scenes that are somehow both factually true in that Vashti can attest to them—she once lived them—and also fantasy, a tripling and quadrupling of the facts, an eruption of desires fulfilled. The more she talks, the more she herself begins to believe. She feels the tent nod and shares in their gladness, absorbs it for herself: Esther, she is convinced, will do more than survive. The child is beautiful, she adds—Esther sleeps with him in her bed. And she has Baraz, too, the most trustworthy eunuch in all of Persia. Vashti pauses, making sure the eyes take him in: his height, his palpable goodness. She has him, that is—and here is Vashti's pivot, here is where she must go gently, as if innocent of her own intention—Esther will have Baraz if he gets back to her before daybreak. She will have him only if they leave in time.

"He can go now," says Itz.

"He's here to help."

"We don't need his help."

Vashti wishes she could stuff Itz in a rug again, just for a while, until they are out. *He's here to help me*, she thinks at him. *I was first, I am still first, I will be first until I am gone. There is no way to change this.*

Itz narrows his eyes. He hears her, maybe. Or he is just a precocious boy, expert in skepticism. "Who are you?" he asks.

Vashti perceives in the upturned faces around her a breath withheld—Itz has planted doubt in them, too. She looks to Baraz. She is a loyal maidservant to Esther; this is the answer she is supposed to give. But in Baraz's raised eyebrows she can see that he agrees with her: Itz will never believe that story. Itz has the power to turn the camp against them.

Vashti looks into the shadows of Itz's eyes and says, "I am Queen Vashti."

The people shift as one. Their awe makes a heat that she can feel, a heat she knows well, so well that for a moment the scene is familiar to her, and her feet press into the earth, lifting her body away, so that she feels herself at a distance. She is pleased, for they want to believe her and she depends upon their believing her, and also ashamed, at how susceptible they are, even these people who are not supposed to worship other people.

But there is no time for shame. And she is not in a position not to take full advantage of them. She says: "If I am not gone by sunrise, if I am found, they'll kill me."

A murmur rises. Marduk reaches for his son's hand and pries his knife from his fingers. But Itz stands unmoved as a statue. "You're Vashti," he says. "Prove it."

Again she looks to Baraz. It's the first time she has known him to look afraid, and her blood grows heavy. She isn't sure what he fears more: her failure to convince Itz or what she will do to convince him. They are both thinking of the same thing, she knows, though it makes only an illusory kind of sense, and though Baraz has spent his career protecting her from such humiliations. But without Itz, they lose the people, and she and Baraz will have to go out into the desert alone, as almost no one does, certainly not a tree-tall eunuch and a woman. They will be caught and killed, the gold sewn into Vashti's robes sliced out and stolen—or she will be recognized, and hauled back, and both will be killed where they began. And in the process Esther will have lost Baraz, as they promised her would not happen.

A shift occurs in the color of the tent's walls, an upturn of hue so slight it might only be perceptible by someone whose life depends on darkness. Vashti, who has not seen the sun in thirty-four months, experiences it as a pulse of fire. She turns her back to Itz and lets her robes fall off her shoulders until she is exposed from nape to waist. A gasp goes up in the tent, followed by silence as they take in what she is showing them: the wings spanning her shoulders, the beak pointing in tandem with her spine toward the sky, the two black eyes that look out from the top of the head.

She begged Baraz for the bird when she still imagined that she might escape aboveground. She had seen high priestesses turn their skin into parchment, had seen dancers in the night station do it, too, ink flowers they had never seen onto their buttocks or breasts. Baraz had balked, then given in—of course he had given in. He must have been relieved that she was no longer raging and pacing, as she had in the early days of her banishment, when she swung between planning ways to kill herself and planning a coup to topple Ahasuerus. *I could do it*, she would declare, *I would win*, to which Baraz would nod—of course. He nodded because he loved her and he nodded because it was true: if she called for it, she would have the loyalty of the guards. Most of them had worked for her father; they saw Ahasuerus as a benign but inferior intruder; they would turn for her if she commanded them to. She went so far as to order Baraz to gather arms.

Then, as suddenly as if she'd run into one of her walls, she was done. A calm fell over her, she lost her appetite for blood; she saw clearly that to wage war on Ahasuerus would be to destroy the kingdom. Her father had raised her too well for that. She knew that her banishment itself, understood by most to be her death, would be enough to confuse the people for thousands of years, and that to reverse it would be far worse, that the course had to be kept. She would have to flee, instead. And so the bird began to take shape in her mind, and soon she wanted it not only in her mind but on her body; she wanted to become it.

Baraz brought substances, some for her to drink, some for her to smoke, as he worked with his needles and ink. The needles were longer than any she had seen, made from antelope horn, he said, and she played with the ones he wasn't using, rubbing their silky lengths against her lips, jabbing their points into her fingertips until she bled. She was high, she was hibernating in highness—and all the while, the heavy air never moved. Then Baraz came with news. His favorite virgin, the one who did not want to be queen, had been chosen. She had turned herself into a beast—no, not metaphorically. She had tried to escape her fate, and failed, and now the palace was thicker with guards than he'd ever seen it; some were new, loyal to Ahaseurus, others brought in from Persepolis, men who'd known Vashti since she was born. Her idea that she would sneak out in costume was unlikely to succeed.

This time, she did not scratch or slam the walls. She thought. If Ahasuerus learned she was alive, he would break. Any equilibrium he'd found—which the new queen was testing, evidently—would be spun into chaos.

And so the fox. Vashti did not know that Esther was above somewhere, in the bones room, working out the same problems, devising parallel solutions. Though she must have known. Esther, too. They must have moved, in moments, as one. Or, it was simply obvious, universal: anyone would think first to fly, above the earth, and, when that didn't work, to go through.

She turns now, baring the fox that crawls across her stomach. One front claw wraps around her waist; the other cups her left breast. Baraz's lines are simple but bold, so that the fox's tail, skirting her ribs, appears to quiver. Itz's mouth is open. Agony sings in Vashti's ears. *Who is this whore*, she thinks. *This whore has swallowed the woman who was called a whore for her virtue.* It does not follow. But of course it does. Of course Ahasuerus hadn't wanted her to be virtuous at that particular moment, because it made her look frigid, and if she was frigid, it was about him, whereas a whore—or a leper, or whatever other conclusions they came to—well, that was about her. She was a woman like that. By the time his drink wore off, she knew, it was too late. She was gone, dead—and he could not change his mind. He could not be seen as weak.

So now, again, whore. Her robes open. Itz is aroused—it would be false to pretend that she can't see his arousal. He does not know that ink is not reserved for the queen. None of them know this. They have never seen anyone's body adorned in such a way, and it is easy to believe, in their stunned state, that only a queen is given these markings. (This is one way people come to think they know things, which they then tell to other people, who tell them to other people, who write them down, and so the thing stands as truth in a book and later on a pixelated screen: "A queen in ancient Persia was marked by animal tattoos.")

They don't approve of what has been done to the queen's body, but they are moved by it. Even Itz. Itz is moved as a rebel and he is moved as an adolescent boy. He confers with his father.

It is easy, after that, to spread word among the other tents. It is easy—they are experts—to pack. They are gone within an hour, leaving only footprints, and these too, are gone by sunrise, when the breeze turns into a wind that sweeps low and fast across the sand.

MANHATTAN

VEE

Summoned Forth, She Kept Her State

The windows need cleaning, Vee thinks, as she follows Georgie back into the apartment—the sun's angle highlights the soot. Can it be three o'clock already? She did not plan for the girl to stay so long. She makes a note about the windows, then sits at the table to take off her shoes. Her arches are tired. Her whole body is tired. She rises to clear off the table, then sits back down, attempts a halfhearted stacking of dishes and cups, and looks elsewhere. Her plants need watering. *Windows. Plants.* The tea has made her hands shaky. She sits, looking out through her sooty windows at the building next door. She should go sit on the couch so she can look at the park. But just as she knew she should say something to somehow cheer Rosemary's daughter, and then failed to actually do it, she stays seated in the chair.

It had been a bit of a shock, at the memorial service, to find that the girl looked nothing like Rosemary. Her brothers shared her friend's fair hair and good tanning skin, but Lily looked like her father, and this disappointed Vee more than she could explain. Today, though, as they talked, Vee began to see pieces of Rosemary in the girl, not in her features themselves but in the way she used them. A slight tilt to her head when she listened. The completeness with which her mouth pulled back when she smiled. The way she moved her eyebrows. Rosemary's had been thick, and Lily's were less so, but they emoted as Rosemary's had, furrowing and lifting and falling as if not quite in her control.

When Rosemary told Vee she needed to leave, it was her eyebrows that betrayed her regret.

What was it Lily said exactly? *Did you ever think to reach out to her?* As if Vee hadn't thought it all the time. Even in recent years, every so often a longing would swell up in her, for Rosemary. But it was not her place, as she said. Alex had asked her to come back; Rosemary had not. And it was apparent from the way Lily's brothers regarded her at the reception that she had not been spoken of with any fondness in their house, if she'd been spoken of at all. To those boys, clearly, Vee had been ruinous.

Vee waters her plants: her jade, her just-emerging amaryllis, her Christmas cactus on its iron stand. She puts away the watering can and crosses out *Plants*. Then she stands in her stockinged feet, picking at a little scale that has grown back on the jade's lower leaves. She steps back. It's a beautiful plant, Vee's for more than twenty years. She has trimmed its branches to encourage breadth over depth, so that it fills the window without claiming too much space. When an individual branch goes rogue, she clips it and gives it to one of the doormen in a mug of soil. The oldest, Mikel, has shown her pictures of his, now two feet tall on a windowsill crammed with figurines of children dressed in some style of Old World European dress. The jade appears to be providing them with shade.

In Vee's palm the black bits she has scratched off the jade

form a little hill, which she carries to the kitchen, Georgie following at her heels. On a usual day, they would go to the park around now, for their longest walk of the day; sometimes they go as far as the Met. But today is not a usual day. She feels at once exhausted and agitated by Lily's visit, overwhelmed by how insufficient her own answers seemed, dropped anew into the shock she experienced the morning she saw the obituary. She had been estranged from Rosemary for longer than they had been friends. Still, it was as if some solid ground had been pulled out from under her, a piece of earth she hadn't realized she'd been walking on. Vee is not a crier, but she took off her glasses and wept, and now, standing in her kitchen with her palmful of scale, she has an urge to weep again. To learn that Rosemary loved her. Or loved Letty Loveless, at least. It made no sense, on the one hand, and it made all the sense in the world, for although Rosemary was consistently loving and kind, she was also consistently curious and open. Of the many memories that have come flooding back to Vee since her death, one has played especially vibrantly: a summer afternoon on Rosemary's porch when they were teenagers, with women's bodies and children's skin, skin that imprinted easily but also rebounded quickly—Vee remembers this because she remembers the lines the porch wood made in the backs of Rosemary's legs and in her palms. They were sixteen; Vee knows because her father was recently sick; this is what she was telling Rosemary on the porch. Rosemary, unlike Vee's mother and everyone else, did not try to reassure Vee that her father would not die. She moved closer to her, so that their hips were touching, and said, *That's rotten luck. That's what it is.* Then, after a while, she said, *Come on*, and pulled Vee up and led her through the lanes to the dank market that smelled of beer and bought two lemonades and stripped Vee's straw and put it in for her, bent in the particular way that Rosemary bent her straws.

Maybe Vee should have told Lily about that. A nice memory of her mother, instead of telling her how much Lily had scared her. That was even worse than telling her about the cross. *Always a little afraid of you.* Why had Vee said such a thing? Because it had found its way out. It was true. But Lily had not come for Vee's story.

Vee tips the scale into the trash. She rinses her hands and dries them in Georgie's fur, though she knows it's a disgusting habit. It's time for a nap. A nap instead of a walk—later, she will take him down to the ugly cabbage bushes to have a pee. In the hallway, she pauses. She has long stopped noticing her old columns, but they strike her now as oppressive, the sheer mass of them, the thousands of words she wrote, never quite as herself. Letty Loveless had been a lark at first, an experiment, a chance she was given through one of the women in the Jewish consciousness raising group, to whose meetings Vee had gone twice more after leaving Rosemary's. Vee was staying at that point in Boston with another old friend, Hannah, whom she'd met at riding camp in Vermont. Hannah had two children and an extra room, and while they weren't especially close, Hannah was sophisticated enough not to believe tabloids, and so it was an easy arrangement, at least as first, with Vee coming and going independent of the family's schedule. At the "CR" meetings—which Vee went to mostly for company, and perhaps a little bit for entertainment, telling herself she would only go until Rosemary was recovered and well enough to rejoin herself—she was warmly welcomed, even by Rosemary's mother-in-law, because Rosemary had of course said nothing disparaging about Vee. Vee was like a pet for the women, an unwitting Vashti they could educate and encourage, and she encouraged them back, telling them what they wanted to hear about her final night in Washington, letting them shake their heads and mmmm. They were more serious than the women's group in Washington had been; there were scholars and mystics and even a rabbi among them who spoke of Judith and Dinah as if they'd been her fellow students at Radcliffe. "Radical empathy" was their thing, and in moments, Vee let them bathe her in it. She would be back in that other bath, after Alex pinned her to the kitchen floor, and feel herself floating up and out of it, held by a web these women spun among them. But most of the time, she could not buy in. She felt as if barbed wire had been strung around her. She stayed fundamentally separate. And soon enough Hannah's husband wanted her to leave, and Hannah said why didn't Vee go live in a hotel while she figured things out, and Vee had plenty of money, so she did and was very lonely.

She began to hate the city then. It was spring and everyone seemed to be kissing someone along the Charles. Part of her missed Washington, where more lies were tumbling down around Nixon each day—she knew it would be an excitement to be in the middle of that. Mostly, though, she missed Rosemary. While she knew other people, old classmates, parents of her friends, people she could have asked to stay with for a while, the barbed wire held her back. Her shame by then felt as visible as a second skin. There weren't just the articles she would have to explain away, there were the things no one knew that sat inside her, things that seemed to her bad, even wicked: nonmissionary sexual acts she had performed with Alex, which may have suggested she'd be willing to do anything; her seduction of the married Benjamin with his house and dog and books and bare windows and the way their sex over that month had worked her shame out of her body; the other husbands. Rosemary's husband. Hannah's husband. Vee had not slept with these men. She had not even kissed them. But she had done other things, unprovable yet palpable things like tying her robe a little loose, or standing by a window as if lost in thought for a beat longer than necessary, or offering extraneous praise for coffee well made, or going barefoot when it was too chilly for bare feet. She had asserted her sex, wanting it to save her. Beyond all this, there was her loneliness now, which was its own failure. So she did not seek out more people. And she did not tell anyone in the CR group that she was living in a hotel. Someone might take her in, as Philip had suggested, and she did not think she could live up to that. Her skepticism would fall out at some point. It would be as if she'd stabbed them.

Then one of the women from the group connected Vee with a woman in New York who was starting a magazine called *The Inez*, after Inez Milholland. The magazine woman loved Vee's story, too, and wondered if she might write something for them?

So she did. Not as Vivian Kent, of course. She called herself Elisabeth Pewter, and she wrote a story about Vivian Kent, comparing her to the biblical Vashti. The woman in New York loved it and published it and said that many of her readers were indeed Jewish, but she also wanted to appeal to a broader range of women, and might Vee have anything else to say?

Vee went to New York to meet with the woman. On the train she wrote down what felt like every thought she had thought for a year. She filled a notebook and then read what she had written and out of it she created Letty Loveless. Letty Loveless would steal everything Vee had thought and seen and done. She would steal equally—from the women's groups and from the senators' wives and from the housewives and from the husbands—and she would judge equally. Manicures and empathy exercises and ugliness and beauty and dish-doing blowhards and pantie girdles versus open-bottom girdles versus no girdles and infidelity and babies and submission and toe hair and booze and hunger and bodies and anything else women needed to talk about. She would not take sides and she would take all sides. She would be only honest.

The magazine woman, who was called Linda Hart, was not sure she liked this idea. But *The Inez* was still nascent; the world was wide open; she was willing to let Vee try.

Vee did not go back to Boston. Rosemary would be well soon—the CR group would be hers alone. The hotel sent Vee's belongings, and she holed up in a different hotel, near Gramercy Park, and wrote her first columns. Linda Hart published one. Then, when new subscription requests flooded in, she published another. Women loved Letty Loveless.

Vee rented an apartment, a studio in Gramercy. She liked its limits; she furnished it sparsely and splurged only on a writing desk and nice sheets. She bought a typewriter and wrote and walked around the city. She became friendly with a woman from the magazine, who introduced her to other women, and to men—there were gatherings, parties, trips to hear music or see plays, men in her bed. Some people recognized her name, so she dropped Kent and went back to Barr, but even those who knew who she was did not interrogate her. People in these circles were curious but only to a point. They were all from somewhere else. Many had been someone else, too.

She felt despair less frequently now. More often she felt determined—to write well, to not be lonely. She succeeded on both counts. The more people she knew, the more she liked being alone. What she liked, she realized, was to know there were people out there, available, should she want to see someone. This was solace enough—often it was better, it turned out, than actually being with people—and usually she chose to remain alone. Sex she could find when she wanted it, either with men after they passed her interrogations vis-à-vis their singleness, or with herself. Her self-sufficiency on all fronts delighted her. She bought an apartment near the one she was renting—dilapidated but with all the original moldings and hardware intact—and managed its renovation. Letty Loveless became wildly popular, and with her earnings, however modest, she was able to cover her daily expenses without dipping too often into the cushion her family had left behind.

Vee received a couple letters at the magazine from the CR-group woman who had introduced her to Linda Hart. Was Vee all right? Did she need help? The letters said nothing about Letty Loveless. If the woman guessed Vee was the author, she might have felt betrayed, or even duped, but as far as Vee knows, she never told anyone.

If Rosemary had known, wouldn't she have tracked Vee down?

The thought hurts—it makes her stop in the hallway and press a hand to the wall. A ripple through her abdomen. A metallic taste under her tongue. There are moments, of course there are, when she feels lonely. She still throws dinner parties, and takes turns with a few others hosting a monthly salon where poets and artists and musicians share their work—Vee herself has written two poetry chapbooks—and she meets friends to see art or theater. But afterward, there is a depression, a literal indent in her mood that even Georgie can't fix.

What no one would believe is that she prefers this to the alternative. No one ever did believe it. When she first made friends in New York, and hosted a number of baby showers, there would always come a moment when she realized that her guests were sliding her looks of pity.

Even the analyst Vee saw could not believe Vee did not want a husband and children. This was the year she turned thirty, when the people she spent time with talked about their "shrinks" as breezily as the people from Vee's old world talked about their boats. She went to a woman another woman recommended, and this woman, Dr. Monmouth, helped Vee create a story out of her life. Everything Vee had done, according to Dr. Monmouth, made sense. She had come from power; she had married a man who above all wanted power. She had come from a family in which sexuality was not discussed; she had married a man who was intensely sexual. She had liked sex and also found it shameful. She had been confused even before that night about her own desires. And then her sexuality had been used against her. Of course she felt lost. Of course she went after Benjamin. Dr. Monmouth believed Vee must have known on a subconscious level that Benjamin was married, and though Vee knew this not to be true, she let Dr. Monmouth believe it because it was easier and did not disrupt the rest of Dr. Monmouth's story, which Vee found comforting. Of course she tried to appear attractive to her friends' husbands, said Dr. Monmouth. All she could do was try to correct for her initial mistake; to stay, she believed, she must seduce. And now, well, now she was living in a way that guaranteed no one would ever throw her out again.

This was not sustainable, according to Dr. Monmouth. Vee would eventually want to have children. She would want a partner, "a lifelong relationship of depth and substance."

After a year, when Vee still did not want these things, Dr. Monmouth continued to insist that she wanted them, until one day Vee said, "I really don't think I do. I've been thinking about it, and I think I did not really want the men so much as I wanted to be the men."

Dr. Monmouth stared at her.

"I want to live alone."

Dr. Monmouth leaned forward, elbows to her wool-slacked knees. "This is so sad," she said. "It's just heartbreaking to me."

Vee leaned forward, too, elbows to her stockinged knees. "Why?"

"You've given up. You met your moment of disillusionment too early. We all have them, but for most of us it's a gradual process, an easing in. Yours, your trauma, and your isolation now, the walls you've built up around yourself . . . Vivian. Just because you'll never be able to worship a man again doesn't mean you can't love one."

Vee sat for a long moment, staring up at Dr. Monmouth's high, white ceiling. Her heart was thudding loudly, because she knew it was time to be done with therapy, and because what Dr. Monmouth had said reached beneath her ribs and squeezed. She said, "I don't think that's true for me." Then she thanked Dr. Monmouth and asked her—*She's the age my mother would be*, she thought, which made it both easier to dismiss her and harder to leave—to put a final bill in the mail.

Even now, more than forty years later, she can summon the queasiness she felt walking out of Dr. Monmouth's office that day. Quickly, it had turned into giddiness. Another spring had come. The leaves in Washington Square Park had unfolded and were sifting a puzzle of light onto the paths and trash and benches, bathing the students and homeless people in a kind of glow. The arch looked brighter than usual, adding to her sense that she had been transported.

In the hallway, Vee summons a deep breath. It fills her. She is fine. She calls to Georgie, and together they go into the bedroom. The room soothes her, as always. There is her bed, and her writing desk, and the art she has chosen, and the drapes—her love of bare windows was short-lived, it turns out—and the old dresser of her father's, one of numerous pieces she got back from Alex once she was finally settled and knew she would not be moving again. She was nearly middle-aged by then, and had come to be grateful that he'd done what he'd done. She would never have found out what she wanted otherwise. She would have had children. Alex would have become more violent. She is certain of this though she has no proof, though Suitcase Wife's charges against him—filed some months after that party—were dismissed. Vee had dismissed her, too, had called her Suitcase Wife instead of Diane Fiorelli, though Diane was her name, though clearly Alex did something to Diane that Diane did not want. Now, Vee suspects, young women would not put up with such behavior from men. Look at them, carrying mattresses around and going into combat—soon Hillary would be president and men would be chastened. But Alex won his reelection, then won again, and again, and now he's the senior senator from Rhode Island. Vee sees pictures from time to time. In a few, Alex, still handsome, is standing with his family, three kids and his wife, the same one he married a couple years after Vee left, or after he banished her and then she refused to come back. The wife wears sweater sets in aqua and peach, but she is beautiful in an understated way, tall and olive-hued. Vee studies the woman's face, but it gives nothing away.

The top drawer of her father's dresser sticks, as it has for years. She tugs left, jiggles right, then reaches into the back for her sew-on-the-go box. Rosemary's daughter, she thinks, is also a second wife, but a different kind, of a different era, with a face that shows everything. It showed Vee that the girl is sad, and confused, and possibly having an affair, and that she is unlikely to take the fabric for her daughters' dresses to a tailor, as Vee suggested. Above all, it showed that she misses her mother. Surely she wanted Vee to offer her something, care for her in some way. And the closest Vee came was rote advice about a dry cleaner, a little tea, and a monologue about how the girl had scared her. Vee snapped at her about not needing company. That was only because it had taken her so long to grow out of needing it—mostly. But how could the girl know that?

Except for the scissors, which rest open and askew atop the other items, the sew-on-the-go box appears as it did when Vee's grandmother gave it to her, the miniature cardboard spools waiting brightly in their rows as if the plastic container has fossilizing powers. Vee can't quite grasp Lily's determination to make the dresses herself—didn't she understand that Rosemary stopped sewing for a reason? What was happening in Brooklyn these days?—but she will send the box via overnight mail, so that Lily has it tomorrow. It's meant only for mending, of course, but she can use more than one color of thread; she can do it at her kitchen table where no one will see her struggle. It will be something.

Vee thinks of her own struggle with the buttons on her collar that afternoon, how much they had seemed to mean and how quickly they had come to mean nothing. How badly she had wanted to be a woman with conviction, and how little it seemed to matter in moments what her conviction was. She could have been a senator's wife if she hadn't seen through the illusion of their armor, or a women's-group woman if she hadn't found them embarrassing. She could have been a mother, like Rosemary, if only she had reached the morning she'd imagined she would someday reach, when she would without hesitation or regret toss her Pill down the toilet. But that morning had not come.

What Vee did not tell Lily—thank goodness!—is that it was Lily and her brothers who made Vee certain that she did not want children. This would sound cruel. But Vee did not feel cruelly toward Rosemary's children. If anything, she felt grateful, as she eventually did toward Alex, because they had solidified for her what she had not yet been able to believe. They were cute. But their cuteness did not outweigh their chaos. And she never found herself asking them questions; she was not interested in knowing them.

Dr. Monmouth said it was different when they were your own. But Vee was decided. No babies, and no men—not at all with respect to the former, and with respect to the latter not for keeps.

More complicated had been women, and the question of how they would appear in her life. Dr. Monmouth did not once ask about that. Would Vee go on stealing from them, and advising them, and berating them, and being loved by them? (Yes.) Would she really get to know any of the ones in her circle, beyond knowing the music and books they liked, whether they preferred wine or weed, where they were born? (No.) Was she ever attracted to them, as the tabloids inferred? (She would like to kiss some of them. That was all.) Would she find a friend again? (Not like Rosemary.)

In the drawer of her writing table Vee finds a cushioned mailer and tape. She opens her laptop. Lily's address is disturbingly easy to find—as her own must be, Vee realizes, for Lily to have found her. She makes a note to find out about changing that, then wraps the sew-on-the-go box in the Arts section, slips it into the mailer with a note, and thinks, No. She'll have a courier deliver it today, so Lily can start tonight.

A half hour later a young man is at Vee's door, in long shorts and a bright-yellow windbreaker. His neck is tattooed, his face bearded. He smiles, a big smile, his eyes sparkling as if he is glad to see her, and for a moment Vee feels as if they know each other. She smiles back. Then he and the package are gone, swallowed by the city, and Vee's thumbs are rubbing at her fingers, feeling the creases the thick tape has left in them. Georgie pants behind her, waiting, and she says, "Yes. Let's go for our nap."

OUT FROM SUSA

VASHTI

Those Who Cannot Fly or Burrow Walk

By sunrise the city has disappeared. They keep walking. There is water, someone says, far but not too far—they can reach it by dark, if they don't stop.

They are down to a few dozen, a diminishment that in the camp they could pretend against. They were not slaughtered in a way that could in a different millennium be tried in some kind of tribunal or court. A few boys who stole fruit off market-bound carts were hanged. A few girls were taken. Some men left. Mostly they died gradually, of hunger, thirst, heartache, heat. Exposed now, they see how minor they are. This and the salt whistling up off the sand urges them on.

Vashti watches the strangers who walk alongside her: the men with tents on their backs and the children hauling skins of water and the women slinging babies and pots and one woman, pitched forward as if against a wind, who is draped so heavily in necklaces strung with bones that she looks like a head atop a white mountain. Esther told her about this woman—the mother of Nadav.

The people are mostly silent, preserving their energy, even the small children on their fathers' shoulders, the babies on their mothers' breasts. Vashti carries all they will allow her to carry, a small skin and one blanket. She should protest, maybe. But her entombment has left her deficient in vitamins and muscle tone, and Baraz has sewn a small kingdom's worth of gold into narrow channels in her robes, and she feels with every step on the verge of sinking to her knees.

She does not sink. As the sun slides across the sky she walks. They all do. They walk as they eat, walk as they drink. The men walk as they urinate. Only the women stop occasionally, squatting behind the pack. Vashti can't bear the idea and so holds herself tightly until the bones woman walks up to her and says, "I can help," by which she means she speaks Persian nearly as well as Vashti—her years of dealings with the palace have trained her well. "You're the mother of Nadav," Vashti says, and so learns the story: that Nadav married the second-in-line-after-Esther girl, the girl from the good family, and that when the girl gave birth to their first child she and the child died and Nadav left—he was one of the few who simply walked away and never returned. Vashti understands now why the woman leans forward as she does, why she appears to be perpetually scanning the far horizon. She asks the woman for her name so that she can call her something other than mother-of-Nadav, and the woman tells her Amira, and Vashti relieves herself behind the tower of bones that is Amira. They walk together. Later, Amira turns to her and asks what Esther's child is called. And Vashti hesitates, because she knows the woman is thinking of her own grandchild. "Darius," she says. And they are silent again, Amira thinking of her grandchild and Vashti of her own shock when Esther told her the boy's name. Esther did not know, of course, that Darius had been the one who gave Vashti to Ahasuerus, that her son's name was for the queen who had come before her. "I see," Vashti said calmly, and Esther began talking of something else, but the boy had turned at his name—the boy looked at Vashti as if he saw through to her thoughts, saw everything.

By the second day, Vashti squats every chance she gets, whether or not she needs to relieve herself. To sweat is a shock. Her calves seize into knots. The skin on her hands and feet burns to the color of cinnabar. She cannot make words, cannot spend the energy to look toward Amira. She sees water where there is no water, clouds where there are no clouds, a cluster of tamarisk where there is only a dune. Her eyes feel singed. She closes them for long stretches, relying on the sand's palpation to guide her forward. She staggers through passages in which she fears that none of this is real, that she will wake soon, in her hole, and others, when the sun flares especially hot, in which she finds herself longing to be in the ground again. She wants Baraz. Late in the afternoon, in a waking dream, she turns around. She approaches the palace gates and uncovers her head. Where is Ahasuerus? Will she be like Esther, going to their king unbidden? No. Esther waited on the floor and shook. Esther got only bones. Vashti is Vashti. She is her father's daughter still. Isn't she? Even without her crown? *Here I am*, she says. *This is mine.*

No one answers. She is herself and she is someone new. She is going out from Susa. Her sandals are full of sand.

MANHATTAN

VEE

In Only Her Diadem

Vee takes off her stockings and dress and slips into bed. But it takes her a while to fall asleep. She worries. She has seen the bike messengers, how they attach themselves by their shoes to the bike's pedals and thread through the cars and trucks on the edge of death. Some ride with whistles in their mouths. Does hers have a whistle? At red lights, does he stop or does he shimmy back and forth, balancing in place? She pictures him in that precarious limbo, his neon-yellow sleeves puffing and deflating as he rocks, the muscles in his calves tensing. She wants to warn him against his refusal to obey gravity, the body, time. But soon, his rocking begins to soothe her, and she slips from worry to drowsiness. Georgie buries his nose in the crawl space beneath her knees, and Vee has the sensation that it is she who is riding the bicycle, she who is at the intersection on her pedals, not falling but rocking, shimmying, rising, as the noise and exhaust swell around her in a kind of salute. She returns the salute. Then the light changes, and she bursts forth, flying through the city like a myth.

SOMEWHERE NO LONGER NEAR SUSA

VASHTI

And All She's Telling You May Be a Lie

Six days out it is decided they will rest. Some kind of water stretches out ahead, a wetly green brush, a scattering of trees. They have stopped before, of course—each time they come to water they drink and fill their skins. On a few occasions they've slept, curling for a few hours into a patch of shade or, at night, into the slope of a shallow canyon. But even in sleep they were preparing to walk again. Even on their Sabbath, after a debate, they walked.

Vashti is not the one who decides, of course. She does not rule here. She gets her news from Amira, the bones woman, who points, her necklaces rattling, and says, "See there? We're making camp."

And a while later: "Are you all right?"

Vashti nods. But Itz, up at the front, is looking back at her, straight at her, as he has not done since they left Susa, and in response her feet have begun to drag. She knows what he is thinking of—his words to her that first night, as they stood together watching the camp's disassembly: "I don't care who you are. When we're gone from here, you'll tell us everything."

She was still dizzy then. But tonight, she knows, once the tents are made and a fire built, it will be time.

"You'll have to translate for me," she says, realizing. "Esther's story."

"Come," answers Amira.

But Vashti is thinking. She thought of the story incessantly the first couple days of their march—what she would tell, what she would leave out. But then she stopped, maybe because she stopped believing that they would ever rest. Who was to say when a people was gone from the place they had been? It seemed to her that they might walk forever. So now she must work to recall what she decided. And now, too, she has walked farther with them. She must consider what she has come to know.

She begins to walk again but slowly; soon the people around her slow, too, adjusting to match her pace. They do so without looking at her, as they've done the whole way, ever attentive to her without admitting their attentiveness, shifting as she shifts, making sure she is never left on the flanks or behind. Whether they think they're protecting her or protecting themselves, she can't decide, or rather she comes to different conclusions on different days. They don't trust her fully, that's clear. And why should they? But now that they're close to a destination she senses in them a new impatience with her, something that borders perhaps on contempt and makes her feel more acutely the demands of her task ahead. They left for her. Or this is what they tell themselves—as little fealty or fear as they should seem to owe her, this is what they need to believe. What will she give them in return?

It's not her story they want, of course. She is only the queen who was banished so their part could begin. She warrants a mention, maybe two. Make way for Esther! They will think they want to know everything. So Vashti will have to make them think she is telling them everything. Esther the maiden in the night station. It will have to be a bowdlerized night station, bawdy but not dark, not depraved. Only as they imagine. Esther the one girl (Lara will be excised; Lara is too complicated) who will not paint her face or tower her hair, whose natural beauty is such that the king is instantly besotted. The king means well but does not have his own thoughts; the king wants above all to be king, to possess and declare; the king is a dupe. They will like this. He is not one of them. But Esther. She will have to do something very brave. Esther had in fact done something very brave, but it was not the thing they would want her to have done—never mind that she became the beast for them as much as for her. In the story, she has to do something that is entirely and explicitly for them, something that emphasizes her virtue (excise Baraz in the linen room, excise the minister's advances, excise anything she may have wanted for herself) and above all proves her loyalty and her good luck. It will be the kind of outrageously good luck that can masquerade as wisdom, the kind of luck that results in triumphs a people can then believe they deserve.

Her trial will involve going to the king unbidden, Vashti thinks. Esther did that, and she will do it in the story. He is harmless, of course. But they don't know that.

She slows further, to think. The story is like tendrils of twine she's trying to braid into rope. Around her the people's frustration at her pace is a palpable heat, and Vashti finds the uncle—Marduk—squinting back at her. Why he hates her she can only guess. Maybe he hates all Persians, or anyone who is higher than him, anyone who makes him feel as his brother did. Maybe he is simply exhausted. He has lost his wife, it seems, and maybe one child—it is hard to tell which children belong to which adults. Or maybe it's simpler than all that. Maybe he does not like Vashti because she is not Esther. Vashti saw how his mouth gaped as she talked about his niece, how when she exaggerated the girl's newfound plumpness, he flinched.

The story, she thinks, lengthening her stride again, will have to prominently and positively feature the uncle. It will begin with him. It did begin with him! The uncle with the idea of sending his niece to the king. The uncle will have to return, more than once.

As Marduk turns away and begins to walk, next to his tall son, the story grows and coalesces in Vashti's mind, not the story Itz asked for but the one he actually needs. Itz will not be in the story. Itz needs a new story, one that has nothing to do with him. But the uncle wants the old story—not as it is but as it might have been. He wants to go back, and do better, and for everything to turn out well. He wants to slay the villain. The villain will be the minister, of course. (The villain is, in fact, the minister.) So Marduk will be a hero, too, along with Esther, Esther who will want what she has. (And she does now, in certain respects, doesn't she?) Marduk and Esther standing atop Persia, grinding the minister's head into the earth. Or maybe not that, exactly, but something like it. A gallows. A hanging meant for one of their own but delivered to another. Reversal, revenge. Yes. Vashti picks up her pace. And other things, she thinks, that would never happen but must happen. Things they don't have the shamelessness for in life. The story doesn't have to be believable, she realizes. It has to be the opposite—so unbelievable that they can believe in it. So far from what they know to be true that they can lose sight of the truth. Rivers of wine. Harlots. A pageant. A parade! Spies and riots and then a party. So much blood shed by their enemies they won't know what to do but howl and dance. Yes. The story is cohering, the story that will become the book is coming into view. Forget the wandering, she thinks. Forget the hole. Burn the records. Hurt with nothing but laughter.

BROOKLYN

LILY

The Spiel

From the wings the empty stage looks vast and dignified, its scuffed floors brought to sleekness by the precurtain light. In the beat before her actors enter, Lily feels almost absurdly stirred. No matter that it's an amateur and melodramatic musical comedy they're putting on, open to anyone willing to make a fool of themselves. Her heart thuds beneath her ribs. And when the curtain rises and Mordecai leaps out crying, "All hail!" Lily finds herself cheering as wildly as the audience, her hands raised high as she claps.

In the program she is listed as the spiel's writer and director, and though in fact what she has contributed on the writing front has been quite minor, she did not correct the proofs. Beneath her name, in italics, is written: *In honor of her mother, Ruth Burnham Rubenstein, the original*. Before she got sick, unbeknownst to Lily—how much had been unbeknownst to Lily!—Ruth had volunteered to write and direct the spiel, and no one was able to bear replacing her before she died. So they waited, then waited a little longer. Then, the day after Lily's visit to Vivian Barr, she received an email from Ruth's friend Susan Levinson—the woman who spearheaded the beautiful platters at the memorial service—asking if Lily would fill the role.

Lily replied, *Sorry, I can't.* She did not say, *I'm still too sad, I'm still trying to figure out how to make my daughters' dresses, I still don't even understand the story, I've got issues with it,* etc. *Thank you,* she wrote, *but surely there is someone else more qualified?*

Thirty seconds later, Susan Levinson wrote back. *Perhaps you're RIGHT. But we would LIKE for you to do it and I know your mother would have, too. Your mother was IRREPLACEABLE, we miss her. We MISS her. Also, you should KNOW that the thing is basically written, we're just recycling it from another temple, so really all you need to do is tweak it in places, a few edits, then help the crew bring it off. They're very enthusiastic just need a boss.*

Lily felt a little hurt then. They weren't asking her to create the thing, just fix someone else's creation. Then she worried. *Boss.* Was she capable of bossing? Then she reread the email and felt the pride and guilt the woman intended her to feel and said, *Okay. Yes. Of course. Thank you.*

And then it had been wonderful! Susan met her at the rabbi's office to show her the script from the other temple, and every wall was lined with books, floor to ceiling; even the back of the door was covered in books, and Lily felt a calm come over her as she sank into a chair and began to read. Then the rabbi walked in and asked if Lily would like to see the original book of Esther and Lily said of course, because what else could she say, and the rabbi—a tall woman in a ponytail and track pants—pulled down the book and said, "We haven't met, but I loved your mother." She walked Lily through the scenes, and the corresponding songs in the spiel, and Lily thought, This isn't something a rabbi is needed for. She must really have loved my mother. And Susan

Levinson kept giggling whenever they went over a funny part of the spiel. Then the rabbi pulled down some other books, full of things people had written *about* the book of Esther, interpretations and arguments and stories, and here is where Lily got lost for a while—she texted the sitter and asked her to stay a little longer.

There was one story about how Vashti's father, who'd been a king, was killed by a candelabrum falling on his head. And rabbis arguing about whether Esther was brought into her uncle's house as a daughter or wife—the language was not clear, and why else would she be described as *shapely and beautiful* in the sentence before the one about Mordecai adopting her? Whole scenes of dialogue had been written imagining what might have happened offstage in the story, including one in which the king, Ahasuerus, finally sobered up, asked where Vashti was, and, when told he killed her because she refused to parade naked in front of his friends, responded: *I did not act nicely.* Then there were people arguing over which woman was really the heroine of the story: Esther saved her people, sure, but wasn't she a coward first, and before that a concubine? Hadn't Vashti, not through outright revolt but simply by saying no, been a pioneer, standing out as *a sublime representative of self-centered womanhood?* But Esther, someone else argued, was the epitome of virtue; when the king made his advances, she was passive, *like the ground.* No, argued someone else, Esther was not frigid, she had used her *feminine wiles* to curry favor with the eunuch Baraz and rise to queen and save her people and she had been right to do so. She had done what she had to do, just as Vashti had done what she had to do. Esther simply had better luck because she was a Jew and it was a story meant to make Jews feel good! She was like Judith, except that in Esther's case she got a lot of help from Mordecai. It was too bad, someone else argued, that Mordecai had to play such a big role.

As for Vashti, wasn't she less a character than an absence? Wasn't it her absence that made the story possible? Sure, but she was also an anti-Semite, according to someone else—she beat her Hebrew servants. Hunh? Come on, wrote someone else. The whole story was an excuse for a carnival, and carnivals were *safety valves that reaffirm institutional control*. Wait, said someone else. Look at how God isn't mentioned, not even once. Wasn't Esther just another version of Scheherazade? Did you never wonder what happened to the maidens who were *not* chosen?

Lily had to tear herself away when her watch beeped. And when she was home and spooning mac and cheese onto the kids' plates, she was still thinking about all she had read, and what she might do with it.

She hasn't figured that part out yet. The temple members now side-stepping and singing "Respect"—Vashti's ballad, of course—will perform basically the same spiel their corollaries performed at a synagogue in California last year, based on the summer of 1967. Ruth had already adapted it a little, and Lily adapted it a little more, writing in a few new lines and one new character, daughter to the wicked minister Haman, who according to one of the rabbi's books may have accidentally dropped a bucket of feces on her father's head while he was parading Mordecai around Susa. Lily is proud of the ditty she rearranged for this particular moment: *Well, here's some poop on you/You're gonna choke on it, too/You're gonna lose that smile*. But mostly she left the script Susan handed her intact and kept what she read in the rabbi's office for herself. For now.

When Esther enters, after Jefferson Airplane's "Somebody to Love," the audience whistles and hoots. Vashti has been disposed of, Haman has received his opening boos; now the real show begins. The crowd is boisterous due to the many Tom Collinses that Lily poured from pitchers as people streamed in. As Esther sings her rendition of "Different Drum," Lily scans the sea of glinting tin groggers and plastic cups. Adam and June and Rosie are in the third row: Rosie on her knees, her dress so bright it could be seen from space, June on Adam's lap. The girls hold not only groggers but also fairy wands from their personal collections, which they insist Esther would want, and gawk in dazzled adoration up at the "real" Esther, a recent college graduate named Blossom Cohen who bops and swishes and flips her long hair as the congregation—many of whom have known her since she was an infant—shimmies along with her. The congregation imagines she is like her name, cheerful and innocent. But Lily has watched Blossom sneak out of rehearsal to smoke weed, and heard her confide to Haman's wife that she's pretty sure she has HPV and may never find anyone to marry her. Never mind that Haman's wife is being played by a thirtysomething woman whom everyone knows has been twice left by fiancés. The girl, like a girl, does not think of the woman. *I'm adulting!* Lily heard her say once as the two headed off to smoke, and it took Lily a moment to realize that she wasn't talking about the vape in her hand but the fact that she was acting in a Purim spiel.

Now Blossom, aka Esther, parades around the stage with a bunch of other maidens singing their rendition of "Piece of My Heart" as Ahasuerus—hands on his hips, fake eyebrows sternly furrowed—pretends to hem and haw. Which one will he choose? June and Rosie point and shout. Adam's mouth is open, his absorption in the show so replete that when a rogue stage light cuts across him the old scar on his cheek looks alive. Last week he was promoted to regional director for East Africa, the step up he's been waiting for, and the depth of his relief, the palpable weight of it in his body, in their apartment, has been a shock; Lily understands now how scared he was before. "Esther!" cry June and Rosie, waving their wands at Blossom. Of course. Lily has indoctrinated them, there is that, but also: if he doesn't choose Esther, how will they come to be? As if on cue, in the opposite wing across the stage, Lily's Vashti winks at Lily and Lily winks back, thinking for the space of the wink of Vira, then finding herself once again swept up in the joy of the thing. She helps one of the unchosen maidens change into her raggedy fasting-Hebrew costume, sings along to Haman's "Purple Haze" (*Excuse me while I kill some Jews!*), and accepts a glass of wine handed to her by Haman's wife, who has smuggled a bottle backstage.

Then something flickers toward the back of the audience. Not a cup or a grogger. Not something anyone else would notice. But Lily notices. It's Vivian Barr's red hair. It's Vivian Barr, sitting at the very end of the very last row.

Lily draws back into the wing. She is conscious suddenly that she is tipsy, conscious that Haman is repeating a verse and that the sound system is crackling. What is Vivian Barr doing here? She has no idea that Lily is directing the spiel. The last contact they had came through a courier: a tiny sewing kit Vivian Barr sent after Lily's visit.

Lily inches forward to peek again at her mother's old friend. She sits somewhat stiffly, not rocking or clapping, no drink or grogger in her hand. A stranger here. And perhaps warier than another stranger might be, Lily thinks, remembering how Vivian Barr said *your father, you know* about Lily's father being Jewish, and how her voice had changed when Lily asked why she hadn't reached out to Ruth. *Do I look like I need company?*

And yet, Lily thinks. She's here.

And here is Esther again, too, entering the king's chambers without his permission, winging her hippie skirt like a flamenco dancer. And here comes Haman, leering, and dopey Ahasuerus, looking confused, and then, in another Lily addition, Mordecai leaping out for a moment to remind the audience to keep drinking, for it's been commanded that they be so drunk by the end of the spiel that they can't tell the difference between him and Haman. "Good or bad!" he cries. "Cunning or true! Who knows? Not you!"

Lily wonders if Vivian Barr can feel Lily watching her.

Clearly she knew that Lily would not take her advice to go to a tailor; hence the sewing kit. Did she also know that Lily would ignore her advice about not going back to the friend who had first helped her, to make the dresses?

Hello I am sorry to have been out of touch for so long I hope you can forgive me went Lily's text to Kyla, because she feared any pause for punctuation would cause her to lose her courage. *I wonder if you would still be willing to help me with my daughters' dresses I have the fabric and the patterns I've chosen very simple ones what do you think?*

Too complicated, Vivian Barr had said, of returning to Kyla. Thinking of Rosemary, maybe, or other failed friendships, or women in general.

But she had been wrong. Within a few minutes came Kyla's reply: *Of course, and please don't worry. I'll be home tonight. Come after 8:30, just text when you're nearby instead of ringing, kids will be asleep*. It was 8:00 already and Adam had just gotten home but he said, *Of course, go*, just as he had said, *Of course, direct the spiel*, understanding already what she was only beginning to understand herself. And Lily thought, that's all right. That happens sometimes. It does not mean I'm a child. It means only that he has imagined what it might be like to be me. He sees that as the emptiness starts to lift, other tides have begun filling in. She took his encouragement, *Of course*, not as fear, but love.

With this softness in her heart she walked to Kyla's. And

when she got there, to Kyla's clean kitchen, all that ran through her was gratitude. Kyla's husband was out, *again*, Kyla said blackly, and Lily, unsure what Kyla wanted—Kyla of the perfect life—did not become paralyzed but said what her instincts told her to say, which was, *Good thing I'm here*, and Kyla laughed. And Lily unpacked her bag, laying out the fabrics, and the patterns, and the box Vivian Barr sent her. *Maybe it's weird*, she said, *but I'd like to include some of this thread in the dresses. Can that work?* Lily was doing this not for Vivian Barr but for her mother, who once upon a time had loved Vivian Barr and, later, loved Letty Loveless. She had used Letty Loveless, Lily had come to see, as a source of courage, so that she could make the choices she wanted to make and not clean the things she did not want to clean—in that sense, Vivian Barr aka Letty Loveless had not ruined but saved her mother. Kyla said yes. They could use that thread in the collars, sew those by hand. She waited until they were sewing—Kyla at Lily's back for a while and then, by the second dress, Lily mostly on her own—to ask if the thread had been Lily's mother's. And Lily told her the story.

Now, a couple rows away from Vivian Barr, Kyla and her kids brandish their groggers like lassos. It's their first spiel. Closer to the front, her mother's friend Susan Levinson laughs, while in the aisle the rabbi dances in a Wonder Woman costume, while not far from her, in the third row, Lily's daughters' dresses glow. When Lily presented them at last with their costumes, they smiled and thanked her. They were oddly serene. It was clear they had expected the dresses, that they never doubted Lily's story that she was making them. They bounce in their seats now, unthinking, aglow. It doesn't matter to them that Lily still doesn't really know how to sew, or that the love she feels for them, so blinding and pure in moments, is obscured from her in others, or that she kissed a man who is not their father, that though she will not kiss him again, will not blow up her life—she does not want to blow it up, this thing she's made with Adam, begun in that bar, this thing with holes they will never patch; she wants it—she may think of him, and desire him.

To a child, maybe, like the child Lily once was, looking at Vivian Barr, there can be only one story at a time.

She will tell her daughters the truth, Lily thinks. Not yet, but sooner than her mother told her. Not the details, but the gist. She will tell them: *The type of woman you imagine yourself becoming does not exist.*

As the spiel reaches its finale, the audience gets to its feet. Even Vivian Barr rises, clapping. After the pageant, Lily will introduce her to the girls. Rosemary's granddaughters. She will make Vivian Barr a stranger no more, and show her the collars, made with the thread she sent. *Perhaps you'll make better use of this than I?* she wrote in her note. *Here it is,* Lily will say, *holding their collars together, turquoise and fuchsia for Rosie, black and white for June. No strand was long enough on its own but together they added up. Thank you.*

She means this. And not only for the sewing kit, but for Vivian Barr's postscript, too: *I did imagine she might read my letters. Of course I did.* And for the thing that has stayed with Lily since she left Vivian Barr's apartment, not yet coherent but cohering: an understanding of Ruth as something not solid but assembled, built of everything she could grab hold of. A Letty Loveless column here, a gathering of women there, a burning cross, a whiff of perfume on her husband's collar, a stray want she could not name, a time of grief. Like a nest, maybe, without a bird—Ruth had to be and build herself at the same time. So of course there could be no talk of sewing, or of Rosemary. A thing put together could always come apart. But Lily, because she did not know any of this, and because Ruth could not tell her, because to tell her would have been to expose her own construction—Lily, who was formed in that nest, believed it had always been. And for so long her own sense that she is still in a state of assembly has made her ashamed.

Soon all Lily can see are the children rushing the stage for the pageant. They surround the cast in a swarm, Vashti in her short skirt and Ahasuerus with his Burger King crown and Haman's daughter with her bucket and Haman with his wickedness and Esther, too, who merely looks like Blossom, the twenty-two-year-old who does not know what will happen next in her life. But who does know? If Lily has been waiting for some kind of transformation, she understands now that none is coming. No new Lily, only herself, moving forward, a little less ashamed. The actors run offstage, leaving the children in their costumes, Esthers and Mordecais and Elsas and Batmen, prancing and yowling beneath the lights, waiting for direction.

It's Lily, hiding in the wings still, who is meant to direct them. And she will, in a moment. She is watching her daughters dancing in the dresses they envisioned, leaping and pouncing with their wands outstretched, making sparks fly. They have forgotten Esther. They are simply themselves, ecstatic. Soon, she will step out, so they can see her.

ACKNOWLEDGMENTS

This book would not exist without two books that came first: the original *Book of Esther*, in all its bawdy splendor, and *The Hours*, whose structure helped inspire my own. Thank you to whoever dreamed up the former, and to Michael Cunningham for writing the latter.

I'm deeply grateful to the friends and sister who read drafts of this book, in part or whole, and provided invaluable feedback. Thank you to Clare Burson, Eleanor Henderson, Marisa Silver, Jessie Solomon-Greenbaum, Rachel Wolff, Gina Zucker, and most especially to Lisa Srisuro, who arrived early and returned as the closer in the final stretch.

To the people who know far more than I do about all manner of things—from the cost of bathroom renovations in 1973 to international humanitarian relief operations today—and who generously shared their expertise and perspective, I offer my humblest thanks. You are Graham Brawley, David Clatworthy, Anne Deneen, Lika Dioguardi, Sarah Ellison, Dr. Ronnie-Gail Emden, Daniel Holt, Kathy Jones, Sheryl Kaskowitz, Aaron Kuriloff, Danielle Lazarin, Iraj Isaac Rahmim, Geoffrey Richon, Dr. Keren Rosenblum, Dr. Dave Shultz, Ellen Solomon, and Michelle Zassenhaus. A special thanks to Amy Gottlieb and my fellow writers in Amy's wonderful Jewish Sources, Literary Narrative class at Drisha Institute. And to Rabbi Rachel Timoner, who opened her office and books to me when I knew almost nothing. Now I know a little more than nothing. Thank you for showing me possible paths.

Numerous texts provided inspiration and information. Those I found myself returning to include *Desdemona: A Play About a*

Handkerchief by Paula Vogel; *The JPS Bible Commentary: Esther* by Adele Berlin; *Surfacing* by Margaret Atwood; *Spinster* by Kate Bolick; *Lilith & Her Demons* by Enid Dame; *Ancient Jewish Novels*, edited and translated by Lawrence M. Wills; *The Feminine Mystique* by Betty Friedan; *The Book of Esther* by Emily Barton; *Good and Mad: The Revolutionary Power of Women's Anger* by Rebecca Traister; and last but perhaps the most influential and the source of "shit and string beans," *The Women's Room* by Marilyn French.

Also on the inspiration front: thank you to Zevey Steinitz for you know what.

Select chapter titles were stolen from Elizabeth Bishop's poem "A Drunkard," Angela Carter's story "The Bloody Chamber," Enid Dame's poem "Lilith," and Elizabeth Cady Stanton's *The Woman's Bible.*

Great gratitude goes to Congregation Beth Ami of Santa Rosa, California, and in particular to Leanne Schy who wrote the fabulous "Purim of Love" script from which I shamelessly and with Leanne's generous permission stole for the spiel in *The Book of V.*

For cheering me on from near and far, feeding me, sending ideas, and being kind, thank you, Bo Abrams, Deborah Barron, Jenna Blum, Judi Campbell, Chris Castellani, Deborah Cramer, Elyssa East, Sarah Ellison, Eve Fox, Abby Greenbaum, Leslie Jamison, Rachel Kulick, Julia Mitric, Rekha Murthy, Britt Page, Eli Pollard, Mitzi Rapkin, Amy Scott, Evelyn Spence, Becca Steinitz, Marina Tolou-Shams, my sister, Fara Greenbaum, and my father, William Greenbaum, who taught me that even old texts—maybe especially old texts—are fair ground for play. To Erika Dreifus, Charlotte Gordon, Celeste Ng, and Sarah Stein for being early enthusiasts when I dared describe my idea to them. For spitballing, thanks to Sonya Larson for the idea and Elisabeth Hamilton, Marisa Silver, Megan Staffel, and Gina Zucker for the spit. Thanks to my students and colleagues at Warren Wilson, Barnard College, and the 92Y for all you teach me. To Heidi Pitlor, Jane Roper, and Gina (again), cheese-loving comrades in self-made retreats. To Lesley Williamson of the Saltonstall Arts Colony, Kathy Sherbrooke of Hemingway House, Scott Adkins of the Brooklyn Writers Space, and Sue Shepherd of her own home: portions of this book were written in the spaces you create. A shout-out to whoever left the bizarre *Ohel Coffee, Product de Persia, Certified for the Court of Ahasuerus, 14 Adar 5773* mug at the Brooklyn Writers Space.

To Lindsay McCune, for all the care you give my children while I work.

Thank you to Julie Barer, whose faith that I could pull off this book kept me from losing mine and whose steady counsel, unwavering reason, and warm voice on the phone help keep my lights on. Also, you are one fine editor. Nicole Cunningham, thank you for all your work; keep dancing.

Thank you to Serena Jones, who embraced this book with open arms and then pushed me to make it a hell of a lot better—your edits and emails bring me joy. To Ben Schrank, whose belief in and care with my story meant the world. To copyeditor Molly Lindley Pisani, who masterfully slayed my commas and left smiley faces in their wake. And to everyone at Henry Holt for welcoming me so quickly and securely into your fold and putting your hearts and expertise into bringing the world to *The Book of V.*, including Marian Brown, Amy Einhorn, Pat Eisemann, Maddie Jones, Jason Liebman, Carolyn O'Keefe, Caitlin O'Shaughnessy, Maggie Richards, and Jessica Wiener.

Thank you to my grandmother, Rose Greenbaum, née Genzuk, who gave me a sew-on-the-go kit that has turned out to be of great practical and imaginative use in my life. And to my mother, Ellen Solomon, who did in fact hang a sampler on the back of our bathroom door declaring *A Well-Kept House Is a Sign of an Ill-Spent Life*, and who was my first writing teacher.

Finally, thank you to Sylvie and Sam for asking tough questions. And to Mike, for cooking me breakfast and keeping me company.

Printed in the USA
PSIA information can be obtained
www.ICGtesting.com
HW040523290823
525LV00003B/273

9 781250 798442